WISTERIA WARNED

Wisteria Witches Mysteries

BOOK #9

ANGELA PEPPER

CHAPTER 1

ZARA RIDDLE
WISTERIA PUBLIC LIBRARY
MONDAY MORNING

I set my second birthday cake next to the coffee maker in the staff room.

I'd been the first to arrive at work that Monday morning, and the building was comfortably quiet around me. I loved the library at all times, but especially in the morning, before we opened.

I heard keys jingling on the other side of the back door, which opened directly into the break room, then the door creaked open. My coworker, Frank Wonder, walked in slowly, his head down. The children's librarian was in his mid-fifties, and extremely fit, with wiry arms, a svelte torso, and skinny legs. Frank dressed to be noticed, often in vintage cords and paisley shirts. His skin was naturally pale, but he tanned outdoors during the summer, often on the beach in a Speedo.

Frank's eyes were wide-set, small, and hooded. His face had a triangular shape due to his narrow, slightly crooked jaw. He had an odd way of talking out of the side of his mouth, but this was a trait most people didn't notice because they were usually staring up at his hair, which he dyed bright pink.

"Good morning, Mr. Wonderful," I called out, using one of his many nicknames.

He gasped and stepped backward, bumping against the closed door. "Zara! I didn't see you hiding over there in the gloom."

I glanced up at the bright lights overhead. What gloom? I looked at Frank more closely. He was typically slow-moving upon arrival, before he got his fix of coffee, but that Monday he was moving less like a former Olympic gymnast and more like a sea turtle. I noticed his hooded eyes were downright wrinkly. He actually looked his age, which was not typical for Frank.

"I brought cake," I said, using a cheerful tone even though "I brought cake" was not a statement in need of embellishment.

He blinked at me a couple times before smiling and saying, "Bless your heart, Zara Riddle. You are a fine woman." His fake Southern accent that he used when he was joking around was back, so he couldn't have been that bothered.

"It's Black Forest cake," I said. "From Gingerbread House. My daughter arranged everything with Chloe, and she customized two cakes, just for me."

Frank dawdled over to the cake and sniffed deeply. "What's that aroma? It's not kirsch."

"It's not kirsch," I agreed. "Chloe made it with orange liqueur, since my enthusiasm for cherry desserts hasn't been as strong lately." Not since the cherry cheesecake at my early birthday party down in the DWM cafeteria. And the subsequent battle to the death.

"Orange liqueur is nice, too," he said. "But can you still call it Black Forest cake without the kirsch?"

"I don't see any pastry police around to stop us."

Frank rubbed his hands. "We should probably wait until coffee break to dig in." He opened the cupboard that held the plates. He had no intention of waiting until coffee break.

"It's a pretty big cake," I said. "We could always have some now, and still have plenty left for later."

"If you insist." Frank's sleepy eyes brightened.

"Just a sliver for me."

"I'll cut you a piece so thin you can see through it." He plated two pieces and handed me a serving, along with a fork.

"Oh, Frank. Do I need to buy you a ruler? This is *hardly* what I would call see-through."

"Oh? I can see through mine. Your eyes must be going, due to your advanced age." He washed down a mouthful of cake with a slurp of coffee, swished his tongue over the front of his teeth, and gave me a small but bright grin. Frank's teeth were supernaturally white, in defiance of all the coffee he consumed. "Happy birthday, by the way."

"Thanks," I said. "And thank you for not making me cram thirty-three candles onto this innocent cake. It's a real fire hazard after a certain age."

"Wait until you get to be my age, and you need a special candle permit from City Hall," he said. We both chuckled, then he asked, "How did your family party go yesterday? I heard some sirens. It must have been the fire department on their way to put out the flames."

"Ha ha." I dug into my slice, careful to take the perfect ratio of chocolate cake and creamy white filling. "No fire, but there were a few drops of blood shed."

Frank grunted and nodded, as though he wasn't listening. I expected him to ask whose blood had been shed, being the gossip hound he was, but he didn't.

"What's going on with you?" I asked. "You seem distracted."

Frank sighed. "My sister is coming to visit."

That explained his distraction. Frank had only one sister, so I knew exactly who he was talking about. Bellatrix Wonder. She sounded like a colorful woman, but then again, Frank did like to embellish stories.

"All the way from London?"

He nodded.

"I'd love to meet her," I said. "Does she know about your big surprise?"

"You mean this one?" Frank set down his plate, winked at me, and shifted into flamingo form.

"Show-off," I said, waving my finger at him while also taking a step back. Sometimes when Frank shifted, he reeked of anchovies, whether he'd eaten them recently or not. It was not his most endearing feature.

Frank-Flamingo let out a loud squawk. Some shifters could speak in human voices while in animal form, but Frank didn't have that ability.

He pecked at the cake on his plate with his comically large beak.

Just then, there was the sound of the back door being unlocked. Uh-oh.

Frank-Flamingo squawked, "KA-KAAAAAA?" The stench of partially digested anchovies hung in the air.

"Yes, it's probably Kathy," I said, trying not to choke on Frank's breath.

The head librarian wasn't scheduled to start her shift until later in the day, yet she was about to walk in and find me sharing not-quite-Black-Forest cake with a giant pink bird that reeked of anchovies.

I waved a hand to direct my magic, and pushed the door shut before Kathy could see us.

"Change back," I whisper-yelled at Frank. "Change back right now, you silly birdbrain."

Frank-Flamingo let out a low squawk, sounding like a kazoo.

"I know, I know," I said soothingly. "You can't shift back when you're nervous." I waited, tapping my foot, keeping the magic pressure on the door.

Frank-Flamingo flapped his enormous wings and flew upward. He landed on the break-room table, his claws scratching for purchase. He knocked an acoustic ceiling tile off its metal grid with the top of his head. The ceiling tile landed on the table next to him, which caused even more panicked wing flapping. He was supposed to have his full human faculties in shifted form, but he sure didn't act like it.

On the other side of the back door, Kathy demanded, "Whoooo is pushing on this door?"

"Nobody is!" I called out. "I think the hinges are stiff!"

She asked, "Should I come around to the front?" Then she immediately answered her own question. "No. I am *not* coming in through the front. I've been at this long enough to know better."

We all knew better. Before the library was open for the day, a librarian couldn't be seen entering. To be spotted would lead to the front door being banged on, and a member of the public demanding to be let in at once, citing facts about whose taxes pay for whose salaries. We librarians loved the public and adored serving them, but not before coffee.

The door rattled with force. Kathy was stronger than she looked. .

I ran over to the door, braced it shut with my body, and tried to calculate a way to solve the current dilemma. What came to mind first were two spells that would only make things worse, but then finally I remembered the calming spell my aunt had used on me a few times.

I cast the spell at the pink bird. "Be calm," I said. To my witch ears, the spell made a sound halfway between a whistle and a hum. The spell worked better if you were holding the person's hand. However, in his current state, my coworker didn't even have hands.

Frank-Flamingo undulated his long neck into a complex curve. He folded his wings against his sides. He seemed less agitated, yet not calm enough to shift back to human form.

I was hit with a sense of déjà vu.

The same thing had happened to us once before, in that break room.

That time, I hadn't been as familiar with shifter magic, so I'd called the local secret agency to help. Three DWM agents had come to our rescue. Two of the agents were bird shifters. They took Frank on his first flight, and had since become his friends.

"Should I call Rob and Knox?" I asked.

Frank let out a long kazoo sound, then the room crackled with energy and he finally melted down into human form. He sat cross-legged on top of the table. His clothes were the same ones he'd arrived in, except his figure-hugging paisley shirt was on inside out.

"No need to call the guys," Frank said, uncrossing his legs and jumping down from the table. "And please don't breathe a word to them about what happened. It's so embarrassing." He waved at the door. "You can let her in now."

"Your shirt's inside out."

Frank looked down and muttered, "What's that all about?" He unbuttoned the shirt and put it back on correctly.

"Magic has a mind of its own," I said.

"She certainly does," he agreed.

While he retucked his shirt, I released the door for Kathy.

The door flew open, and the head librarian appeared in the doorway like the physical embodiment of an accusation.

Kathy Carmichael was short and sturdy, with dark skin, and brown hair that coiled in ringlets. She always dressed in shades of brown, gold, and red, like autumn leaves. She'd been the head librarian since long before I had started working there, and was forty-four, midway between my age and Frank's. That Monday, her round, dark face was shiny from exertion and her light brown eyes were active, flitting left and right, and up and down behind her gold, wire-rimmed glasses.

"Sorry about the door, boss," I said. "I'll put in a call to maintenance."

"I smell seafood," Kathy said, her tone accusatory as she remained steadfast in the doorway. Her back was to the sunny outdoors and her face was in shadow. She looked a little scary to me, which was saying a lot, because I'd seen many scary things, several of which tried to kill or eat me.

Frank and I exchanged a look, then Frank said, "Zara brought cake."

"I did bring cake," I said, smiling like a ding-dong.

"You two must take me for an idiot," Kathy spat out.

Frank and I exchanged another look. His eyebrows climbed so high, his eyelids pulled straight and his eyes were no longer hooded.

What was going on? Kathy had her foul moods, but they were usually directed at the nameless miscreants who dropped "surprises" into the overnight book return.

The head librarian stepped into the break room, moving like a simmering cauldron, and let the door slam shut behind her.

"Honestly," she said, in the irritated tone of someone who did *not* want to hear an explanation just yet. I'd never seen her so blustery.

Frank's wide eyes widened even more as he spotted something on the floor. A trio of pink feathers.

"Honestly," Kathy repeated. "Whooo could possibly tolerate being lied to, day in and day out, by her subordinates?" She blinked furiously behind her round glasses.

"It was me," Frank said. He took a big step forward, placing his foot on top of the three feathers.

"It *was* Frank," I agreed, hoping he had something good in mind.

"I was playing one of my classic pranks," he said. "That's why they call me Franker the Pranker."

I shot him a look. Nobody called him that. Mr. Wonderful, yes. The Frankinator, yes. Even Pinkie. But nobody called him Franker the Pranker because, despite being true, it just wasn't catchy.

"This ends right now," Kathy blustered.

In unison, Frank and I asked, "What?"

"I'm tired of you two going silent whenever I walk into the break room," Kathy said. "Or worse. Changing the topic to some boring thing I know neither of you are interested in. I'm not an idiot."

"Fair enough," I said, nodding. "We will stop all the pranks. No more plastic spiders or fake book requests."

"That's not what I meant," Kathy said.

In unison again, Frank and I said, "It's not?"

Kathy shot us a dirty look that was so powerful, it actually forced her glasses to slide down her narrow, pointed nose. She grabbed the glasses mid-air without looking at them.

"This calls for a demonstration," Kathy said, her tone acidic.

Frank and I started to ask what she meant, but we stopped when we saw what happened next.

Kathy tilted her head back, let her jaw drop open, and released a snake from her mouth.

Or at least that was how it looked.

The snake was not a snake at all. It appeared to be her *tongue*.

Kathy Carmichael, the head librarian, had a very long, prehensile tongue. The tongue snaked toward us, then lashed its way around my birthday cake, like a long bullwhip. Kathy's mouth opened to an impossible size, then the tongue snapped like a whip. Into her mouth went an entire cake, minus two slivers, neat as can be. She didn't drop a single chocolate curl.

Frank and I stared at Kathy in stunned silence.

"Now you know my secret," Kathy said, sounding less blustery and more like the regular Kathy. "I'm not going to insult your intelligence by pretending I don't know about both of yours." She put her glasses back on and peered at me. "Zara, you are a witch, just like your aunt."

I said nothing. It would break witch code to confirming someone else's powers as a package deal with mine. I wasn't the best at the supernatural rules for discretion, but I was trying.

Kathy walked over to where Frank stood, crouched down, and plucked one of the pink feathers from under his shoe. "And I believe this belongs to you, Mr. Wonder." She straightened up and waved the feather under his nose. "Or should I call you Mr. Flamingo?"

Frank said nothing while keeping a poker face. But then he sneezed from the feather tickling, and his grin gave him away.

"You got me," he said to the head librarian. "How long have you known?"

"My family has known your family for a long time," she said, which didn't answer his question, but seemed to satisfy him anyway.

"That's quite the tongue," I said. "What sort of shifter are you, if you don't mind my asking? An anteater?"

"Ew," she said. "I'm not a shifter. I'm a sprite."

A sprite? That was not a word I'd expected to hear. I put my hands on my hips. "A sprite?" She had to be messing with us. "Are you sure you're not something else?"

"Such as?" She put her hands on her own hips, mirroring me.

I had to ask. "Such as... an owl shifter?"

"No." Her face scrunched up in confusion. "Why would you think that?"

"Maybe because of all the hints you've been dropping since the day I started working here? Owl shifter was my best guess."

"That was your *best* guess?" She smiled now, her irritation over being locked outside apparently forgotten. "You witches and your *feelings*. Your type puts far more stock in your hunches and whims than you do in cold, hard facts."

"My type?" I didn't know if I was supposed to be offended, but I was.

We stared at each other.

This was why we hadn't exchanged our supernatural identities before now. There were so many politics involved. Even though we were all interconnected and shared common issues, some supernaturals fixated on the differences between kinds instead of the similarities. Or they took on the prejudices of their ancestors.

Our silent standoff was broken by a strange gurgling sound that filled the room. It sounded as unappealing as Frank's anchovy breath smelled. It sounded like trouble coming our way. I glanced over at the break room's sink.

"Was that the sink?" Frank asked.

"I hope the plumbing isn't backing up," I said.

"Oh, dear," Kathy said, patting her midsection. "That sound was me, I'm afraid."

"Wow," Frank said. "How many stomachs do you have in there?"

Kathy's dark cheeks turned a deeper shade as she blushed. "Never mind about my insides."

Frank caught my eye and made a face. I looked away quickly, before he could give me the giggles.

Kathy kept patting her midsection. The gurgling decreased to a milder sound that was almost relaxing, like a water fountain.

"Oh, fluffernuts. I shouldn't have eaten that whole cake," Kathy said. "Now we've got a big problem on our hands."

"We do?" Frank took a step back, as though the head librarian might explode.

"We do?" I echoed.

"A huge problem." Kathy held her fist to her mouth and let out a burp. "The cake's all gone. What are we going to have at coffee break?"

CHAPTER 2

DINNER TIME

"A sprite?" My sixteen-year-old daughter, Zolanda Daizy Cazzaundra Riddle, also known as Zoey, wrinkled her lightly freckled nose at me. "If a person has a freakishly long, prehensile tongue, that would lead me to believe that person is a troll."

"It does sound exactly like the troll descriptions in the magic books, but Kathy Carmichael informed me that there's *no such thing* as trolls, therefore Kathy Carmichael, with her freakishly long, prehensile tongue, is actually a *sprite*."

Zoey squinted and slowly nodded. "I think I see where this is going. She's a troll, but she doesn't want to be called a troll."

"Nobody wants to be called a troll."

"But that doesn't change the fact she is a troll."

"But is she? Really? If nobody calls them trolls anymore, are they still trolls?"

Zoey frowned. "I don't know."

"Wow. Now there's a phrase I don't often hear coming out of your adorable lips." I turned to address the fluffy white cat who was weaving around my ankles in a figure-eight pattern. "Did you hear that, Boa? I've stumped my genius daughter with a philosophical question."

"It's more of a linguistics question," my clever teenager said, correcting me. "Or a crossover between philosophy and linguistics," she further corrected herself.

I chuckled. "You should have seen the way Kathy put away that cake. One enormous bite and it was all gone."

"What a waste. She didn't even taste it?"

"Not unless sprites have taste buds in their stomachs. I already phoned Chloe to order another replacement cake for tomorrow."

"That will be your third birthday cake, or your fourth if you count the cherry cheesecake."

"What else am I supposed to do? I deserve to get at least one big slice, to be eaten in peace, and allowed to fully digest. My official birthday cake got ruined when *your father* knocked it on the floor. I wasn't going to eat floor cake."

She smiled. "Since when are you too good for floor cake?" Her smile faded to a frown. "And what do you mean by 'your father'?"

"Archer Caine *is* your father. I could call him 'the genie' if you prefer. Or 'the demon,' or 'the devil' with a lowercase d."

The wrinkles on her brow deepened. "You said 'your father' as though him being my father was my doing, somehow. Archer Caine being my father wasn't my doing."

"You're right. It was the doing of a six-pack of Barberrian wine coolers." I took a breath. "Or so I believed, until I read that prophecy scroll with your name in it, and now I'm not so sure."

She raised two red eyebrows. "I caused myself to be conceived?"

"Well, kid, you are part genie. How should I know how genie magic works? When we moved here, your father was out and about, floating around inside people's heads, or in the ether, or who knows, and then he made himself a body out of spare Chet Moore parts. That sounds an awful lot like what you did inside me."

She rolled her eyes. She was half genie, but she was also a quarter witch and a quarter fox shifter. Only the fox shifter aspect had manifested so far. The teenager aspect superseded everything else.

I went on. "Ask your father how genies get out of their bottles and into new bodies. And find out of the bottles are actual bottles or just a metaphor. I'm pretty sure he was the guy I heard talking to a disembodied Dorothy Tibbits inside Josephine Pressman's head. In fact, I'm ninety-nine-point-nine percent sure it was him. Then, after he got that new body of his, he dated the poor girl up at Castle Wyvern, and got her killed." I shook my head. "I know it was Morganna Faire who got the genie-melting poison from that nasty little gnome, but Josephine wouldn't have drank it by accident if she hadn't been mixed up in their genie business." I let out a low whistle. "It's a good thing Jo's spirit has moved on, or he'd always be looking over his shoulder for an angry ghost."

Zoey opened her mouth, but I cut her off, talking faster.

"Ask your father about the prophecy, too. That old scroll they have at the DWM. Get as much information out of him as you can. You've got your deadbeat dad back in your life at the moment, for better or for worse. Why not make the most of it?"

She shook her head. "That's enough, Mom. You've made your point. He's connected to a lot of bad people and unfortunate events. He may even be directly or indirectly connected to everything weird that's happened to us since we moved here."

I shrugged. "Maybe you shouldn't have let him into our lives."

Her jaw dropped open. She blinked at me furiously. When she regained the ability to speak, her words came out fast and angry. "I let him into our lives? Me?" She thumped her chest with an open hand. "I wasn't the one who invited him to your birthday party. It was your wish that brought him into our lives." She pointed her finger at me. "Your birthday wish."

"But my wish was on your behalf. I had to do something. Whenever the topic of your siring comes up, you always look at me with those sad puppy-dog eyes."

"My *siring*? Don't you dare distract me by using a weird, old-timey verb."

I waved a hand, accidentally casting a spray of iridescent magic sparkles. "All I did was blow out some candles and wish that you could have a better relationship with your father than I had with mine. A mother always wants the best for her child."

"And I appreciate that. I do. But I barely found out about Archer being my father before suddenly he was at our front door. I think I would have preferred more time to get used to the idea that my father looks exactly like our next-door neighbor, Mr. Moore, due to the fact he made himself a body using Mr. Moore's spare parts." She sighed. "Why Mr. Moore, anyway?"

"We think he snuck in there, on a physical level, when Chet was stuck inside that fleshy mind-erasing horror in the Pressman attic during the incident that you pretend to know nothing about."

"Right. I certainly didn't listen in on you talking to Auntie Z about it, because that would have been wrong."

I sighed. According to the DWM's internal investigation, Archer Caine had likely been in his non-corporeal genie form the last sixteen years. Morganna Faire, his sister, used his essence to power some diabolical machines they were going to use to erase minds, so the genies could be immortal without having to lose their memories every time they were reborn as babies. But then Archer had jumped ship into Chet Moore, like a virus.

"It's a lot to process," Zoey said. "My father, the body snatcher."

"You should probably call him a genie," I said. "Or Djinn with a capital D. Or djinn with a lowercase d. All I know is they don't like being called demons." I turned away from her, opened the oven, and pulled out the casserole I'd made with various leftovers, covered in cheese.

"Hmm," was all she said.

"Just like how trolls prefer being called sprites." I floated the hot casserole dish over to a trivet. Witches didn't need oven mitts. "Speaking of trolls preferring to be called sprites, don't you love it when a conversation naturally comes around full circle?"

"Hmm." She swished her lips from side to side.

A wyvern flew into the kitchen and landed on the back of a chair.

Most people would scream at the sight of a mythological creature flapping into a room, but it was a regular occurrence in the Riddle household. And this mythological creature wasn't that terrifying, since his body was all of seven inches long and his head resembled that of a large seahorse. Like a dragon, the wyvern did breathe fire, some of it in the shape of colorful ribbons. That was how he'd earned his name, Ribbons.

Ribbons the Wyvern spoke telepathically into my mind and Zoey's. "Did someone say floor cake?" The wood of the chair squeaked under the pressure of his claws. Having a wyvern as a roommate was as hard on the furniture as it was on the grocery bills.

"There's no floor cake," I said.

"I know." He preened himself. "I heard the entire conversation from the moment you arrived home from work, Zed." He communicated in his unplaceable Old Europe accent and semi-formal syntax. "But was it not delightful how I chose that particular phrase with which to make my entrance?"

"It was pretty cute," I said.

He snorted, emitting a sulfur smell, like a struck match. "Ribbons is not *cute*. Ribbons is delightful, and charming, not to mention handsome."

Zoey said to me, "He's extra cute when he refers to himself in third person, isn't he?"

"So cute," I agreed. "Someone should make a line of greeting cards with Ribbons saying all of his cute little catchphrases."

He snorted again, this time emitting a delicate ribbon of orange fire. "I will eviscerate anyone who dares capture my image for commercial purposes. I will rip them limb from limb, and spread their entrails across the land with great speed while their heart still beats. They will have no choice but to bear witness to their disembowelment, for I shall begin my revenge by removing their eyelids."

Zoey and I exchanged a look.

"So cute," we said in unison.

Zoey giggled. "The word 'entrails' always cracks me up when he says it with that Count Chocula accent."

"It is your choice how you hear my voice," he said wearily. "Stop hearing me as Count Chocula and choose something more dignified."

"You know I've tried," I said. "There was that whole day I heard you as Pierce Brosnan, but it didn't stick."

Ribbons puffed up his chest. "Pierce Brosnan is one of the finest actors who has ever lived. He made an excellent Bond."

"You know who Pierce Brosnan is? Ribbons, you cheeky wyvern. You always claim you don't know the names of any celebrities. What's that thing you say? 'The affairs of humans are of no more interest to wyverns than the affairs of an anthill matter to a dolphin.' It's one of my favorite catchphrases."

Ribbons unfurled one wing and made a rude gesture at me with one of his claw-like fingers. Then he tucked in the wing, hopped onto the kitchen island where we ate most meals, and inspected the contents of a large bowl.

After a loud sniff, he asked, "Are these cabbage entrails?"

Zoey said proudly, "I made coleslaw using the food processor Gigi gave us as a housewarming gift."

Ribbons wrapped both wings around the bowl possessively and gave us a malevolent grin, exposing sharp fangs. "My favorite. Cabbage entrails with Dijon and maple syrup dressing. But what are you two going to eat?"

Zoey jumped off her chair and grabbed a second bowl from next to the sink. "I made two bowls, so you get your own bowl, all to yourself."

"Like popcorn night," he said, sounding downright touched by my daughter's thoughtfulness.

Boa howled at my feet and pawed at my leg, as if to say, *What about me? Is there a special bowl for me?*

Boa presumably didn't speak or understand English—she was a regular cat as far as we all knew—but her timing could be eerie.

"There's a bowl of you-know-what for you," I said to her adorable whiskered face.

I looked up at my daughter, who was already putting Boa's special dinner in the microwave for the optimal amount of warming—thirteen seconds. The thing about heating cat food was you always knew it was warmed to the right temperature when the smell made you gag. It wasn't as noxious as Frank's anchovy breath, but it came close.

Zoey set the bowl on Boa's floor place mat. "Here's your you-know-what, Boa." She tapped the side of the bowl, and the cat trotted over, white tail in the air like a flag pole.

My daughter and I avoided saying the specific brand name of the cat food because it made Boa go crazy. And also because it was a really stupid name.

We finished getting the human food ready, and sat for dinner. The conversation flitted between genies and sprites, Zoey's father, and my boss.

"You both have learned many secrets in a short period of time," Ribbons observed as we reached the end of the meal. "Now you know what weaknesses your foes have. You can use this knowledge against them in times of battle."

"Kathy's my boss, not my foe," I said.

"She is your *work foe*," he said.

"He's not entirely wrong, Mom," Zoey said. "You do complain about some of the things she makes you do. And her rules."

"She can be unreasonable at times. I mean, she actually wanted me and Frank to throw out our Cynical Librarian Bingo cards, and I was *so close* to getting five in a row."

"Sprites have many weaknesses," Ribbons said sagely. "They are agitated by changes in routine, and by underlings not following their rules. Also, they have a powerful addiction to popular food-borne toxins such as those found in commercial snack products."

"Addiction to snacks? That sounds like a lot of regular people," Zoey said. "Are you sure it's specific to sprites?"

"Do not question my wisdom," he said tersely, shreds of coleslaw escaping his mouth. As much as the pint-sized creature enjoyed salad, it was difficult for him to eat, due to his teeth being designed for shredding rather than chewing.

"What about genies?" I asked. "What are their weaknesses?"

"As you know, they can be transformed into their gas and liquid essence—"

"He means melted down," I cut in, for Zoey's benefit. I explained further. "Archer's sister, who I suppose was technically your aunt, was killed with a poison made from red wyvern venom." I looked over at our resident wyvern.

"It's a big mystery how someone got red wyvern venom, seeing as how they're extinct, but we'll have to take Ribbons' word for it that he hasn't seen any red wyverns around in millennia."

"So tragic," Ribbons said. "Completely extinct."

A likely story.

I set down my utensils and folded my hands on my lap for a somber moment. "Zoey, I'm sorry for the loss of your aunt or whatever she was."

"She was just a spooky old lady who cut my hair one time."

"In any case, I am sorry."

"Don't be. That old kook was building a machine to wipe people's brains," Zoey said. "Don't take this the wrong way, but I'm glad she's gone. She was a bad influence on my father."

I felt my eyebrows raise. "Is that what he told you last night?"

She stared down at her plate. "We didn't talk for very long. He was bleeding pretty bad from the puncture wounds he got when your boyfriend tried to eat him."

"Bentley apologized for that." I didn't correct her on the point about the reanimated detective not being my boyfriend. "He only attacked because he thought Archer was here to hurt us."

Zoey shook her head. "He didn't think that. He wasn't thinking at all. He just reacted."

"Reacting is a form of thinking. Sort of. Okay. Not really."

Zoey pushed her chair back and stood. "Do you mind if I do the dishes later? I'd like to be excused to my room."

"Are you mad at me?"

She groaned. "Not everything is about you, Mom."

I started to say something, but Ribbons cut me off with a private message. "Let it go, Zed."

I looked over at the wyvern, who was licking his coleslaw bowl with his long, purple tongue. *Let it go, Zed?* For someone who claimed to not care about human affairs, the wyvern could be quite the family counselor when needed.

"Don't worry about the dishes," I said softly. "I'll clean up."

She turned to leave, still not meeting my gaze.

"I love you," I called after her.

She left, and I listened to her light footfalls on the stairs, followed by Boa's even lighter hops after her. The only thing Boa loved more than a bowl of lightly nuked you-know-what was being in the same room as her favorite person.

I wondered if I should follow them up to Zoey's room and make things better.

Or worse.

"Give her space, Zed," the wyvern spoke in my head. "Even the strongest need some solitude."

And, right on cue, he left the kitchen to go spread wisdom and cause trouble elsewhere.

The wyvern did have a point.

Even the strongest needed solitude.

But they also needed each other.

I picked up my phone and scrolled through my contacts, to the letter C.

All three of the triplets were there: Charlize, Chessa, and Chloe.

I noted with amusement that their names all started with the same two letters, yet were pronounced differently. The English language was not without its quirks. I'd always been good at spelling, but even I had to look up a few words, such as Caesar, as in Caesar salad. I also had a funny urge to spell the word dilemma with a letter N, as in *dilemna*. I couldn't explain it, but that word in particular felt like it should have been spelled that other way.

I wondered if I was living in an alternate timeline, and there was another Zara Riddle, in another universe, where everything was exactly the same, except dilemma was spelled differently.

I send a text message to my gorgon friend, Charlize: *Have you ever thought the word dilemma should be spelled differently?*

She wrote back: *Yes! Dilemna with an N. You're not the only one!*

I smiled as I replied: *You totally get me. I like you. What are you doing?*

Charlize: *Hanging out with the girls for a late dinner. We have five bottles of wine for three of us. Do you think that's enough?*

Me: *Probably not.*

Charlize: *Chloe's still breastfeeding, so she'll only have a sip.*

Me: *You might be okay then.*

Charlize: *If not, there's always tequila. You should come join us! We're in Chessa's cottage, behind Chloe's house. Just the girls. You could sleep over again.*

Me, struggling to come up with an excuse: *I have to be at work bright and early in the morning, so I'll have to pass.*

Charlize: *You're not still worried about Chessa, are you? You big chicken. Relax! Her bark is worse than her bite.*

I'd rather not find out, I thought, and I politely declined.

We sent messages back and forth for a while, chatting about life and making silly in-jokes. Then she had to sign off and interact with her sisters, so I wished her a fun evening without me.

Then I cleaned up the kitchen.

I resisted the urge to go upstairs and bug my teenager. Instead of causing more trouble, I retired downstairs to the basement to do some reading.

With nothing specific in mind, I flipped open a magic book at random and found the story of the Four Eves. I recognized it as the same tale I'd been told by Morganna Faire, albeit in more formal language.

I read about the four sister-wives who'd shared the original man, Adam. In one part of the story, the four women, Quenya, Mahra, Dinara, and Amora, bickered over who drank all the honey wine. It had been Amora, the lover. The text didn't come right out and say it, but drinking all the honey wine was such an Amora thing to do.

As I turned the pages and read more tales about the Four Eves, I kept thinking about Charlize and her sisters. At that moment, they were gathered in Chessa's chic white living room, inside her chic white cottage. The woman's cottage stayed perfectly chic and white because she stayed at the Moore house most of the time.

I wondered if the sisters were getting along tonight, or if the inevitable bickering had started up.

CHAPTER 3

THE TRIPLETS

COTTAGE OF CHESSA WAKEFUL

Across town from the Riddle house, in a chic white cottage, three blonde sisters gathered in a chic white living room.

"Use a coaster," said the owner of the cottage, Chessa Wakeful. She was the fairest of the three. Her wavy platinum blonde hair was practically white, and her pale skin was luminous. She was the oldest of the triplets by one hour. Family legend had it she emerged from her mother's womb, stood up on the birthing table, and reached in to help haul her sisters out by the hand.*

*It should be noted that family legends in the Wakeful clan were often exaggerated. For example, some people believed that Grandmother Diablo was a time-traveling demon/goddess from another world, and had a brother who could turn himself into a volcano.

While Chessa was elegant and ethereal, like an elf in a Tolkien novel, Chloe was the more mundane of the sisters. She was always trying to figure out the rules—the rules about how to be the best cheerleader, or the best daughter. After high school, she moved away from

Wisteria for a while, but had come back to run a bakery. Naturally, it had to be the best bakery, with the best pastries. Now that she had a baby, she had to be the best mother.

"Coaster," Chessa repeated. "Now, Chloe." There was ancient power in all of Chessa's commands, even the minor ones.

Chloe jerked forward and grabbed a coaster as per her elegant sister's order, but not before shooting an exasperated, she's-doing-it-again look at their other sister, Charlize.

Charlize, however, didn't notice, because she was staring at her phone while chewing her fingernails. As Charlize gnawed away on her short, tattered nails, Chloe felt bile roll up her throat. What a disgusting habit. Charlize was, by far, the least refined of the three. She was like a wild creature who'd been raised by animals and introduced to society too late in adolescence to be properly socialized. At least that was how Chloe saw her.

Charlize had never been terribly concerned about the rules. Unlike Chessa, who considered herself regally above and beyond such earthly things as rules, or Chloe, who was obsessed with them, Charlize only took enough notice of the rules so she could be amused by the ones she was breaking.

Of the three triplets, Charlize had always been the most physical, the one most comfortable in her body. Her body was her friend, her ally. It never gained three pounds after she ate a few ounces of pastries, unlike Chloe's body, which was defying all attempts made by its owner to shed the pregnancy weight.

Charlize and her body danced through life. She dressed her body in clothes that sparkled and moved without restriction, clothes that could keep up with her whims and energy. And she chewed on her nails as though nothing else in the world could be as interesting as herself and her own body.

A moment ticked by. Chloe grew more and more irritated that Charlize was chewing her nails and looking at her phone instead of participating in the sisters' social night. How rude of her! Chloe had made sacrifices to be there, sacrifices that were not being appreciated. To think, she could have been next door, in her large and comfortable house, relaxing and making cookies while Jordan Junior snoozed in his bassinet. He loved being in the kitchen while his mother baked, and Chloe had some new cookie cutters she was dying to use.

Chloe snapped her fingers, trying to get Charlize's attention. When that didn't work, she summoned her powers. Of the three, she was the least powerful, but she could get someone's attention if she wanted to. She narrowed her eyes and shot her rude, nail-munching sister a special look—the kind that would not be ignored.

Charlize yelped as her hand turned to stone. Before she could turn it back to flesh, Chloe grabbed the phone from her hand.

"What's so interesting on here?" Chloe demanded. She tried to read the screen, but it was, like Charlize's hand, currently made of marble.

A few seconds later, when the phone turned back to regular electronics, it requested a lengthy password. Chloe shook the phone accusingly. She didn't need to read the message to know what Charlize had been distracted by. The phone still resonated with a witch energy. A Riddle energy.

Chloe demanded, "Were you complaining to Zara about us again?"

"No," Charlize said guiltily. "I was just checking in with her. She's got a lot going on right now, with Zoey's father back in the picture."

Zoey's father. The genie.

Suddenly, Chloe was back in high school, back with the cheerleading squad, about to dive into some hot gossip.

Just like that, her irritation at her sister about the phone usage and the nail biting melted away.

Chloe sat, leaning forward, and asked, "Do you think they're going to hook up? A genie and a witch would be quite the power couple. Plus, it would be nice for Zoey to have both parents in her life. Children need stability. If I were in Zara's shoes, I would want the father of my child living under my roof with me and my child."

"Zoey's sixteen," Charlize said. "Practically an adult."

"Family is family," Chloe said with an air of smug superiority.

Charlize rolled her eyes, turned sideways in the white armchair, and dangled her legs over the side, teenager-style. "You've had a baby for a couple of months, and now you're the expert on everything."

"Excuse me?" Chloe's voice pitched up. "I think that having a family of my own is precisely what makes me an expert. What exactly are you an expert on? Besides sparkly jumpsuits and not cleaning out your car, like, ever?"

Charlize reacted to the criticism on a gorgon level. The magic snakes that resided between another realm and Charlize's golden curls began to wake up and hiss.

Charlize hissed back at her sister, "Since when doessss it matter what I have inside a car that'ssss one hundred percent *my car* and not yours, sisssssster dearessst?"

Chloe retorted, "Since there wasn't any room for me to safely buckle in Jordan Junior's car seat yesterday!"

Charlize's hair snakes settled down. "You should have thought about that before you asked me to drive you all over town running your stupid errands."

Now Chloe's hair snakes woke up. They twined around each other, still short-tempered from her haircut.

"Errands? We were spending quality time together," Chloe said. "I thought that was what you wanted! Besides the trouble with the car seat, we had a lovely day. You have to admit I was extremely patient when you tried on all those weird outer-space jumpsuits at that store you like."

"Patient?" Charlize snorted. Three hair snakes snorted as well. "You call that patient? You paced outside of the dressing room the whole time, telling me to hurry up."

"I wasn't pacing. I was walking. To calm the baby. And then I politely asked how long you thought you might be."

"I was trying on clothes, sisssster dearessssst. I was only taking the normal amount of time a person takes to try on clothes. I'm not like you, when you're looking at cookie cutters. Now, that's something that could take hours." She tossed a smug look at Chloe. "You'll notice I've started packing a lunch and bottled water whenever you drag me to the bakery supply store."

Chessa, who'd been quiet for a moment, giggled and joined in. "She's right," Chessa said to Chloe. "You do take forever at your favorite baking stores. And, as for your obsession with cookie cutters, it may be time for an intervention." Her pale, ocean-blue eyes twinkled.

Chloe pointed at Chessa, finger wagging accusingly. "Don't you dare take *her* side. Not now! Not when I'm barely hanging onto my sanity by a thread! Not when I'm getting by on three hours of sleep a night!"

Chessa smiled knowingly—like always—as she picked up the bottle of wine and poured some into a clean wine glass. She handed it to the new mother.

"Drink this," Chessa said with gentle authority. "Junior is already sleeping, and I know you won't have to feed him again for hours. It'll be fine."

Chloe narrowed her eyes at Chessa but accepted the wine anyway. She took a sip, then another, and relaxed back into the sofa.

Chloe snuck another she's-doing-it-again look over at Charlize, who caught it that time, and understood.

Charlize understood how much Chloe hated it when Chessa gave her "permission" about anything regarding the baby. The infant was Chloe's, born from her womb, yet the egg had come from Chessa. That meant, at least to someone as sensitive to rules and criticism as Chloe, that everything Chessa said about the baby had a double meaning. "That should be fine for the baby," actually meant, "That should be fine for *my* baby, who is with you on loan, for now, until such time as I decide to reclaim him for myself, the way I did with young men who struck my fancy when we were growing up."

Charlize offered no comment on the giving of permission. It was between the other two.

Charlize leaned over the mirrored coffee table, grabbed her phone back, and stuffed it into the chest pocket of her favorite silver jumpsuit. She refilled her own wine glass, and settled back into the chair.

Charlize smiled as she looked at her two sisters. A warmth went through her entire body, and it wasn't just from the wine. This evening was going so nicely! She'd expected her sisters would be in an argumentative mood, but things were going much better than usual.

After a few minutes of comfortable silence, in which all three gazed at the television, which was tuned to a baking channel but muted, the fairest and most powerful broke the silence.

"What do you think about moving?" Chessa asked.

Chloe's forehead furrowed. "You mean into the kitchen?"

"She means away, dummy," Charlize said. "You really need to get more sleep. Why don't you just nap when the baby's sleeping?"

Chloe's face reddened. Her short-bodied snakes writhed. "Why don't I jump across this table and just—"

"Calm down!" Chessa raised one fair hand and flashed her power through the room.

Both sisters fell silent and froze. When they moved, it was only enough to sip their wine. Calmly.

"This is exactly why I can't move away," Chessa said, sounding exasperated. "The two of you would kill each other without me around to calm you down."

The other two spoke at the same time, sharing dissenting opinions.

"You can't move away," Charlize said.

"It might be good for you," Chloe said.

Charlize narrowed her eyes at Chloe. Of course Chloe wanted Chessa to go away. That would leave her to raise Junior without any interference or the passive-aggressive giving of permission.

Chloe narrowed her eyes at Charlize. Of course Charlize wanted Chessa to stay. Chessa always took Charlize's side in the big fights.

"This town has so many painful memories for me," Chessa said. Her voice was light, ethereal, but almost weak. She spoke with none of her usual power. The other two took notice and listened quietly.

Chessa went on. "When I see people who know about what happened, I can't stop their thoughts from flooding into me. They're all so curious, their minds prying at mine, clawing to get inside me, desperate to know what happened." Her ocean-blue eyes glistened. "What is it about the worst things imaginable that makes complete strangers want to know every detail?" She shook her head and went on. "But the worst has got to be the pity. I hear them thinking, 'Oh, you poor thing. You poor, poor thing.'" Her eyes deepened in color, and her voice took on an edge. "As if I am a *thing*. As if I am some creature, some pathetic, helpless creature, to be pitied." She finished with a low, gravelly roar. "As if I am some poor, poor thing."

The sisters said nothing.

Chessa refilled her wine glass and tossed it back in one gulp.

"But I can't exactly pick up and move," she said, her tone more conversational. "I wouldn't dream of going anywhere without my darling Chet. But, like it or not, he comes with the other two. Grampa Don's determined to stay in that house until he dies, and with the way he's going, it doesn't look like that's going to happen time soon. His mind is repairing itself, and his memories are coming back. And then there's..." She gripped the name in her mouth before releasing it. "Corvin."

Chloe let out a nervous giggle. "And then there's Corvin," she said. She was doing everything right, by the rules, to make sure her precious Jordan Junior didn't turn out strange, like Corvin.

"Shut up," Charlize warned her sister. "It's not funny."

"Yes, it is." Chloe finished her wine and shook the last drops into her mouth. She hiccuped, then said, "It's literally the funniest thing that has ever happened to anyone in our family. Chet went out one day to pick up a stray dog, and he came home with Corvin." She giggled again. "Surprise! Your new dog is a hellhound. Oh, and it's also a weird little boy. Congratulations. You've got an insta-family."

"Shut up," Charlize said again. "Corvin's just a kid. He's not a joke. He's a kid who wants to be loved, just like any kid. Why don't you practice some of those maternal instincts you have on him instead of treating him like he's some stray dog?"

"You shut up," Chloe shot back. "I can find it funny if I want to. It's my business."

"It's not your business," Chessa growled. The decorative items on the fireplace chattered. Everything in the room was shaking from Chessa's power.

The other two both shut up.

"Forget I mentioned anything," Chessa said, her voice light again. "As long as Corvin is in our lives, we can't move away. I know my darling Chet would do anything to make me happy, but I can't ask him to uproot his father and his child just because I can't handle a few intrusive questions from the ignorant." She straightened her back, taking on a regal air. "I'll have to find another way."

The timer on the oven dinged.

The nachos were ready.

All three jumped up and ran for the kitchen, bumping into each other and wrestling to be the first through the doorway. One triplet got the giggles, and it became contagious, just as it had in the old days. All three became delightfully and happily stuck in the doorway, giggling as they struggled and wrestled against each other.

And, just like that, they were sisters again. Although they bickered, it was only because what ran between them mattered, for they were the whole world to each other.

Eventually, the three broke free of the doorway and gathered around the hot nachos at the kitchen table. They ate and laughed over shared memories of their greatest fights. Oh, the wars that had been waged over things that had seemed so important at the time, but that, in hindsight, didn't matter at all.

CHAPTER 4

ZARA RIDDLE
WISTERIA PUBLIC LIBRARY
TUESDAY

I picked up another cake Tuesday morning, and everyone at the library enjoyed it as much as they enjoyed the tired jokes about birthday candles, and special permits, and fire alarms.

At lunch time, Frank and I printed out fresh Cynical Librarian Bingo cards and started our game again.

Kathy had banned the game previously, but she'd been in a much better mood since sharing her supernatural secret, so Frank and I decided take our chances.

By the end of Tuesday, Frank had one square filled: patron makes a "check out" pun.

I had two squares: patron mentions it won't be long before the internet puts libraries "out of business," and patron exclaims that librarian jobs must be easy because all we do is "sit around reading books."

* * *

WEDNESDAY

I set up a new account for a young woman named Persephone Rose. With a name that unique, I knew she had to be the same Persephone Rose who worked at the Wisteria Police Department and had a girlish crush on Detective Theodore Bentley.

She had to be at least twenty-five, to be working for the WPD, but her long, dark hair and thick bangs made her look like a young girl my daughter's age. Peering out from under the bangs were big, brown, sad-looking eyes that drooped down at the corners. She had a round face, pale skin, and rosy cheeks.

A real English Rose, I thought. How appropriate for someone with the last name of Rose.

As I handed over her new library card, she asked, "Are you, um, Zara Riddle?"

"All day, every day."

"I think you might be friends with a man I work with. Theo Bentley."

"You mean Teddy?" I smiled like the shark on the cover of Barracuda Magazine. Her use of the shortened version of his first name didn't sit well with me, so I'd one-upped her by calling him Teddy, which I never did. "You could say we're friends. Why do you ask?"

"Do you..." She trailed off and fidgeted with her thick lashes. They were false eyelashes, detaching slightly as she tugged on them.

I glanced over at my pink-haired, narrow-jawed coworker. Frank was watching the interaction with great interest while disinfecting a stack of hardcover books that a patron with a bad summer cold had just returned.

I turned back to Persephone Rose and asked, "Do I *what*?" My tone was snappier than intended, and she took two steps back from the counter.

"Nothing," she squeaked.

I held out my hands for the books she was clutching to her chest.

She slowly came back to the counter and handed me the books she wanted to check out.

I completed the transaction. It took me three tries to hit the right keystrokes.

Nothing, she'd said. Was it really nothing? By the way she was fidgeting with both her bangs and her false eyelashes at the same time, I guessed she hadn't stopped by the library for "nothing."

"What did you want to ask me?" I prompted, deliberately making my tone sweet. "Is it something about Detective Bentley?"

The roses on her cheeks deepened to scarlet. "I don't know. He seems different lately."

Being dead will do that to a person.

"I hadn't noticed," I lied. "Maybe you didn't know him that well in the first place."

She blinked those big, droopy brown eyes twice. "Did you two, um, break up or something?"

"No," I answered honestly. I didn't clarify that the reason we hadn't broken up was because we hadn't been dating.

She bit her lower lip. "Good to know." She swayed from side to side girlishly.

"Is there anything else I can help you with, Ms. Rose?"

She shook her head and transferred the books into her canvas book bag. She'd borrowed some thriller paperbacks as well as a hardcover, all seemingly random selections from the New Arrivals table.

She thanked me, and left without another word.

I glanced over at Frank, who said only, "Meow."

I thumbed my chest. "Me? Are you implying I was catty just now?"

"Meow," he repeated. "Does kitty want a saucer of milk?"

"Mind your own business." I waved at him to get busy. "You worry about removing all the sneeze residue from those books, Mr. Wonder."

"Oh, it's more than just sneezes." Frank tapped a second pile of books. "These ones came in courtesy of a sweaty gentleman in a tank top who was holding them under his arm. He must have walked a long way, because every single one of them reeks of armpit."

"Isn't that one of your bingo squares?"

He beamed. "It sure is. Armpit books. Bottom-right corner." He waved me over. "Come here. Smell."

"I will do no such thing."

"You know you want to."

"Every single book reeks of armpit? I suspect you are exaggerating, Mr. Wonder."

"Maybe I am. Maybe I'm not. Come over here and smell these books. You know you want to."

I couldn't resist his charms and my own curiosity. An acrid, musky smell hit my nostrils. He'd been right.

We looked at each other and sighed in unison.

"We are so lucky to be librarians," I said.

He nodded. "All those degrees are really paying off." He glanced around to make sure nobody was reading a book within earshot of us, then asked, "Who was that big-eyed girl with the bangs who got your kitty-hackles up?"

"Her name is Persephone Rose, and she works with Detective Bentley." I smirked. "She says he's been acting *different* lately."

Frank snorted. "Being dead will do that to a person."

I shushed him, because he'd been getting loud. I could have cast a sound bubble, but I tried hard not to cast spells at work, tempting though it was. I could have deodorized the armpit books in five seconds flat using a spell, but I'd promised myself I wouldn't. Also, the spell did create a visible stench cloud that floated six inches off the floor and took hours to dissipate.

In a quieter voice, Frank asked, "Do you think she's more than just a coworker?"

I put on my old-fashioned Southern accent. "Whatever do you mean, Frank Wonder?"

He blinked rapidly. "Like how you and I have been smitten with each other since the day we met?"

"She might love him, like I love you, but it's a puppy sort of love. Their bond can't possibly be as strong as ours," I said with a straight face.

His expression grew serious. "How different is he, exactly? How does becoming a vampire affect a person?"

I threw my hands in the air. "How should I know? I barely saw him on Sunday before he tried to eat Zoey's father." I held one finger in the air. "But he did seem to have more of a sense of humor. Oh, and his eyes weren't gray anymore. They were silver."

I turned to get back to work, but Frank stopped me.

"Hang on. I want to try something." He held up a popular graphic novel featuring a tough but beautiful blonde who reminded me of the gorgon triplets. "What's this girl's name?"

"Buffy."

"Buffy the... ?"

"Buffy the, uh, Slayer."

"It's Buffy the Vampire Slayer." Frank shook his head. "You still can't say *vampire*, can you?"

"Apparently not."

"You should get your new beau to bite you, or put you in a thrall, or whatever it is they do. See if he can reverse what your mother did."

"Right," I scoffed. "I'll get right on that. *Please, Bentley, bite my neck for scientific reasons.*" I tugged down the collar of my blouse, exposing my neck.

Frank's eyes flashed with mischief. "Or for personal reasons."

I rolled my eyes and got back to work.

* * *

THURSDAY

Mid-day, I got scolded by Kathy for constantly checking my phone.

She pushed her glasses up her sharp, narrow nose, which still looked owlish to me even though she'd been revealed as a sprite, not an owl shifter, and said, "I expect this sort of obsessive phone-checking behavior from the teenaged pages, but not from my librarians."

I nodded for her to follow me into the break room.

Once we were alone, I explained to her my very good reason for obsessive phone checking. My daughter, who was still on summer break from school, was having lunch with her father, the genie. I relayed to Kathy how I was feeling every kind of emotion imaginable, all at once. I was happy she was getting the gift of another parent, but fearful it would be a crushing disappointment. I was curious about what information she would find out about genies, and Archer's past, but also angry they hadn't invited me along. I could have taken my lunch break early and met up with them, if anyone had asked.

"You're a good mom," Kathy said after I'd poured my heart out.

"Well, duh," I said, then, quickly, "I mean, thanks."

"Does your phone vibrate when you get a new text message?"

"Yes."

"Then leave it in your pocket. Taking it out and looking at the screen isn't going to make your daughter report back any sooner."

"You say that, but can either of us, knowing what we know about magic, really say for sure that looking at my phone *doesn't* have some effect on her messaging me?"

One of Kathy's golden-brown eyes twitched behind the round lens of her glasses. "What do you mean?"

"There's a witch I know who has a psychic ability about phones. She can sense when someone's going to call her, a few minutes before they do."

"Is it your aunt, Zinnia?"

Oops. I only knew a handful of witches in town—three, to be precise. Aunt Zinnia, Dreamland Coffee owner Maisy Nix, and her niece, Fatima Nix. Kathy knew I was a new witch, so she must have known my witch social circle wasn't wide. I hadn't even been invited to join a coven. This was exactly why supernatural people didn't gossip about powers.

"Just a witch I know," I said breezily.

"Zinnia and I have been friends for years. You have my permission to reveal to her my secret. You can make official introductions when you have hers."

"Good." *Because I probably would have told my aunt regardless.*

Kathy peered up at me, her lips pursed. "But you were going to tell her anyway, weren't you?"

I pursed my lips right back at the head librarian. Were sprites mind readers? *Kathy, are you reading my mind?*

She cocked her head to the side. "Why are you making that face?" Kathy asked. "Did your phone buzz?"

If she was a mind reader, she was an equally good bluffer.

"No, but I should probably check it, just in case it buzzed while we were talking and I missed it."

She pointed to the charging station, where we kept cords and chargers for every type of phone. "Check it one more time, then leave it in your pocket or keep it back here at the charging station."

"Yes, boss."

As she walked away, the screen lit up with a new message from Zoey: *Lunch with Mr. Caine is going well. The waitresses thought I was his date! He introduced me as his daughter, and now they are all flirting with him like crazy. One of them offered to be my new stepmom.*

I typed out a few choice words then erased them.

I was so full of confusing mixed emotions that a full minute passed and I hadn't been able to compose a response.

A second message came through: *I'm going to put my phone away now. I just wanted to let you know everything is fine and you can stop checking your phone obsessively. Have a great day at the library! Boost those circulation numbers!*

CHAPTER 5

FRIDAY

As I shelved books about family relationships, I thought about Zoey's relationship with her father, whom she referred to as Mr. Caine. She would probably come up with a goofy nickname for him soon enough, but he was Mr. Caine for now.

In addition to having lunch together, Zoey had spoken to her father, the genie, on the phone a few times.

According to Zoey, his powers were pretty much what we'd known about. He had the ability to bend and manipulate time, but only in small pockets.

Other than that, the genie who'd sired her was, in Zoey's words, "basically normal." She'd gone on to say that despite his age, he was immature. His body was the same age as Chet Moore's—thirty-seven—but he acted like someone thirty-seven going on sixteen. He seemed to Zoey less like the fathers of her friends and more like the teenaged boys she went to school with. This was mostly due to his interest in massive multiplayer online video games. At their lunch meeting, he'd talked about his gaming system and playing strategies "pretty much non-stop." He'd also acquired the phone numbers of not one but two waitresses.

"Two waitresses," I muttered to myself as I shelved books about self-improvement.

"Two waitresses," I huffed as I shelved books about knitting, and gardening, and origami.

"Two waitresses," I snorted as I was logging into the computer system to help a patron at the self-checkout.

I probably would have thought about Archer Caine getting the phone numbers of waitresses for my entire shift, except I was finally startled out of my thoughts by the name on the self-checkout patron's library card: Jasmine Pressman.

Pressman! Alarm bells clanged in my head.

She was the ex-wife of Perry Pressman, and the mother of Josephine Pressman. Both of them were now deceased, thanks to their involvement with Archer Caine and his genie sibling. Before he was getting phone numbers from multiple waitresses, he'd been involved in dealings that lead to several deaths.

I turned toward the woman at the self-checkout slowly. "Jasmine Pressman?" I had spoken to her on the phone once before, but we'd never met—that I knew of. Until now.

"Yes," she said cheerfully. "That's my card, all right. Would you like to see my ID to make sure it's me? You probably do. Here. I'll grab my driver's license for you." She rummaged in her purse, humming a happy tune under her breath, then produced her driver's license. "That's me. I know it says Jasmine Carter on the license, but it's actually Carter-Pressman, with a hyphen. Or at least it is now. After my divorce, I went back to my maiden name, but then," she paused to inhale rapidly, "earlier this year, after my ex-husband and my daughter both passed away unexpectedly, I decided to add the Pressman back on to keep them alive, so to speak. To keep them with me."

I looked her in the eyes and struggled for an appropriate response. I couldn't let her know what I knew, but I wanted to say something.

"I'm sorry for your loss," I said. There was genuine sadness in my voice, courtesy of my memories of her loved ones.

Jasmine Carter-Pressman, however, only shrugged.

"That's how things go," she said, smiling and being quite chipper for someone who'd suffered such terrible losses so recently. Was it medication? Magic? Or was she simply one of those remarkably resilient people?

She was a petite woman, much shorter than her daughter. She had big eyes, olive skin, and acne-scarred cheeks. Her hair was long and dark, and very sparse. She was practically bald at her temples. Her makeup was heavy and her eye shadow was a jarring shade of turquoise that matched the turquoise in her earrings and necklace.

I caught myself staring, and quickly looked down at the driver's license in her hand.

She followed my gaze down, and her smile broke as she frowned at her driver's license. "Look at that silly photo of me," she said, then immediately returned to smiling again. "Such a shame anyone checking my license has to see this dreary old mug looking up at them, don't you think? Did you know they don't let you smile? It's a security thing, they say. It's hooey, if you ask me. Nobody looks like themselves in a photo if they're not smiling. They might as well ask us ladies to remove our makeup, too! What are they thinking over there at City Hall, at the DMV?" She waved the driver's license card between us, then stuck it into my hand. "Horrible, isn't it? Well, there you go, now you've seen it. I suppose it serves me right for not coming in here more regularly!"

I passed back her card and hoped she didn't notice the tremble in my hand. I'd been pretty tough, emotionally and physically, even before my witch powers kicked in, and I was even tougher now, but I wasn't made of stone! My emotions caught me off guard sometimes. My hand trembled because I'd had the spirit of the woman's ex-husband inside me, as well as that of her daughter. I'd been a vessel for their personalities, as well as their memories. I'd experienced their most precious moments as vividly as my own.

Even after my successful rezoning spell, fragments of these experiences were around, like how dust stays around, no matter how well you vacuum. Standing next to this woman who felt like a wife and also a mother threw me for a loop. I didn't know her, yet I had all these feelings for her. I had genuine love for her.

"You should come in more regularly," I said, smiling my love at her. "To the library, that is. We'd love to see you."

She smiled back at me, though it was hard to see her face due to the tears welling in my eyes.

"Sweetheart, you look like you could use a hug," she said, and then she had her arms around me.

Mom, I thought, even though she wasn't my mother. I hugged her tightly, then I finally overrode the residual feelings and took a respectful step back.

Jasmine looked me up and down. "You must be going through something difficult right now," she said.

I had to laugh. "You could say that." When was I not going through something difficult? Really, when was anyone?

"You should come to a meeting sometime." She dug around in her purse. "Darn. I don't have any of the fliers, but we do meet once at week at the community center. It's a self-help group for people dealing with life changes." She glanced up and beamed at me. "We don't say *loss*. We say *life changes*."

"That sounds like a wonderful group." It did sound like a wonderful group.

She took my hand and squeezed it. "You're welcome to drop in any time. We call ourselves The Ducklings." She tilted her head back and laughed. "That's just a joke.

We're actually called The Awakenlings, but that's kind of a mouthful, so some of us call ourselves The Ducklings."

"The Awakenlings," I said, nodding. "Or the Ducklings. I'll keep that in mind."

* * *

I was ready for the weekend.

At the end of Friday, before we went home, Frank and I put on a magic show for Kathy to demonstrate some of our powers.

While our little performance of witch and flamingo tricks was good for a few laughs, the whole thing also felt cheap. As though I'd sold myself out, artistically.

I looked forward to some time away from the library, away from Kathy's expectations that everything was different now, and that the three of us would share everything with each other.

I liked Kathy, and I respected her, but she wasn't like Frank. I didn't want to talk to her about my confusing feelings or petty jealousies.

I told myself it wasn't because she was a sprite. I had nothing against sprites, no matter how long and weird their tongues were. My discomfort was only due to the fact the woman was my boss. No matter how many times she insisted that the library's patrons were our only true bosses, we all knew it wasn't true. The patrons had never scolded me for looking at my phone. I couldn't stop feeling self-conscious whenever Kathy was looking over my shoulder, supervising. I didn't want her doing the same with my personal life.

After I left the library, I picked up some Thai takeout from Kin Khao on my way home.

As I walked up the front steps of my house, I heard a dog barking. The sound seemed to be coming from inside a house. My house.

I opened the front door and listened. My senses tingled. Not my witch senses, but my regular mom ones.

The dog barked again. It was almost certainly a dog, though Zoey did make some similar yips when she was in fox form, especially if Boa and Ribbons were successful at getting her riled up.

"Zoey?" I called up the stairs.

There was a scuffling sound from the vicinity of my daughter's bedroom.

I dropped the takeout bags and practically flew up the stairs. I banged open the bedroom door and found four creatures in a standoff, growling, glaring, hissing, and breathing fire.

They were, respectively, an enormous black dog, a red fox, a white cat, and a wyvern.

I demanded, as any mother would, "What the hell is going on in here?"

The fox shifted back into the human form of my daughter. She gave me a sheepish look. "We didn't hear you come in," she said.

"And who, exactly, is *we*?" I widened my eyes and nodded at the dog.

Zoey settled onto the edge of her bed and said to the dog, "You can change back now. I promise you won't get in trouble for the mess."

The mess?

I surveyed the room. There was a pile of dirt, greenery, and broken pottery in one corner. The cute potted plant that had been growing on Zoey's windowsill was in bad shape. Next to it was the lamp Aunt Zinnia had given us for a housewarming gift. Alas, the flowered monstrosity had survived the fall and was perfectly intact. Shame.

"Change back," Zoey urged the newcomer.

The large dog gave me a guilty look, and then shifted into the form of a human. Specifically, the human form of a ten-year-old boy.

"Corvin Moore," I said.

He looked up at me slowly, his dark green eyes as big as ever. "You were a ghost," he said in a monotone, staring at me unwaveringly in that creepy way of his. "I saw you."

Zoey lurched forward and punched him on the arm. "Stop saying that, you little jerk. She might be a witch, but she's not a ghost."

Corvin shifted back into dog form and started barking at her. The barks were so loud, I had to clap both hands over my ears.

Zoey shifted into fox form again, and chased him out of the room and down the stairs. Boa ran after them, fluffy white tail in the air, looking anything but frightened.

I turned to Ribbons, who'd remained in the room. He looked guilty, but then again, he always looked guilty. It was the beady eyes.

"I didn't start it," he said.

"What happened in here?"

"Is it not obvious?" He nodded his scaled head toward the pile of dirt and broken ceramics. "The hellhound knocked over that plant with his big tail. Unlike some of us, he has no control over his tail."

I put my hands on my hips. "Corvin may be a bucket full of strange, but calling him a hellhound seems cruel."

"That is what he is, Zed."

"What?"

"His kind guards the gates between worlds. That is why he was able to see you in spirit form."

Corvin wasn't a wolf shifter? Or even a huge raven, as I'd suspected, based on his name? I connected a few dots. "Does that mean Chet Moore is also a hellhound? He looked like a regular wolf to me."

"The boy is adopted," Ribbons said.

"Adopted," I said. "Huh."

"Haven't you noticed how the wolf shifter always seems confused whenever you refer to Corvin as his son?"

My hands flew to the sides of my face as I gasped. "I thought that was out of embarrassment for the kid's weirdness." I gasped again. "Now that you mention it, the hellhound thing makes a lot of sense." I let go of my face, crossed my arms, and glowered at the wyvern. "It would have been a nice family courtesy if either you or Zoey had mentioned to me that our next-door neighbor is the adoptive father of a hellhound."

Ribbons raised his brow ridge. "I would be happy to trade information with you, Zed, if you brought me something besides your tedious stories about the boring customers at your bookstore."

"It's a library, not a bookstore, and you know it."

He flipped up his wings. "We must go downstairs immediately."

I jerked toward the door in a maternal panic. "Why? Are they fighting dirty? Do I need to break it up?"

"Let them sort out the pecking order for themselves." Ribbons flew for the doorway, arced through the hallway, and gripped the balustrade to slide down.

"What's the hurry?" I called after him.

"The Thai food is getting cold."

CHAPTER 6

SATURDAY

So the neighbor's kid was a hellhound. Just when I thought I couldn't be surprised, I was. Between Kathy and Corvin, that was two big supernatural secrets revealed in a single week. And, as my aunt always said, secrets revealed were trouble unsealed.

I wondered what trouble would be coming my way.

Whatever fate had in store for me, I didn't want it to happen while I was still wearing my housecoat and slippers.

I cast the usual outfit-locating spell on my closet. I'd been using the spell so regularly, I'd nearly forgotten it was meant for finding pages within books, not clothes in a closet. A modified spell—*home brew*, as the other witches called it—could be dangerous. My spell seemed stable enough, but I suspected that had more to do with my house's own magic than with the syntax of my home brew.

Once, I'd tried the spell on someone else's closet—Frank's—and the casting hadn't gone so well. Instead of spitting out the perfect outfit for Frank to wear for the day, Frank's closet had twitched and emitted ominous noises. Then one of Frank's faux-leather belts had slithered off a shelf, hit the floor, and snaked its way across the room, hissing angrily as it hid under his bed. We eventually coaxed the belt back out again, but the its color had changed from white to a sickly purple-brown that didn't go with any of Frank's pants.

That Saturday morning, my home brew spell worked perfectly, as I expected it would within my own house.

The day's outfit consisted of a dark blue tank top with a star pattern, a gray pencil skirt, and matching kitten heels.

"This seems overly dressy for a lazy Saturday," I said to the closet. I had been expecting a pair of stretchy yoga pants to not do yoga in. The navy top with the gray skirt was so conservative. It looked like something Bentley would approve of.

As I stood there, wondering what the day had in store for me, the closet burped out a pair of earrings.

"Thanks," I said. What else do you say when your closet burps earrings at you?

I shimmied into the pencil skirt and tank top, then tidied the front of my hair with a couple of bobby pins. If I was picking up on the hint from my house correctly, Bentley would want my help on a case today.

The doorbell rang.

"Ding dong," yelled my daughter from downstairs. "I think it's Bentley!"

So much for a lazy Saturday of wearing yoga pants while not doing yoga. Aw, shucks.

* * *

Bentley drove his car, and I sat in the passenger seat. I tried not to stare at him in profile, but I was overwhelmed with curiosity about outward signs of his recent life change. I kept sneaking peeks. His hair was darker—still streaked with gray, but not as much gray as before. His jaw looked wider, more square, and more determined.

Back at my house, he'd explained that the day's assignment was a simple nuisance call. It would take a few minutes for us to deal with, then he'd have the rest of the day off. His silver eyes had twinkled as he'd explained that I might get a kick out of this particular call, which was why he'd invited me along. Also, we could go for lunch afterward and discuss "recent events."

"Nice weather we're having," Bentley commented.

"What did you expect? It's the last weekend in July," I said, feeling a little contrary.

"And no forest fire smoke. We can all breathe easier now. Those light rain showers we had during the week certainly helped the firefighters."

I let out a bark of laughter. "That little spritzing didn't help nearly as much as a couple of witches on broomsticks," I said knowingly.

He broke his focus on the road to give me an eyebrow raise. "Witches on broomsticks," he repeated. "You're pulling my leg."

"Bentley, would I lie to you?" I waved a hand. "Don't answer that. I know I used to pull your leg all the time, but not anymore."

"You used to steal my donuts, too."

"That's all water under the bridge." I held up my hand. "I don't lie to you anymore. I mean, I won't. My word is my bond." The air shimmered as my pledge took hold. "Honestly, Bentley, there were witches helping the fire crew put out those forest fires. They flew around doing controlled burns on the mountainside. I saw a demo, week before last. I went flying. On a broomstick. Just like a real witch!"

"You never told me that."

"We were busy with the Greyson case."

He returned his attention to the road. We turned onto a quiet street, and parked in front of a cute, multi-story house that was similar to my own, except painted a sun-yellowed white instead of Wisconsin Barn Red.

"Speaking of the Greyson case," I said, "did everything get squared away? Did Carrot Greyson and the rest of the family buy the cover story?"

"What do you think?" His tone was prickly. So much for his big life change improving his sense of humor.

"I don't know what to think. That's why I'm asking you, Detective," I said, also prickly.

He turned off the car engine and turned toward me slowly. "I apologize for my brusqueness," he said.

"That's a first," I said.

"We'll have plenty of firsts," he said. "Everything is different now."

"Because we're brother and sister, sort of? Your maker is my mother. Your head is all clear now, right? You remember Zirconia Riddle?"

A slow smile spread across his lips. "My head is perfectly clear. Did Zirconia tell you why she wanted to spend so much time with me?" He waggled his dark eyebrows.

"Ew." I held up my hand. "Gross. No. And I do not want to hear about any of the weird sex stuff you did with my mom."

Patiently, he said, "The reason she wanted to spend time with me was to program me to protect you, Zara. She knew that if you stayed in Wisteria, you would be getting into all sorts of trouble, and she wanted you to have a guardian." He glanced out the car window at the white house, then back at me. "She made me your bodyguard."

I snorted. "Some bodyguard you are."

"Are you snorting in reference to the incident in the cafeteria? Do you not recall the fact that I did save your life?"

"I remember, all right. But I wouldn't have been in danger in the first place if you hadn't dragged me into the Greyson investigation."

His silver eyes twinkled. "Nobody's perfect."

I tore my gaze away from his handsome face, and looked at the white house. My cheeks were hot and getting hotter now that the car's air conditioning was off. "We should probably deal with this nuisance call," I said flatly.

My door opened from the outside. Bentley was holding it open, his other hand extended to help me step out.

I whipped my head back to the driver's side seat. Were there two of him? No. Just one very speedy Bentley. I hadn't even heard him move.

Maybe he was right.

Maybe everything would be different now.

CHAPTER 7

RESIDENCE OF TEMPERANCE KRINKLE

Our nuisance call was a sweet old widow named Temperance Krinkle. She plied us with cookies and tea, and assured us she wasn't wasting our time, even though it was becoming more clear by the minute that she definitely was. At least being plied with cookies and tea wasn't a bad way to waste some time.

Temperance Krinkle was ninety-three, with a round face, rosy cheeks, and a mass of curly white hair. The lenses on her eyeglasses were different prescriptions, which gave the illusion that one of her green eyes was twice the size of the other. She spoke with a charming English accent, and while she'd lived in Wisteria for eighty years, she spoke of life in her old village with wistful clarity. Sometimes she imagined an alternate life for herself, she said, one in which her mother's psychic premonitions hadn't inspired the family to emigrate overseas before the start of World War II.

Temperance's mother, Matilda, was always drawing and scribbling in journals like a woman possessed. When the Spanish Civil War began in 1936, Matilda declared that it was a sign; one of her prophecies was coming true. It was time for the family to make a new home in a better place. It took a few years to make arrangements, and then they left England, hoping to make a fresh start in a town that was young in comparison to their old village.

I became so caught up in the woman's story, I barely remembered to eat my gingersnaps, which were delicious and homemade. The tea was an herbal blend, which Temperance apologized for, saying she didn't keep caffeinated tea in the house because it was bad for her nerves. The way she talked about black tea made it sound like the mere presence of caffeinated tea bags in the house might keep her up at night. I didn't press for details.

After the woman's oral history reached her early twenties, and the issue of the family business, she excused herself.

Bentley murmured, "She says her mother had psychic premonitions. Do you suppose it's true?"

"They did leave their village just in the nick of time before it was turned to rubble during the Blitz. If you consider three years *just in the nick of time*."

"I'm not sure I *would* consider that the nick of time." He picked up a gingersnap, tapped off the crumbs, then set it back down. "Do you believe in prophecies?"

I took a big breath before answering, because it was a big question. "If prophecies are real, that would mean we don't have free will. And I'd rather believe in free will."

"So, you *choose* not to believe in prophecies?" He raised an eyebrow. "Like how some people choose to believe the earth is flat?"

I blinked rapidly. "Oh, the earth is very flat. Have you not looked around outside? It's flat, flat, flat. Do you know about the wall?"

"Yes," he said dryly. "I'm familiar with the theory that the earth is a flat disc, and Antarctica is an ice wall around the perimeter."

In a serious tone, I replied, "The ice wall keeps the boats from sailing off the edge." I smiled. "Detective, I could carry on this conversation all day. My work at the library brings me into regular contact with *all* the local crackpots. I'm fully up to date on the popular conspiracies. Do you know about Planet X? Of course you don't. Nobody does. Because Planet X doesn't exist." I winked. "That's what NASA wants us to believe."

"Keep going," he said. "This is all quite amusing coming from the mouth of a woman who flies around town on a broomstick."

That was when Temperance Krinkle returned with more cookies and tea.

Bentley leaned back and widened his shoulders in the manner of someone forcefully changing the topic of conversation. "Mrs. Krinkle, are you a world traveler?" He gestured to the artwork on the wall. The large pieces of art were neither paintings nor prints, but glued-together jigsaw puzzles depicting great monuments around the world.

"Not yet, but soon, I should think," the woman said excitedly in her English accent. "There are so *many* places I'd rather like to see." She turned and stroked the nearest puzzle, which showed pyramids, bright and rust-colored against a saturated blue sky. "I expect Egypt shall be first."

While she focused on the puzzle, Bentley and I exchanged a look. *Egypt shall be first?*

The woman was in her nineties. Most people her age were joking about not buying green bananas, and here she was talking about embarking on a world tour? Aside from the physical demands, international travel wasn't cheap. I knew you couldn't judge a book by its cover, but the people I knew who glued jigsaw puzzles together to make art for their walls did not have international travel money.

"Now, about the issue of the store," Temperance Krinkle said, returning to the anecdote she'd been telling. "My sister and I did take over the hardware store when our father passed, as it turned out. However, because there was already another hardware store in Wisteria, we decided to turn ours into a haberdashery. That's an English word, in case you don't know. It refers to the small items used in sewing, such as buttons, zippers, and thread. All of the little, wee things." She held her wrinkled hands up, the palms a half inch apart. "Oh, how we both loved the smallest items, my sister and I. But we also had our disagreements, as sisters do. She felt the new store should be called Wisteria Haberdashery, but I told her people around here wouldn't understand what that meant, and that we should call it Wisteria Notions." She paused, then asked, "Can you imagine what we did to resolve this dilemma?"

Bentley answered flatly, "You put up two different signs over the storefront's two doors, and let people choose."

The old woman gasped. "How did you know?"

Bentley glanced over at me, looking mildly embarrassed, then said, "I have an interest in local history." He'd taken up that interest during the stressful time period after which he'd become suspicious about the strange things happening in Wisteria, but before he had gotten proof he wasn't simply going crazy.

Temperance Krinkle smiled. "If you are, indeed, a local historian, then you already know that my sister and I kept both names for many years, until such a time as we had to close, sadly, due to the changing times. People today no longer need notions, because everything comes fully finished from the store. Such a pity. And then, just when an item such as a garment or a shoe is starting to show some character, rather than repairing it, they throw it away and get a new one that is of even lower quality."

Bentley gave me a look, as if to ask, *Is this exactly as much fun as you hoped it would be?*

I smiled, as if to say, *Yes, this is fun. This woman is like a great historical novel begging to be read.*

The old woman went on. "I also have a bit of an interest in history, Detective. In fact, I've been learning about genealogy." She pointed to an old but still humming laptop that sat charging on the sideboard next to a stack of papers and an old-looking, leather-bound book. "I've recently connected with a distant cousin who lives overseas, in an English village. His name is Cole, and he has the most wonderful ideas about our family tree." She giggled and covered her mouth. "But I shouldn't talk about such things. After all, a family's secrets are kept hidden for a reason."

My gaze lingered on the book, and my fingers twitched. I couldn't read the tiny words on the spine, but I wanted to grab that book and crack it open. Being a librarian wasn't something I could turn off completely on the weekend.

Bentley spoke again, less patiently this time. "Mrs. Krinkle, if it's all right with you, I'd like to discuss the matter about which you called the police department. Over the phone, you said you knew something about a missing person?"

The white-haired woman looked at her watch, then gave us a sweet smile. "That's right. A missing person. She's a woman with two young boys." She pursed her wrinkled lips. "But I'm afraid I don't know her name."

Bentley gave me another look. I gave him a small shrug. It was a nuisance call, all right, but at least the cookies, tea, and conversation had been pleasant enough.

In the silence, Temperance Krinkle reached across the table and stroked one finger across the top of my hand. I was startled, but didn't jerk my hand away. Her fingertip felt dry and smooth, more like a pink eraser than a finger.

She looked straight at me, with her one magnified green eye that looked twice the size of the other, and asked, "Tell me, dear, are you friends with the Gilberts?"

"Sorry," I said, shaking my head. "I don't know any Gilberts."

"Are you sure? They're a very old family who have lived here for many generations. Everyone knows a Gilbert."

"I'm not from around here. I'm new in town, just like Bentley. I got here in March, and I've been busy with work ever since." Busy with work, and magic, and all sorts of things.

"Oh," she said, sounding disappointed. "Then it wasn't you I saw last month—no, back in May, it was—at Queenie Gilbert's memorial. I could have sworn you were there. Not many women have your beautiful fine features and stunning red hair."

I grinned at Bentley. This visit hadn't been a waste of time at all.

The woman murmured, "I could have sworn you were there."

"You must be thinking of Zara's aunt," Bentley said. "The two are what you English folks would call the spitting image of each other. You'd think someone put Zinnia Riddle in a copy machine and made a duplicate."

"A younger duplicate," I said. "Much younger. And more fun."

Temperance Krinkle rubbed her chin, which was covered in a soft-looking white fuzz. "That must be it. My old eyes are not what they used to be." She waved her finger at me. "But I can still spot a stunning woman, and both you and your aunt are very special, indeed."

I fanned my face with my hand. "Why, thank you. Now, as much as I'd love to sit in your charming dining room all day, eating gingersnaps and getting accurate compliments, we should probably get on the case of this missing woman you called about. If she's a mother, her children must be missing her. Is there anything you can tell us that might be helpful? If not her name, then maybe a detailed description? Or the location where she was last seen?"

Mrs. Krinkle pushed her chair back and stood. "The location question is easy," she said. "She was last seen in my attic. I'll take you there now."

She turned and led the way out of the dining room.

Bentley looked at me.

I mimed both of us being stabbed by a giant knife in the attic.

Bentley stared at me, wide-eyed.

I mimed both of us being shot at point-blank range.

Bentley shook his head, then nodded for me to follow him up to the attic.

I mimed calling for backup on the radio.

He stopped and said, "We'll go for lunch soon enough, Zara. Do you ever stop eating?"

"This is the radio," I said, holding up the mimed object in my hand. "As in, should we call for backup?"

"Backup to go into a sweet old widow's attic? What's she going to do? Bore us to death with more stories? I'll take my chances. Come on."

I held up both hands. "All right, but if she does anything alarming, promise you'll bite her on the neck."

He grimaced, pretended to gag, then turned and led the way.

CHAPTER 8

As I followed Bentley up the creaky, narrow, seldom-used attic stairs, I silently cast a threat-detection spell. Bentley had his backup, and I had mine.

The spell was the magical equivalent of entering a scary, dark room and calling out, "Hello? Is anyone there?" It didn't detect much, but it was better than nothing. The spell would highlight the most basic traps or monsters.

In fact, as the spell spread out in its wave, it highlighted the form of Detective Bentley with an eerie red glow. *Monster detected.*

He paused on the steps and peered back at me. "Did you say something?" He narrowed his silver eyes. "Or *do* something?"

"Nothing to be concerned about." I waved him onward. The red glow would only be visible to me, the caster.

My head popped above the floor of the attic, and I immediately saw another object glowing. It was an oversized metal chair. I guess it was either a rustic throne or a fancy garden chair. It glowed amethyst.

Neither Bentley nor Krinkle showed any sign of having seen the glow on the chair.

When an object glowed amethyst after a threat-detection spell, it meant the object had magical properties. If the properties were strong, it was called an? Animus. My aunt had demonstrated the spell on a special writing pen she wouldn't let me touch. This chair's glow was less than one-quarter the brightness I'd seen on the pen.

If an object had magical properties, that didn't mean the object itself was good or bad. But any object could be used in good or bad ways—like the jinxed table that Maisy Nix had stuck my hands to.

Krinkle flipped a light switch, and multiple strings of festive patio lanterns flickered on, lighting the dusty attic. The edges of the space were lined with storage boxes, of the type you'd expect to find in an attic. In the center of the room were two ping-pong tables next to each other, holding up a miniature town.

"This is neat," Bentley exclaimed, looking over the miniature town. "It's so lifelike!"

Krinkle let out a knowing chuckle. "Even the most mature man turns into a little boy when he sees a train set." She leaned over the table and clicked something. "Wait until you see this."

A model train emerged from a cave, and noisily wound its way through what appeared to be a scale replica of the town of Wisteria, albeit a version that was over a hundred years old. The buildings were old fashioned, and the space where the City Hall building would eventually be constructed was still an untouched patch of forest.

I leaned over the town, looking for what any woman in my kitten heels would have looked for: my own house.

And there it was, standing on its corner, painted a cheerful shade of red.

Bentley, who'd apparently forgotten our search for the missing woman who was last seen in the attic, said, "This model should be on display somewhere."

"In a museum," I said.

"Or somewhere nicer than a museum," he said. "This model is amazing. Someone worked very hard on this."

"My husband built the whole thing," Krinkle said. "I helped with a few details, learning as I went, but he was the one who spent many a happy hour up here. Do you really think it's amazing?"

"It's the finest town I've ever seen," Bentley said. He couldn't take his eyes off it. Krinkle was right about the toy houses bringing out the little boy in him.

Krinkle said, "Some of our friends felt my husband should have made a contemporary version, even updating it as new buildings sprang up. But my husband, rest his soul, stuck to his vision. He wanted to hold onto a time period that represented the best of our beloved town, back when it was more wholesome and pure."

Wholesome and pure? Bentley and I exchanged a look across the model. He flashed his eyes at me, as if to warn me not to ask the old woman what she meant by pure.

"What do you mean by pure?" I asked.

Bentley slapped his hand to his forehead.

"Before television, of course," she said. "Television, the internet, video games, Polaroid pictures."

"Right." I didn't point out that Polaroid pictures had been replaced by the powerful cameras everyone carried around as part of their phones.

We talked about the model for a while, with Krinkle pointing out town landmarks, and Bentley admiring the detailed craftsmanship. They reset the train and ran it through its whole course several times.

Eventually, begrudgingly, Bentley brought the conversation back around to the missing persons report.

"She didn't go missing from this town model, if that's what you're implying," Krinkle said, sounding offended.

"Of course not," Bentley said. "That would be crazy. You're a fine, upstanding citizen, Mrs. Krinkle, and you wouldn't waste police time looking for a tiny wooden model."

"Of course not," she repeated, indignant. "The woman didn't disappear from the town model. All of those people are glued down, and they're so small you can barely tell if they're male or female." Krinkle stepped back from the two ping-pong tables, and turned toward a dark corner of the attic. "She went missing from this house over here."

Krinkle whipped a dust sheet off another model. This one was on a larger scale, and only a single house. It was a classic dollhouse, with one wall missing so that all the rooms were visible.

Bentley and I joined her in the dark corner to get a closer look. Mrs. Krinkle was not playing with a full deck of cards, so to speak, but if the dollhouse was as well crafted as the town, we both wanted to see it.

The house had three bedrooms and two bathrooms over three levels. Unlike the town model, the house was contemporary. Inside it were scale model furniture as well as three dolls. There was a man—the father, presumably —and two small children. The father stood by the front door, as though greeting a visitor. Deeper inside the house, one child sat at the dining room table, next to a stack of books. He appeared to be doing homework. The other child stood in the kitchen, rummaging in the refrigerator, which had a working hinge on the door. Upstairs in the master bedroom, there were female clothes shown in the closet—not actual clothes, but a drawing of dresses and feminine outfits, glued to the closet wall. There was no female doll present.

"You're right," I said to Krinkle in a professional tone. I was, after all, a "special consultant" who worked with the detective. "The mother has gone missing."

Bentley gave the dollhouse a serious inspection, poking his finger into dark spaces and opening the doors with hinges. "Ma'am, I can't promise it will be a top priority, but I will look into the matter of your missing person." He managed to keep a straight face.

"You two don't need to humor me," Krinkle said. "My mother didn't raise any fools. I would never waste your time looking for a two-inch-tall wooden doll."

"You wouldn't?" He gave her a sidelong look.

"It will make more sense if I show you," she said.

Krinkle waved us over to a shelving unit. She whipped the dust covers off three more dollhouses of a similar scale.

"I made all of these months ago," she said.

The first two were crime scenes that I recognized immediately. The third was a location I wasn't familiar with, but guessing by the puddle of fake blood—I hoped it was fake—on the carpet, it was also a crime scene.

I kept my mouth shut. I snuck a peek over at the iron chair. The amethyst glow was all but gone.

Bentley said, "You made these months ago?"

"Yes," she said, then stepped back to give us space.

Bentley pulled a flashlight from his pocket, and shone it over the dollhouses. The attic was dim where we stood, and the bright beam of the flashlight passing over the tiny homicide scenes made them only more gruesome.

First, there was a replica of a single room—a bathroom. In it was a picture that told the story of a crime. A woman lay motionless in an old-fashioned clawfoot bath tub, a toaster next to her in the water. I touched the water carefully. It was hard. A clear resin.

Next, there was a stand-alone garage with a car inside the garage, and an apartment on the upper floor. In the apartment, sitting on the tiny black leather sofa was another doll. It wore a man's clothes, and had no head. The top of the cut neck had been painted red.

The third model was an office interior with several desks, and a dark-haired woman in a green dress lying in a pool of blood.

"I know the first two," I murmured to Bentley. "The first one's my house, and the second is the Greyson case."

"Yes."

"Do you know the third one? You don't suppose it's something that's going to happen, do you? We have to stop it. We have to save that lady."

"It's too late," he murmured back. "That one has already happened. I told you I read the whole report. It was the one your aunt—"

Krinkle interrupted, speaking sharply. "You do understand what this means, don't you?"

We did? I didn't.

Bentley, with a poker face, said, "I'd like to hear it in your own words, if you don't mind."

Mrs. Krinkle spoke as she folded the dust covers. "The images come to me in dreams. I can't sleep or focus on anything else until I've built the models that show the images from my dreams. It's a psychic gift I have, the one that runs in my family. You'll remember I told you about my mother, and her journals."

Bentley nodded for her to go on.

She explained further, enunciating each word carefully, almost as though she was giving us a rehearsed speech, or lines from a play.

"I built the first model, of the woman on the office floor, and then, a few days later, I read in the newspaper that someone actually was murdered in one of the offices at City Hall. I told myself it just a coincidence. But then I build the second one, and it happened again. And the third." She squinted, squeezing out a single tear that gleamed down her wrinkled cheek. "Oh, Detective Bentley! You simply must do something. You have to stop the fourth one from happening. I couldn't live with myself if it came true."

Bentley and I wordlessly returned our attention to the dollhouse with the allegedly missing woman.

"This isn't like the others," I said. "There's no body. It doesn't even imply that a crime has happened. There are three living people in this house, and no body. No blood."

"My partner is right," Bentley said to Krinkle. "By the logic of the other models, if something were to happen to the woman from this family, you would have built a model showing *that*."

"But magic isn't logical," Krinkle said. "Don't you know? Magic has a mind of its own." She looked directly at me. "That's something my mother used to tell me. I didn't believe her, of course. Not until now. Not until I finally became old enough and wise enough to understand that she was right about everything." She patted her chest with one wrinkled hand. "Magic is real, and it uses all of us as its agents."

Bentley stared at the dollhouse a solid minute before asking, "How long do we have? When will this woman go missing?"

"Soon," Krinkle said faintly. "It's just a feeling, like my dreams, but I believe she'll be taken soon."

"I'll put a crime scene team on the case," he said. "Our first step will be identifying the residence and the potential victim." He reached for the base of the model.

Krinkle shrieked and put her small body between Bentley and the dollhouse. "This can't leave the attic. Please don't ask me to explain how I know. I just do."

He looked at me.

I shrugged.

He frowned. Some help I was.

I shrugged again. Magic dollhouses were way out of my areas of expertise.

Krinkle asked sweetly, "Can the crime scene people come here?"

"They'll have to," Bentley said. "I'll tell them they have to keep the dollhouse here, in the attic."

She looked at her watch again. "How soon can they get here?"

CHAPTER 9

TWO HOURS LATER

Once again, Bentley and I sat with Temperance Krinkle in her dining room. The gingersnaps were all gone. I was getting really tired of looking at glued-together jigsaw puzzles.

Two floors above us, a forensics team of three people—one who knew about magic, plus two junior investigators fresh out of school—did their work. The two who didn't know about magic had been told the dollhouse was a training exercise to teach them lateral thinking. The person leading the team, the one who knew about magic, was Dr. Jeremiah Lund, a coroner with the DWM.

Dr. Lund had set up the on-site testing equipment in the attic, then left the other two to work while he gave Mrs. Krinkle a brief physical exam. He had declared the elderly widow to be in sound physical condition. She'd taken this as good news, happily proclaiming herself fit to begin her world travels. Lund was eager to continue testing the woman. A little too eager. He had pulled out an enormous needle to draw blood when Bentley put a stop to Lund's plans.

I was left wondering if Bentley's objection was about the drawing of blood in his presence, or that taking such physical samples was far beyond standard protocol for examining a witness who'd allegedly witnessed a future crime in her dreams and built a dollhouse to tell the story.

Krinkle refilled my tea cup. The pot had gone cold, but we were both sipping it anyway. Bentley hadn't touched his.

"What an odd little man," Krinkle commented about Lund. "Or do you suppose all doctors are like that these days? I wouldn't know. I haven't been to a doctor in decades. 'Stay away from hospitals,' my mother always told me. 'That's where they keep the diseases.'" She took a dainty sip of her cold herbal tea. "I do calisthenics every morning to keep my bones strong. It works. You heard the odd little doctor. I have very healthy bones. Not one single break."

Bentley shifted in his chair. An ugly expression crossed his face.

"I would hate to break a bone," Krinkle said, as though answering a question, though one hadn't been asked. "It must hurt terribly. I can't even imagine."

Bentley picked up his tea cup, which looked even more delicate when encased in his big hand, and slurped back the cold tea in one swallow. "Broken bones are no picnic," he said, setting the cup on its saucer with a soft clink.

He would know. My stomach twisted at the memory. He'd gotten nearly every bone in his arms and legs busted by a rampaging iguammit. The vial of blood he'd taken to give him supernatural strength had fixed the breaks, yet it hadn't erased the memory of the pain. It must have been excruciating. I almost felt sorry for the guy.

There was a loud clatter in the attic, then the sound of Lund yelling at his underlings to be more careful.

If the clatter had come from my attic, I would have run upstairs to find out what was ruined, as well as which animal—fox, wyvern, or hellhound—was responsible for the damages.

Krinkle, however, seemed unconcerned. If anything, she appeared pleased to have so many visitors within her house. She had greeted Dr. Lund and the CSI techs warmly, as though she was running a Bed and Breakfast and they were day guests, arriving right on time as per their reservation.

Bentley leaned forward and sniffed his empty tea cup. "Were there rose petals in the tea?"

"No." Krinkle fanned her face with one hand.

"I smell roses."

Krinkle's magnified green eye twitched behind her thick eyeglass lens. "That must be my perfume you smell."

"It smells familiar," he said. "There must be someone at my office who wears the same brand."

"That's not possible," she said, laughing haughtily. "It's a custom blend given to me by my dear friend, Queenie Gilbert, rest her soul. It's a blend of rose, magnolia, bergamot, and something she claimed to be otherworldly."

The doorbell rang.

Both of Krinkle's hands flew to her cheeks. "Oh, dear! That must be my friend, Louis. In all the fuss, I completely forgot! He must be here to take me to the meeting."

She excused herself and went to the front door, moving quickly for a woman her age.

Bentley and I followed, in case the visitor was another crime scene technician, or someone there to tie up loose ends from a kidnapping.

Standing on the front step was a tall man in his sixties. I didn't know him. He had a long, leathery face, and a bulbous, pockmarked nose. He had jet black hair, worn back in a low ponytail, and an equally dark goatee. He wore black trousers and a black shirt, despite the summer weather.

He looked at us with surprise and said, "Temperance, you have company!"

"It has been quite the morning," she said. "These are the police. I called them about my visions, the ones I told you about. Now they're conducting a very important investigation, thanks to me."

He winced. "Temperance, you didn't."

"Louis, I told you. My visions are real!"

The man looked past her, at Bentley, and said, "I apologize on behalf of my friend. I've been taking her to meetings at the community center to get her out of the house and away from that imagination of hers. I hope she hasn't wasted too much of your time."

He hadn't been addressing me, but I cut in, asking, "What meetings?"

He looked down and shuffled his feet. "It's, uh, sort of a group for people going through life changes."

"The Awakenlings," I said.

All three of them jerked their heads and stared at me.

"I hear things," I said enigmatically.

Bentley fixed his silver-eyed gaze on me. "How do you know about this group?"

"One of the library patrons invited me. A woman named Jasmine Carter-Pressman."

His nostrils flared. "Pressman?"

Louis said, "I know Jasmine. She's a good woman. Been through a lot this year. She makes my problems look like nothing at all." He rubbed his black goatee and glanced over his shoulder at a black car that was double-parked in the street. "Temperance, let me park the car, then I'll come in and help straighten things out."

"No, no, no!" She pushed him out of the doorway. "Don't you dare trouble yourself with my business, Louis. You go ahead to the meeting. Say hello to everyone for me. I'll be fine here on my own. Trust me."

He tried to get into the house despite her protests, but she playfully swatted him on the arms until he agreed to leave.

We went back inside with Krinkle, sat at the table, and went over the same questions. She still didn't know any more about the missing woman than when we'd arrived.

After a while, my phone buzzed. I checked the screen, and all my thoughts about Krinkle and the dollhouse left my head. My mom priorities completely took over.

Bentley, leaning over to look at my phone, asked, "What is it?"

I held the phone to my chest. "Nothing to do with our current business."

"You made a noise when you read the message. What does it say?"

I showed him the screen. "It's just my daughter. Asking about the spare tire for Foxy Pumpkin."

"She's got a flat tire?"

I patted him on the shoulder. "You figured that out from my clues? I can see why they made you a detective."

He groaned.

"I'll be fine here on my own," Krinkle said. "You should go and see about that... Did you say pumpkin?"

Bentley wagged a finger at the woman as he stood. "You have my card and all my numbers," he said. "Don't let Dr. Lund examine you again, and don't go anywhere with him. Do you understand?"

She giggled, as though it had been a joke. Krinkle didn't know how serious Lund could be about the research aspects of his career. I'd heard him talk excitedly about taking apart bodies to see what made them "tick." He was looking for physical connections to magic abilities. I secretly hoped he wouldn't succeed.

We said goodbye to Krinkle, and left the house.

Zoey's flat tire had happened near the museum, so I told Bentley, and we headed there.

"Don't think I forgot about your promise of lunch," I said once we were driving.

"I would never think you forgot about lunch," he said.

Or a promise you made, I thought.

CHAPTER 10

CHET MOORE
MOORE RESIDENCE

Inside his kitchen, Chet Moore placed a glass of chilly orange juice on a serving tray. He wiped the condensation from the glass off his fingers with a tea towel. The meal was almost perfect. All it needed was a finishing touch.

He stepped out to his back yard, walked over to the flower garden, and selected the loveliest peony blossom. He'd forgotten to bring the pruning shears from his potting shed, so he glanced around to make sure nobody was watching, then shook his hand to shift two fingers into sharp claws. He rotated one finger, forming scissors, and neatly clipped the blossom. A bird screeched overhead. A snail shell crushed beneath his shoe.

He returned to the kitchen, where he nestled the short stem into a bud vase. Peonies were not Chessa's absolute favorite—she preferred the crisp symmetry and pointed petals of white dahlias—but she would appreciate the peony because she loved all white flowers. And she loved Chet. Or so she said.

It was funny, how she'd never felt so distant from him as she did now, after her return. Perhaps she had been gone too long, and everything that wasn't Chessa had changed too much while she stayed the same. He, Chet, her loving fiancé, had changed too much. He had changed in spite of holding on so tight, making himself so rigid against change while he waited for her to return.

Chet's upper back ached as he rearranged all the items on the tray, swapping the position of the orange juice and the bud vase with the peony, and then swapping them back again.

He held one hand over the waffles. They had been steaming, emitting a delicate vanilla scent, but now they had grown cool. Not distant and cool, like Chessa, but cool nonetheless.

He looked over at the bowl of batter and the still-steaming waffle iron. He decided to make another batch of fresh waffles.

Ten minutes later, he once again found himself rearranging the items on the tray. The waffles were cooling. He was stalling.

Get it together, he told himself. *She needs you to be strong for her. Don't wimp out now. Not when life is finally almost good again.*

He picked up the tray, and felt the creak of stiffness in his neck as he did, along with the rigidity in his rib cage.

Breathe, he told himself. At his age, his body should have known to keep moving his diaphragm, to keep working his lungs, to keep bringing fresh oxygen into his body without him having to think about it. And yet, a dozen times a day or more, Chet Moore felt the dimness creeping up his head. It was like a long shadow falling over his mind. Before passing out, he would realize the dimness and the long shadow was from lack of oxygen. Then he would order himself to breathe. He would tell himself to relax—not that it did much good. How could he relax, knowing as much about life as he did? The only people walking around happy and relaxed were the ones who had no clue what was actually going on.

The fools.

The damn *lucky* fools.

With the tray in his hands, he marched up the stairs and into the master bedroom.

The love of his life lay crumpled within the bed linens, folded into herself like clean but forgotten laundry. Her platinum hair looked heavy, as though soaked with water.

Chessa appeared to be fast asleep, but as soon as he drew near the bed, her ocean-blue eyes flashed open. She pushed herself upright at once.

"I thought I smelled breakfast," she said sleepily.

"More like brunch," he said.

They both glanced over at the room's clock.

"You shouldn't have let me sleep in," she gently scolded.

He started to say she'd looked like she needed more sleep, but he bit his tongue. He had learned not to speak about her sleeping habits. It was far better to suffer through her yawning and grumpiness. It was easier for everyone if Chet pretended that it was reasonable for her to cut short her sleep every night as a way of stealing back the time that had been taken from her during her year in a coma.

"I made waffles," he said, stupid though it was to state the obvious.

She pushed herself further up the bed, until her back was resting against the tufted headboard. She licked her lips and looked over the food as Chet folded down the tray's legs at the sides and placed the tray over her legs.

"That peony is lovely," she said.

"There's a whole garden full of them. Would you like me to take everything outside, to the back yard?"

"No," she answered, sharply and quickly. "Eating in bed sounds luxurious."

"That's what I figured."

"These waffles smell heavenly," she said. "Everything is perfect. You must have done this without

Corvin *helping*. Whatever did you use to distract the boy and keep him out of the kitchen?" She used the dessert fork to stab pieces of fruit in the bowl.

"No distractions," he said. "He's with the dog walker for the whole day."

She looked up from fruit stabbing and raised an eyebrow. "You certainly are a clever one, *Mr. Linklater*." She put extra stress on the fake name Chet had been using to make arrangements for Corvin. "Am I to presume that I will be spending an entire romantic day alone with you?"

"Like it or not, I am yours for the whole day. No work. Just the two of us, doing whatever we want on a lazy Saturday."

She wrinkled her nose. "Don't say that. You'll tempt fate."

"Oh, Chessa."

"I know I shouldn't be superstitious, but every time you say you-know-what, the office calls."

"What? You're imagining things."

She let out an exasperated sigh. "I swear they must have a magical alert on you saying the phrase 'lazy Saturday.' All you have to do is say 'lazy Saturday' three times, and you immediately get called in for some crazy emergency."

He frowned at her.

Just then, both of their phones rang with the tone that indicated exactly such an emergency.

"This is your fault," she said in mock anger. "Your fault, *Mr. Linklater*."

He gave her a guilty look as he answered his phone. "Chet Moore," he said. "What's up, Knox?"

* * *

The news from the Department of Water and Magic had not been what Chet Moore would have deemed an emergency, if he were the person in charge of such things. But he wasn't in charge. The mayor was. And when

Mayor Paladini declared an emergency, people reported to the office, whether it was their "lazy Saturday" off or not.

Chessa, who would be on sick leave for a week due to her surgery on Wednesday, had gotten a courtesy update rather than a call to come in. She'd expressed relief that she could stay in bed "for a few more hours." Chet knew she would probably still be there whenever he managed to get home again.

His platinum-haired fiancée had been camped out in the master bedroom since coming out of surgery on Wednesday. Her reluctance to get out of bed had nothing to do with the actual procedure, which she had recovered from—physically, at least—almost instantaneously. In fact, her body was so strong, the surgeon had to use magic spells and ancient instruments to remove Chessa's damaged ovaries. Dr. Lund had been beside himself with excitement, though he tried to mask it. Chessa had been awake and conscious for the entire procedure. Chet couldn't imagine what that must have been like. But it had been her idea to stay conscious. She insisted on destroying the biological material herself, and never having any part of her leave her possession. Not again.

It was such a horrible procedure, and for such awful reasons, yet she had calmly prepared for the surgery as though she were a regular person getting a cavity filled at the dentist.

After the procedure, however, had been a different story. All the sadness she'd been holding back was able to burst through the dam. She'd lain in bed, listless.

Her sisters came to visit on Thursday, which was when they'd been given the news. Chessa hadn't prepared the girls during their last get-together, because she feared one or both might talk her out of taking such drastic measures.

After receiving the news, Charlize and Chloe bickered in the bedroom for hours. Chessa didn't put a stop to their arguing.

It was Chet's father, Don, who finally stopped the racket. He barged into the room and told the three sisters he'd rather have his brain eaten by brainweevils all over again than have to listen to their fighting for one more minute. Charlize and Chloe left in a huff.

Chet had been anything but sad to see the two go. They meant well, he supposed, but they were also *the worst*, always drawing Chessa into their petty rivalries.

Charlize wasn't so bad on her own—Chet considered her one of his best friends, along with Knox and Rob— but when those three got together, it brought out the worst in them. He suspected Chloe was the problem, that she was the one with the toxic personality that infected the others, but he'd never had any reason to spend time with her on his own, and he wasn't curious enough to try.

Chet accepted that he would never understand their complicated family dynamics. He was an only child, and had always been glad of it, except it did leave him completely clueless about sibling rivalry.

That Saturday afternoon, as he arrived at the underground headquarters and reported in for debriefing, Chet kept thinking about Chessa, and how her depression showed no sign of lifting. Things had been bad before the surgery, and now her heartbreak had only gotten worse.

* * *

As the suited man from the mayor's office talked about the new Magical Calamity of the Week, Chet struggled to sit upright in his chair and keep his mind focused.

The whole hullabaloo was about a valuable book that had been stolen from the archives. The book had since been recovered at a civilian's house, so tracking it down was not the issue. The problem was that the theft had been an inside job.

Chet rubbed his temples. All this fuss, for a book they had back on site? There hadn't been this much fuss over the last couple of agent-on-agent homicides.

Another person in a suit interrupted the presentation with an update on something unrelated but important.

There were some technical issues regarding Codex. That was the new AI software that had been forced upon them without enough testing. Charlize had warned that it wasn't ready, but Charlize wasn't in charge of implementation. Just programming. And the AI's irritating personality. That was all Charlize.

Chet rubbed his forehead and pretended to be listening.

The IT department technician turned the microphone back over to the young man who worked under the mayor. What was the fellow's name? Alistair Something? The kid tried his best. He'd even brought visual aids: images projected onto the viewing screen in the gallery. It was always nice to have visuals at a debriefing, but photographs of a boring old leather-bound book couldn't hold Chet's attention.

Chet felt like shifting into a wolf and howling for the meeting to end. He couldn't pay attention to any more of this crap.

And it was *such crap*. All of it. Or, in his father Don's wise words, *What the wing-dang-doodle was all this bullcrap?*

If the DWM didn't keep such valuable archives in the first place, agents like Chet and his friends wouldn't be sitting ducks on top of a tempting bunker full of valuable books, and prophetic scrolls, and various objects with powers beyond comprehension. There were millions of dollars in gemstones alone. These were exactly the sort of things that evil forces—the bad guys—were constantly trying to steal.

The Department must have been spending close to three-quarters of their resources on internal security alone.

It was wasteful, and stupid. It was like keeping your sugar bowl inside an ant colony and constantly holding emergency briefings about how the ants were trying to get the sugar again.

Whatever happened to the good ol' days, when magical objects were scattered hither and thither? Sure, some encursed gemstone or magicked-up dune buggy or evil, indestructible lamp popped up every now and then, causing trouble, but that was what made magic fun.

Keeping everything in one storehouse was asking to have security breaches. *Of course* someone stole a book of ancient deity resurrection spells from the archives. The temptation was too much for most people to withstand.

What was that other expression his father used to say? *A wise man knows better than to flash his Rolex in a dive bar.* Don's expressions were becoming more and more likely to pop up in Chet's head as he grew older. He was becoming his old man. Who knew? Soon he'd be cutting deals for extra slices of bacon. Now that was a funny/sad idea.

And he *liked it.*

He liked being a little bit sad all the time. It helped with his guilt over not having been able to protect his fiancée.

The weight of guilt felt better when it mingled with sadness.

The man sitting next to Chet Moore in the gallery leaned over and elbowed him.

It was Agent Rob, who said in a low voice, "If it's a dusty old book that's gone missing, what are the odds your witch neighbor has something to do with it?"

Chet's thoughts returned to the present. He sat up straight in his chair. Rob had a point. This weekend's so-called emergency did have the hallmarks of Riddle shenanigans.

"I'll talk to Zara," Chet said gruffly.

Rob grinned. "That's not what I'm asking, Moore. I mean, what are the *actual* odds? Do you think it's three to one? A few of us have a betting pool on the go."

"Good one," Chet said.

It was a good one. A betting pool that Zara Riddle was somehow involved in the new Magical Calamity of the Week? Now, that was a game that could pay out in both cash and entertainment value.

Chet Moore wanted to laugh, but the anxiety-related stiffness had returned to his back, plus he'd forgotten to breathe again.

CHAPTER 11

ZARA RIDDLE

By the time Bentley steered the car into the museum parking lot, Zoey had apparently already dealt with the flat tire.

I saw my daughter sitting on the bumper, watching for us to come in the entrance. She waved as we pulled up alongside the 1986 Nissan 300ZX known as Foxy Pumpkin.

"Don't you look fresh as a daisy," I said through the open window.

"Why, thank you," she said, grabbing the rim of her wide-brimmed sun hat and tipping it toward us. "You didn't need to come. I told you I already dealt with the flat tire."

Bentley turned off the engine and stepped out. He went straight to my daughter, knelt in front of her, and began examining the palms of her hands. "These hands didn't change a tire," he reported back to me over his shoulder.

Zoey pulled her hands away, laughing. "I dealt with the flat tire a different way," she said. "Griffin changed it for me."

Bentley stood and put his hands on his hips. "Don't you know how to change a tire? You should know.

Someone should have taught you. Here, I'll show you now." He waved for her to open the trunk.

"I know how to change a tire," she said, not moving from her seat on the bumper. "I only sent Mom that text message because I was confused about the spare being one of those skinny ones, but Griffin and I figured it out together. I would have been able to change it myself, but Griffin insisted on doing it for me so I didn't get my hands dirty."

Bentley looked over at me. "What do we know about this Griffin person?"

I opened the passenger door, stepped out, and counted off the main points on my fingers. "Griffin Yates. Age seventeen. Works here, at the museum. No felonies on his record."

"What about misdemeanors?"

"I don't know about misdemeanors."

"Didn't they tell you when you checked him for felonies?"

I looked down and kicked a pebble across the asphalt of the parking lot. The sun was causing heat waves to radiate up around us. "To be honest, I didn't check for felonies. But I did see him dressed in a cave man costume, and he didn't have any visible tattoos that would cause a mother any concern."

Zoey jumped in. "He's just a kid, you guys. A regular kid. I know him from high school."

"Just a kid," Bentley mused, then asked, "Are you two serious?"

She let out a nervous laugh. "We're serious about *just being friends*." She looked at me. "Is he always like this?"

"The new and improved Bentley is full of surprises," I said. "Apparently, your grandmother programmed him to be some sort of guardian for us." I squinted at the tall detective, cocking my head to the side. "It was for both of us, right? Package deal? Two Riddles for one big, strong guardian?"

"I told you that in confidence." He shook his head. "You two don't keep anything from each other, do you?"

Zoey said, "She tells me way more stuff than any daughter should ever know."

"I believe it," he said.

More heat waves rose up around us from the dark asphalt. A road-paving crew was working a block over, and I could smell the even hotter asphalt they were laying down.

Bentley walked around the side of Foxy Pumpkin and kicked the skinny spare tire. He continued around to the driver's side, opened the door, and folded his tall body into the seat. Once seated, with the top of his head touching the top of the car's interior, he started turning knobs and adjusting mirrors.

Zoey asked me, stage whispering, "What's he doing?"

"My best guess is a safety inspection. Remember, he was programmed to be our butler." I shook my head. "I mean guardian. No, wait, that's not it." I struck one finger in the air. "Bodyguard."

"Gigi made him promise to protect us?"

"Using her special zombie magic," I said. My mother didn't like being referred to as a zombie, but she preferred it to "the evil undead."

"That was nice of her," Zoey said.

"Nice. Sure." I glanced around the parking lot. "Nice in the way that it makes me wonder what other 'nice' surprises she left behind for us."

"Mo-o-om," she moaned. "Why can't you accept that Gigi is back in our lives and wants to do nice things for us?"

"Because her nice things always come with strings." I pointed down to the car's tail lights, which were flashing on and off as Bentley tested the hazard lights. "For example, now we're going to have to put up with Bentley safety testing all our vehicles."

"We only have the one car."

"What about all the brooms? And when he's done with the car and the brooms, then what? He's going to find the stuff we have at the back of the fridge and declare our whole house unfit for habitation."

"You may be overreacting." She took off her sun hat and used it to fan me. She'd noticed I was starting to perspire in an unladylike fashion. She was such a sweet kid.

Zoey asked, "What happened with your nuisance call, anyway?"

I gave her a quick recap of our fun Saturday morning at Temperance Krinkle's house.

When I was done, she said, "Dollhouses always gave me the creeps. Thank you for not getting me one when I was little. All those tiny plates, and bowls, and coffee mugs with their too-thick rims." She shuddered. "They're even more disturbing than those child-sized tea sets, also with their too-thick, not-to-scale rims."

"You were such a weird kid," I said. "You didn't go through the usual development stages other kids do." I clapped my hands together. "Speaking of which, say 'hang-a-burger' for me. Please. Just once."

She refused, as usual. Weird kid. Sweet, but weird.

Bentley stepped out of the car and declared it to be "safe enough," given its age. Then he asked Zoey if she wanted us to follow behind her while she drove to a garage to get the flat tire fixed.

"There's a garage about two blocks away," she said. "I think I'll be fine." She turned and glanced at the museum. "Actually, I'm not leaving yet. Griffin says I should apply for a summer job here. He says I'll have more fun hanging out with him and his friends who work here if I'm in on all their jokes."

My heart swelled. I gave her a look of motherly pride. "You're applying for a job so you can learn more in-jokes? I've never been more proud of you."

Bentley frowned in the direction of the museum. "Why would you want to work here? The building's modern enough, but all museums do is glamorize cult leaders and pagan worship."

I let out a bark of laughter. Bentley turned his frown from the museum to me.

"Oh," I said. "You're serious. What did museums ever do to you?"

He relaxed his expression as he turned back to Zoey. "Don't mind me," he said gently. "If you want to work here, then by all means, work here. You can use me as a personal reference."

She raised an eyebrow. "You won't tell them about my felonies?"

He mimed zipping his lips.

Zoey stopped fanning me with her sun hat and returned it to her head. "I'd better get in there soon, before I get too sweaty from standing out here in the parking lot."

I hugged her goodbye, then stood where I was.

I watched my sixteen-year-old daughter walk toward her first job application. She would get the job, of course. I'd encountered a number of local teenagers through the library, and there wasn't a single one of them who came anywhere near as perfect as my daughter was for this or, well, any job. But it was possible love had clouded my vision.

Bentley patted me on the shoulder. "She's growing up fast, but she still needs you. Just wait and see. When this Griffin boy breaks her heart, she'll come running to you."

"I know," I said, my voice sounding hoarse. My throat was so tight.

"Let's get that lunch I promised you," he said. "How does Dreamland sound?"

I wiped some stray parking lot sand from the corner of one eye and then the other. That darn parking lot sand.

"Sounds good," I said. "They do make a decent lunch."

"Plus, we can ask your friend Maisy Nix what she knows about dollhouses."

I agreed that it was a good idea on both counts.

CHAPTER 12

DREAMLAND COFFEE, TOWN CENTER LOCATION

Maisy Nix wasn't in the coffee shop, but the store manager assured us she would be returning shortly.

I looked over the lunch menu, and asked Bentley what he thought looked good.

"I'm not hungry," he said.

"You always say that, but then you put away food like you've just come home from the health spa."

I ordered something on his behalf. I knew his kind ate regular human food, thanks to sharing meals with my mother, whose appetite after her big change had diminished no more than her love of bossing around waiters.

We sat, choosing a non-jinxed table, and he dug into his potato chowder and beef dip sandwich with gusto.

As for the blood part of Bentley's diet, I'd assumed he had been getting a synthetic compound from Dr. Ankh at the DWM. He reluctantly confirmed that this was true while dipping his beef dip in his soup.

We talked about the possible missing person's case as we ate lunch. He'd received an update from Lund that the student technicians were tackling the project eagerly.

"Doesn't that worry you?" I asked. "They have no idea what they're dealing with."

"This is how investigations work," he said. "We have to rely on each other as a team." He gave me a steadfast look. "That doesn't mean I don't still attempt to handle everything on my own." His silver eyes twinkled. "And get myself deep into trouble."

I nodded and pushed my chair back. "Can you stay out of trouble while I use the washroom?"

He glanced around the busy coffee shop. "I can if you can."

* * *

Maisy Nix walked into the women's bathroom while I was washing my hands. The alarming part was that it was a single-user bathroom, and I had definitely locked the door. But, when it came to witches, there was no such thing as a locked door.

"How was your lunch?" Maisy asked.

"Lunch was excellent." I turned off the faucet using magic, and then dried my hands using a spell. I could have used the paper towels that were next to the sink, but I wanted to impress my fellow witch.

"Good," Maisy said.

"The roasted turkey I had in my sandwich was surprisingly tender and moist."

She quietly stared at me in a way that said she didn't care how tender and moist my turkey had been.

Maisy was an intimidating woman, even to a powerful witch like yours truly. She was over six feet tall, slender, and strong-looking. She had medium-brown, perfect skin, black hair, and equally dark eyes. If there was one thing about her that wasn't perfect, it was that her upper lip was bigger than her lower lip—but both were still beautiful.

The last time we'd seen each other, she'd been dropping me off in my back yard after taking me on my first broomstick ride. In order to give us super speed on our flight back into town from the mountainside, she'd borrowed my powers. Without asking. Ribbons felt that her power theft had been a violation that deserved violent retribution, but then he was always looking for an excuse to talk about violent retribution. Me, I had been bothered by the way she'd drained my power without asking, but not nearly as much as I was bothered by the way she'd walked in on me in the bathroom without so much as a knock on the door.

"Are you and the detective working on a case?" Maisy asked. She had her feet spread wider than her shoulders. A fighting stance.

"How'd you guess?"

"It's either that or you're on a date. Are you on a date?"

I mimed pushing up my sleeves, even though I was wearing a tank top with no sleeves. "All right, Maisy. How do you want to do this? A magic duel? Arm wrestling? Or just a basic girl fight where we pull each other's hair while crying hysterically?"

She blinked twice. She didn't move from her wide-legged stance. She was blocking the only exit.

"Listen," I said. "It's become quite clear to me that you're interested in the detective."

No response.

"And you can do whatever you want with him," I said. "That's between you two. I'm not his girlfriend."

"I didn't think you were."

"I may not be his girlfriend, but you should know that he has pledged his allegiance to me."

She narrowed her dark, pretty eyes. "In what way?"

"As a bodyguard."

"Why? How?" She looked me up and down, then repeated, "Why?"

I kept my mouth closed and crossed my arms. I wouldn't discuss my mother's reappearance in my life, let alone how she'd given Bentley the gift—or curse—of a second life. But something—the look on her face, probably—told me she already knew enough to piece together the rest.

She broke the silence. "Do you always let your mother turn men into vampires who are sworn to protect you?"

Ziggity. She was good. Even so, I wanted to correct her. Technically, the first thing had only happened as a result of the second thing. Bentley bit into his vial of emergency blood because he had to save me, along with a few other people.

She pushed out her fat upper lip as though preparing to drink from a straw. The gesture was cute yet disconcerting.

I uncrossed my arms. "I didn't 'let' my mother do anything. If you knew anything about Zirconia Riddle, you'd know she never asks for permission."

Maisy's fat lip recessed and spread into a smile. A genuinely friendly smile. "Mothers," she said with a chuckle. "Yours sounds exactly like mine. Except for the part about being a creature of the grave. Mine is a witch, naturally."

"Mine was too, originally."

She scrunched up her face and unfocused her gaze, as though putting together a mental model of my family tree. Then her expression relaxed and she said, with an air of generosity, "You can have him. Fully and completely." She held up one hand as though swearing an oath in a court of law. "He is yours, Zara. My word is my bond."

She was giving me Bentley? How, um, generous.

I said, "Isn't that up to him?"

She sniffed. "You're funny, Zara."

"What makes you think I even want him?"

She gave me a knowing look, her dark eyes flashing wide.

Behind her, the door handle started to turn. Without so much as a glance over her shoulder, Maisy flicked her finger, and the door locked. She spoke to the person on the other side, in an eerie, magic-infused voice. "You want to use the other washroom."

From the other side of the door came the muffled sound of a woman saying, "I think I'll use the other washroom."

The walls of the tiny washroom seemed to be closer now. Being trapped in close quarters with a witch who wasn't family finally got to me. I shifted from one foot to the other. "Maisy, are we going to be in here much longer? Bentley might wonder what's taking me so long. I'd hate for him to come crashing through that door in a heroic burst of chivalry."

"How long we're in here is up to you. Ask me about whatever it is you're after. I know you didn't come here just for the roast turkey sandwich. Stop stalling."

When Maisy Nix told you to stop stalling, you stopped stalling. "What do you know about dollhouses that predict the future?"

"Are we talking about voodoo dolls?"

"Not exactly," I said, and I explained what we'd found at Temperance Krinkle's house.

When I finished, she said, "The Krinkle woman doesn't have any powers that I know of. It's possible she was meant to be a minor mage, like her mother, but her powers were suppressed. Do you know about Animata transfer?"

I waved one hand in a level gesture. My knowledge was *so-so*. Zinnia told me a witch with suppressed magic could accidentally imbue the objects around her with her own life energy. This was why it was important for witches to never give names to objects, or talk to objects as though they were alive. It was also why she'd been so concerned about my daughter's powers not manifesting on her sixteenth birthday.

Maisy gave me a refresher on Animata transfer, then concluded, "The answers may be inside the dollhouses she builds. You must focus your investigation there."

"Bentley has a team working on that already. Dr. Lund is supervising."

Maisy wrinkled her nose.

I picked up on her reaction—was it disgust?—and said, "I know, right? What is up with that guy?"

"He means well, but silly Jerry is trying to map things that should not be mapped." She reached into a leather bag that was slung over one angular shoulder. "That reminds me. I found this map in the back room. If it's not your aunt's, I'm sure she will pass it along to the appropriate party."

I took the map and unfolded it. It was a simple map of the town—the kind given out to the small number of tourists who passed through during the summer months. One segment had a nasty burn mark right through it, and the whole thing was stained brown by what smelled like coffee.

"The map has no intrinsic value," Maisy said. "But your aunt may wish to keep it for sentimental reasons."

"I'm sure there's a great story that goes along with this map."

Maisy said nothing.

I refolded the map. I'd left my purse at the table with Bentley, so I slipped it into the side pocket of my pencil skirt. "Thanks for your advice about the dollhouse. We'll look into your Animata theory."

"I have some advice to give you about dating a vampire."

"Uh..."

"Get him to bite you as soon as possible," she said, not waiting for my permission. Typical Maisy. "Get it out of the way so the game of will-he-won't-he isn't hanging in the air. Then you can move on to the more fun games." She gave me a knowing eyebrow-waggle.

"You've dated a... creature of the grave?"

She puffed up proudly. "I've dated every kind of creature. Even Jerry Lund."

"Why?"

"Oh, Zara." She turned to smile at herself in the mirror as she rubbed her pinkie finger across her enlarged upper lip. "Some creatures are more fun than others."

I stayed quiet. I struggled with the idea that gorgeous Maisy Nix she had dated Dr. Jerry Lund, the creepy coroner. Aside from the fact he looked like a bullfrog, the man had to be twenty years older than her.

Still smiling at herself in the mirror, Maisy said, "Zara, make sure that door's locked, and I'll tell you a few more things about dating supernaturals."

CHAPTER 13

When I got back to the table, I found that Bentley had stayed out of trouble, unlike me—not that getting supernatural dating tips was trouble. Not necessarily.

Bentley caught me up on the investigation, though there wasn't much to tell. The team still hadn't identified the house, or its residents.

But, on the positive side, the WPD hadn't yet received a new missing persons report.

Bentley began talking more quickly, moving his hands animatedly as he told me about his new theory: One of the children in the dollhouse seemed to be doing homework, with books spread out on the table, therefore we still had plenty of time before the kidnapping happened. Kids were currently on summer vacation.

"And kids never do homework in the summer," he said.

"You can't say never. Zoey does homework in the summer, if she can get the textbooks for the next semester."

"But most kids do not. As a detective, I have to focus on the general rules of human behavior, not the exceptions."

"I guess you would have to." I tilted my head thoughtfully. "Okay. I see your point. We have at least a month to crack this one."

He leaned back in his chair. "And I'm glad to hear your daughter is so dedicated to her studies. I was a good student myself, always striving to make the academic list, but I never considered doing homework on summer vacation."

"Zoey's a special kid. I got lucky." Movement outside the window caught my eye. A group of people in colorful fitness clothes jogged past. Dreamland Coffee's downtown location was well situated along a popular jogging route. Many exercise groups used the large cafe as their endpoint, and Dreamland's delicious desserts as their rewards.

My thoughts drifted to my daughter.

After a moment of daydreaming, I asked Bentley, "What do you think the starting wage is at the museum? They probably hired her on the spot."

He turned to follow my gaze, then kept turning, watching Maisy Nix as she walked by with a bus pan full of dishes. He rotated back to face me and said, in a low tone, "Maisy Nix is back. You can take the lead on asking her for information."

"Already done. We had a chat in the ladies' room."

"You did? Without me?"

"It was in the ladies' room."

"Even so, I would have liked to have been present." His nostrils flared, and his fingers twitched as he reached for his coffee mug.

"Trust me, Bentley. You would not have wanted to be present for that conversation."

He took a sip of black coffee, then leaned forward as he looked into my eyes, his silver irises gleaming. "You promised not to keep things from me. Your word is your bond."

A chill traveled down my spine. "I promised not to lie to you. And I'm not. It was better that you weren't in there, and not just because it's a ladies' room." I felt my cheeks flushing. "Let me make a bubble, and I'll tell you every word she said."

He leaned back, seemingly satisfied by this.

I cast a sound bubble for privacy, then shared Maisy's theory about Animata, how the energy might be powering the dollhouse to make its predictions.

There was one detail I wasn't sure about. "Did Krinkle say there had been a mother doll originally, and it disappeared from the house? Or did she make the house without the doll?"

"There was a mother doll," he said. "When she assembles the dioramas, it doesn't show a crime yet. Then, while she's not looking, the crime happens. That's what happened with the others. The woman in the green dress got her throat cut, the toaster fell into the tub, and the young man on the couch was beheaded."

"If this Krinkle woman was serious about preventing crimes, she would set up a camera to catch the killer."

"I'm not sure we'd be able to make a positive identification. The dolls are only two inches tall, and the faces aren't detailed. Besides, the evidence would never hold up in a court of law."

"I wasn't serious about the camera."

"Why not? Like you said, if the woman was serious about preventing crimes, it's the next logical step."

"I like how you apply logic to things that defy logic."

"Krinkle could come out of retirement and head up a new department at the WPD. A pre-crimes department."

"Wow. You're really running with this idea."

He rubbed his chin thoughtfully. "Of course, it would generate new legal and ethical issues. Can you charge someone with a crime they were going to commit before you stopped them?"

"No, but you could still stop the crime."

"But if they aren't charged with anything, what's to prevent them from trying again the next day?"

I nodded. "Sounds like this pre-crimes division of yours could turn into a glorified criminal-babysitting operation."

He rubbed his temples. "And to think, at one point I was blissfully in the dark about magic. I had no idea how lucky I was."

"You don't really feel that way, do you?"

He frowned. "It doesn't matter. You can't go home again."

My phone buzzed.

"It's Zoey," I reported. "The museum offered her a job on the spot." Just as I'd predicted.

Bentley grumbled, "They didn't call me to check her personal references."

"Not everything is about you," I teased.

"Tell her congratulations," he said. "I'm proud of her."

He was proud of her? Someone took his job as bodyguard very seriously.

The joggers who'd run past earlier filed into the coffee shop noisily. Even through the sound bubble, they were loud. It wasn't just their voices, it was their energy and their bright clothes.

Bentley slugged back the rest of his coffee, then said, "I wouldn't mind dropping by the community center to check out that support group. The Awakenlings."

"That's a great idea. You should totally do that. Even if you can't tell them all the gory details about your big life changes, you can get some emotional support." I shook my fist at him in a congratulatory gesture. "Good for you, admitting that you're not too big and tough and masculine to get some help with all of your feelings."

He stared at me steadily, the muscles around his mouth and eyes twitching, as though his face couldn't decide if he was annoyed or delighted.

"For the investigation," he said flatly. "We should find out more about The Awakenlings as part of the investigation. Krinkle's spouse has been gone for years, but in the absence of a spouse, a good detective looks into a suspect's affiliations."

"Krinkle is a suspect?"

"She's a person of interest." He got up from his chair. "A third party may have been using the group to gain access to Temperance Krinkle."

"Why didn't you say so?" I grabbed my purse and followed him out. I turned to wave goodbye to Maisy, but she was busy making hot drinks for the joggers and didn't meet my gaze.

CHAPTER 14

We reached the community center ten minutes too late to catch anyone from the group meeting. The front lobby smelled of chlorine from the swimming pool, and was full of people.

"They normally run for a couple of hours," said the woman at the front desk. "But it was a smaller group today, so they must have gotten through their business faster than usual."

A noisy family ran by, a squealing toddler in a bathing suit in the lead.

"Their business?" Bentley asked. "Tell us more about the group."

The receptionist stared at him blankly. "They bring in a lot of donuts," she said dully. "If you'd like to know more, sir, I suggest you attend a meeting."

I elbowed Bentley. "Did you hear that? Donuts." I smiled at the woman behind the desk. "What about donuts with the rainbow sprinkles? Do they bring in those ones?"

She frowned. "I believe they bring in a variety. That's what most people do. They usually bring in far more food than needed. I'm always throwing out donuts at the end of the day."

"What a waste," I said. "Now I'm hungry for donuts."

Bentley raised an eyebrow. It was the you-just-had-lunch look.

The receptionist said, "If you go to the large meeting room right now, you can help yourselves to whatever's left over."

"Perfect," I said, heading toward a hallway that was full of people with white-painted faces and striped shirts.

"It's the other direction," she called after us helpfully. "Up the elevator, on the top floor."

I changed direction, as instructed.

Once the elevator doors closed, Bentley said, "Tell me what's going on. Did you cast a spell? What did you find out?"

"I didn't cast any spells," I said. "Don't you want a donut?"

He didn't find this very amusing.

"It's a gut feeling," I explained. I remembered what Kathy had said about witches putting too much stock in feelings, and brushed the insult aside. I had my reasons, and my logic. It just happened to manifest as an intuitive feeling before I figured out the rest.

Bentley was giving me a skeptical look.

My brain finally caught up to what my gut was thinking, and I understood my impulse. "A couple of people might still be up there," I said. "If I know anything from the community meeting spaces at the library, it's that people love to linger after a meeting. The receptionist said everyone from the meeting left already, but how would she know for sure? This place is a zoo, between the art classes and the pool, and whatever those people in the mime makeup were doing."

"They were miming," he said.

"But not very well," I said.

"Well, no. But not everyone is excellent at everything they do." He paused. "Not like some of us."

"Was that a compliment umbrella that you just opened over both of us?" My gaze dropped from his silver eyes to his mouth. His very attractive mouth. The elevator hummed as it climbed up three floors. I couldn't stop looking at the detective's mouth.

Bentley must have noticed me staring. His voice low and husky, he said, "What else did you and Maisy talk about in the ladies' room?"

"Witch stuff."

"Such as...?"

The elevator dinged, and the doors open. I charged out, skipping toward the meeting room. Bentley followed in a brisk but professional walk.

I pushed open the door to a big room. A big, empty room. "They're all gone," I said dejectedly. "So much for my gut feeling."

I walked over to the refreshments table. Some donuts had been left behind, but none of the good ones with the rainbow sprinkles.

Bentley walked toward the large window. "Zara," he said, his voice tinged with excitement. "What's that over there?"

I joined him at the window and followed his gaze. Immediately, I saw what he meant.

From the third floor of the community center, we had a perfect view of several residential streets lined with houses, including one that appeared to be missing a wall. Someone had built the house—or renovated it—to have one side that was almost entirely glass. From where we stood, we could see directly into the home's back yard and the house itself.

I gasped. "That looks exactly like a dollhouse."

"And not just any dollhouse. It's the same one we saw at Krinkle's house." He squinted, then took a step back. "Do you see what the family is doing in there?"

I squinted, but squinting could only do so much. "No."

"I can."

"Then your eyesight must be a lot better than mine. There's too much glare on the glass for me to see inside."

He turned and looked at me. "My eyesight *is* better than yours." His cheeks rippled as he clenched his jaw.

My gut felt heavy. My arms were heavy at my sides. He'd seen something bad. I'd been joking about donuts, and staring at Bentley's mouth, and I hadn't been thinking at all about that family in the house. That poor family.

I asked, "Did you see the mother inside the house?"

"No. Just the father and two boys." He looking out at the house again.

I turned and squinted. I still couldn't see past the glare on the glass. My head felt dizzy. In half an hour, when the sun shifted, I might have been able to see inside. But we probably didn't have half an hour.

I remembered the enchanted sight-enhancement gel I kept in my purse. I could apply the goopy gel to a pair of sunglasses, and that would allow me to see past the glare, but there was no need. Bentley could see for me. He was my seeing-eye-creature-of-the-grave. All I had to do was ask.

My voice was hoarse. "What are they doing now?"

"One of the boys is sitting at the dining room table. He has stacks of books next to him."

"But it's the summer." I pressed both hands flat against the meeting room's window, framing the dollhouse between my thumbs and fingers. "The summer! He shouldn't be doing homework. This isn't right. We were supposed to have more time. You promised we had more time."

"I don't know what to tell you," he said, then, "It's happening."

It was happening.

CHAPTER 15

The glass-walled house was within walking distance of the community center, but we took Bentley's car so we would have it in case we needed to leave the house in a hurry.

While he drove, he called in to the WPD and gave an update about where he was heading.

"The address is 2319," he said to the young woman on the other end of the call.

He cruised slowly past the house, which we'd had to identify from the alley side, since the front looked just like the others up and down the block. He parked up the street, out of sight of the residence. The block was lined with sturdy-looking trees—the kind that had thick branches perfect for hanging rope swings. In fact, the tree we parked under had a rope swing on the sidewalk side.

The person on the other end of the call was Persephone Rose, the junior officer who'd come to see me at the library earlier in the week. She answered over the car's speakers. "Why does that number sound familiar?"

I said softly to Bentley, "It's because she looked it up on a license plate for the Greyson case." I remembered it clearly because 2319 was my favorite four-digit number. When viewed in a mirror, it spelled the word PIES. Sometimes I remembered the number incorrectly, as

5319, which was almost the same, but with a backwards S.

Persephone Rose asked, "Is there someone else in the vehicle with you?"

"Yes," Bentley said. "Ms. Zara Riddle is assisting me this morning."

"But you told me—"

He cut her off with a gruff command. "Do you have that name for me?"

There was the sound of keys being tapped, then, "The residence at 2319 Aubergine Street belongs to William and Veronica Tate."

"Anything on them or the address?"

"Looks like the house was vandalized two years ago."

Bentley gave me a look, then told her, "Go on."

"It... was... nothing," she replied, her voice having that flat detachment of a person multitasking, skimming text, and summarizing. "Halloween before last, some local teens hit the trees in front of the house with toilet paper. It wasn't targeted at the Tates. The kids did half the block before Detective Fung rounded them up with the help of Old Man Wheelie."

"Thank you for that," Bentley said. "I'll report back after I speak to the Tates."

"Wait," she said hurriedly. "Do you really think someone's going to kidnap that woman? I'm so confused about what's going on. Is this a training exercise or not?"

"I don't have a crystal ball," he replied tersely, then he looked over at me.

I held my hands up and mouthed the words *me neither*.

"Detective Bentley?" Her voice was weak, fragile. She sounded like a kid asking their parent for one more glass of water, stalling for time because they're afraid of the dark and the monsters in the closet.

"What is it?"

"I've seen things in this town that can't be explained," she said. "Strange things."

I pressed my lips together to keep from making noise.

"And?" He shot me a look of dry amusement. It was funny, in a cruel sort of way, to be in on the town's secrets when other people were not.

"Never mind," she said. "I'll keep going through the files to see if there's anything else connected to the Tate family."

He thanked her again, and ended the call.

Without further discussion, we both stepped out of the car and walked up to the front door.

My imagination fired up a playful image of something happening across town at Temperance Krinkle's house: a pair of two-inch-tall wooden people suddenly materializing on the front step of the dollhouse that Lund and his technicians were analyzing. Wouldn't that be a surprise!

The door opened. The man who opened the door, presumably William Tate, took one look at us and said, "We don't want any, thanks."

He closed the door.

Bentley knocked again.

The man called out, "And we're atheists."

Bentley, who had apparently received this sort of treatment before and wasn't at all surprised, knocked on the door a third time.

On the other side of the door, the man groaned. "Seriously?"

"Sir, we are with the Wisteria Police Department," Bentley said. "We are canvassing the neighborhood about a non-emergency matter. We're following up on the incident from Halloween before last. May I trouble you for a moment of your time?"

The door opened again. "Hang on," the man said. "Now the land line's ringing. Everything happens at once around this place." He yelled over his shoulder, "Billy? Luke? The phone's ringing. Can't you hear anything over that video game?" He shook his head and said to me,

"They have one job: answer the phone and the door. Do you think I can get them to do either?"

Before I could answer what was probably a rhetorical question, Mr. Tate retreated into the house, waving us to follow him in. He grabbed the ringing phone from a hall table.

I stepped inside, then turned and looked back at Bentley. Would he be able to enter the home without a verbal invitation?

Just then, Tate called out, "Come on in." He spoke into the phone with an agitated, "Hello. Tate residence. William Tate Senior speaking."

Bentley stepped inside and closed the door behind him.

The interior of the Tate house looked exactly as it had in the dollhouse version of the home, right down to the color of the flooring, which was an amber-hued type of bamboo. I hadn't seen many bamboo floors. It was very modern, though some parts of the house felt old. They must have had the flooring installed at the same time they'd removed the back wall of the home and replaced it with glass. Most of the walls were a pale cream, but one had been painted a deep purple. *Aubergine*, I thought. It was a nod to the name of the street, the sort of whimsical thing an interior decorator might think of.

The dollhouse also had an aubergine accent wall. Had the wall been a clue? Were the crime scene technicians supposed to have seen the purple wall and connected the home to Aubergine Street? The idea was awfully far-fetched, but magic did have a mind of its own—as well as a wicked sense of humor.

We stood and listened to one side of Tate's phone conversation: "No, she's not back yet." There was a short pause, followed by a light laugh. "I'm sure they got held up at the off-leash dog park. It's a beautiful day, Mr. Linklater. And, now that I think about it, Veronica did mention she was meeting with a new client this morning. An extra dog can slow down the routine."

A longer pause. "Yes, I understand your dog needs special medication, and that you're on a tight schedule. My wife is quite aware of that." Tate shot us a wide-eyed look to let us know that the person on the phone—his wife's dog-walking client, by the sound of it—was being needy.

Tate continued, "I'll have my wife call you the minute she gets home. In the meantime, you should check your back yard again and see if your dog isn't hiding under something." Another pause, then, "Listen, I'd love to help you out, but now isn't a good time. Someone from the police department is here." He turned to lean over and hang up the phone, but paused. He straightened up, frowning at us. He listened for a moment.

Then he slowly took the phone away from his ear and held it out toward us.

Frowning, Mr. Tate said, "He asked to speak with you."

Bentley took the phone and identified himself to the caller.

I waited all of two seconds before losing my patience and doing what any witch would have done if she were in my kitten heels.

I cast a spell to listen in on the phone call. It was an inversion of the sound bubble. My home-brew version acted as a tunnel, or a funnel, depending on the size of the source. It carried some—but not all—of the sound vibrations from the source, which in this case was the caller's voice coming from the phone speaker—directly into the caster's ear.

The spell cast without a hitch, and I was in, so to speak. It was now a conference call, witch style.

"I had a feeling something like this was going to happen," the male caller was saying. "Corvin has been careless lately. He shouldn't have revealed himself like that. Did Zara tell you all about it?"

I understood at once that the caller was Chet Moore, and the dog he'd been phoning about was Corvin. The bad feeling in the pit of my stomach spread.

"No," Bentley said. "This is... the first I've heard about this matter."

"He shouldn't have told anyone," Chet said, sounding frantic. "I know he's close to Zoey, and she's like a sister to him, but he still shouldn't have done it. Not without permission from myself and Chessa. Now his secret is getting out all over the place, and, wouldn't you know it, he's gone missing. This better not have been his idea. When I get him back. I'm going to redefine the concept of being grounded."

My heart raced as the whole picture clarified. Veronica Tate, a dog walker, was missing, along with at least one client's dog. That dog was the hellhound shifter who lived next door to me. Questions bubbled up. Why did Chet have a professional dog walker taking Corvin for walks? Was it because he couldn't be seen with a dog but no son some days, and a son but no dog on others? That made sense to me, a woman who refused to leave the house with her daughter in fox form.

Bentley continued to listen to Chet, giving only short answers due to the proximity of Mr. Tate, who was now pacing nervously. Tate breathed heavily and alternated between pushing one hand back over his hair and checking his cell phone in the other.

On the phone, Bentley calmly assured Chet that he understood the gravity of the situation, and that everyone at the station would be put on the case immediately. "All resources will be directed to the case," Bentley promised.

"What case?" William Tate demanded. "There's a case? Has something happened to my wife?" He gave me a pleading look. "What's going on? You two aren't here about the Halloween toilet papering, are you?" He suddenly grabbed my hands in his. "Talk to me," he demanded.

At the instant his fingers made contact with mine, I lost the sound tunnel connection with the phone call. But I'd already heard plenty, and now, like Bentley, I also understood the gravity of the situation.

Veronica Tate had disappeared, along with Corvin Moore.

CHAPTER 16

Once Bentley and I discovered that Krinkle's crime prediction had come true, the WPD "training exercise" turned into a full-blown missing persons investigation.

I did what I could as a witch. I cast threat-detection spells around the Tate residence and neighborhood, kept an eye open for ghosts, and even used my bluffing spells to question Mr. Tate and the two boys, with Bentley's assistance.

None of the three remaining Tates knew anything about the disappearance of Mrs. Tate, or the identity of the new client she had been planning to meet that day. The only secret the family was keeping involved an incident in which someone intentionally soiled the guest bathroom's frilly towels. It had been the younger boy, and both the older brother and father knew about it, but none had discussed the matter until my magic had unsealed their secrets. Disgusting though it was, if the towel thing was the Tate family's darkest secret, it didn't seem likely the woman's disappearance was related to any criminal family dealings.

After a few fruitless hours at the Tate home, Bentley had to take some meetings without me, and sent me off on my own. I didn't want to go home, because who could just go home when a child was missing? But I did have magic books at home, and research could be helpful, so that was where I went.

I planned to look up information about Animata, dollhouses, hellhounds, and anything else that might be connected to the Tate investigation.

* * *

Zoey's wasn't home when I got to the house, and the resident wyvern didn't show his scaly face.

I found Boa upstairs, curled up on Zoey's bed, and told her I was home. She twitched one ear as if to say that was all well and good, but she hadn't noticed I was gone in the first place.

I made a pot of coffee, noticing how much the simple act of following the routine to make coffee put me at ease. It was no wonder people were always offering each other cups of tea or coffee during stressful situations. The world could be crashing down around you, but a steaming cup in your hand said that maybe things weren't so bad. Night would come, and then daybreak, and then more simple routines to pull you back into your life.

I fixed up a big mug of coffee, and went downstairs.

Our house hadn't had a basement when I'd purchased it. But my house was no ordinary house. Rooms rearranged themselves without notice. The basement had manifested without warning, conveniently enough at the same time a certain dark-loving wyvern had been looking for a new hangout.

The dungeon-like space had resisted all attempts to make it brighter. With Zoey's help, I had applied two coats of heavy duty primer to the stone walls, only to have the primer disappear overnight, slurped back into the walls.

We changed tactics, hanging big decorative canvases on the stone walls, only to find them missing the next day, and a pile of ashes on the floor.

That was when I'd sensed a novel way to solve another problem. After Zoey had gone to sleep, I snuck her hideous floral lamp down to the basement. However, unlike the two coats of primer and the decorative canvases, the lamp had been perfectly intact the next morning. Not just intact, but gaudier and more floral than ever. It even seemed to be heavier. Before, it would have rated a seven out of ten for bludgeoning, but now it was closer to an eight.

Zoey realized the lamp had gone missing from her bedroom, stomped down to the basement, and scolded me as she repossessed the monstrosity.

And so, besides the addition of a few more books, the basement lair remained exactly as dungeon-like as the day it had magically appeared.

I settled in at my desk and dove into research mode.

I took a brief break when Zoey got home. I broke the news about Corvin to her, had a light dinner, then settled back in for more reading.

At some point, I must have dozed off.

I woke up to the sound of something ringing. I jerked my head up quickly, and nearly fell off my chair.

My basement lair was cozy enough despite the decoration, but the darkness did lead to napping. And one of my reference tomes in particular amplified the nap factor. In fact, the onset of sudden napping was a known side effect of consulting *Zarnov's Big Book of Mythical Bedtime Tales*. The book's stories were equal parts terrifying, informative, and—weirdly enough—sleep-inducing. Also, the pages themselves puffed up to form a pillow whenever they detected contact with a face.

The ringing sound that had woken me grew more insistent. It was my laptop, sitting on top of a stack of old books. The sound was an incoming video call from my aunt.

I answered groggily.

"Zara?" The redheaded older woman on the screen leaned forward, her familiar features taking up the whole display. "Are you in some sort of dungeon?"

"Just down here in my new-old basement," I said.

Zinnia had been there several times, so she readily accepted my explanation about where I was.

With the mystery of my location resolved, my aunt peppered me with new questions. "Why do you look so tired, Zara? What's happening there? Why did you let me go away on vacation for so long? Don't answer that, actually. I don't want to know. Where's Zoey?"

"One question at a time." I yawned and stretched on my chair. "It's been a long day, and I'm afraid good ol' Zarnov's took me down about half an hour ago." I slapped both of my cheeks to wake myself up.

"Where's Zoey?" Zinnia repeated.

I didn't want my aunt to worry, but there was no point in lying to her. After hearing the news about Corvin, my daughter had run out, too anxious to stay indoors when she could be looking for him.

"She's sniffing around town, checking the Moore boy's favorite hangouts. I'm afraid he went missing earlier today."

"Floopy doop," she said, just like I knew she would.

"Don't make me laugh, Aunt Zinnia. This is serious." I paused to double-check that our communications link was secure. It was, so I continued. "Corvin was in his animal form when he went missing. He's a hellhound, by the way. Did you know about that?"

"A hellhound? How interesting. That does explain a lot about the Moore boy."

"I know, right?" I went on to tell her about how Chet had been dropping off his adopted son, in dog form, with Veronica Tate for regular outings. Chet did it so Corvin could freely trot around town while spending quality time with a dog pack. According to the boy's father, it was beneficial for Corvin's social skills as a human to spend time with other dogs, even if they weren't hellhounds like him.

I backtracked, telling Zinnia about that morning's meeting with Temperance Krinkle, and confirmed that my aunt didn't know the woman personally. If anything, Zinnia was offended by the idea that she would be acquainted with someone like Krinkle. It might have been the way I described Krinkle as being around Zinnia's age. *Zara tries to be a good witch, but Zara enjoys teasing Aunt Zinnia about her age.*

Once she'd calmed down about the age thing, we covered what happened after we'd identified the missing woman as Veronica Tate, and the dog she'd been walking as Corvin. I relayed the result of my spells, leaving out the specifics about the Tate Family Guest Towel Soiling Incident.

The full WPD would be working around the clock, using their standard missing person protocols. They were canvassing all of Veronica Tate's family, friends, and dog-walking clients. So far, Tate appeared to be as normal as a person could be, considering she lived in Wisteria.

Veronica Tate, age thirty-nine, didn't have any known enemies, addictions, or financial problems. She was a hard-working mother of two who ran a dog-walking business during the day. She had several university degrees, specializing in antiquities and ancient languages, but hadn't done much with her degrees except have them framed for the wall.

Phone records revealed she'd recently had a few incoming calls from a pay phone. The pay phone was situated in her neighborhood's grocery store, right next to the bulletin board where she advertised her dog-walking service. All of the dogs she had been walking that day were back with their owners, except for Corvin.

"For all we know, the kidnapping had nothing to do with Tate," I said to my aunt.

Zinnia made a soft noise of agreement.

I went on. "She could have been an unfortunate bystander during a dognapping—or, should I say—a hellhound-napping."

"And there's been no ransom demand?"

I shook my head. "But on a positive note, at least I haven't seen her ghost yet. Let alone—" My throat tightened. Let alone the ghost of Corvin Moore. *Perish the thought!* As much as he gave me the creeps, I'd gotten used to the little guy. The idea of something bad happening to him made my whole body hurt.

"Just because you haven't seen her spirit doesn't guarantee she's still alive," Zinnia said sharply.

"I know!"

Then, softer, she said, "But I understand what you are saying, Zara. That is a good observation. We ought to always stay positive and not give up hope." She gazed down and touched the corner of her eye with one finger. "That poor little boy. He must be so frightened."

"What should I do next? Should I consult all the others in the coven?"

She looked up, directly into the camera. Her lips pursed. She said nothing.

"You know that I know there's a coven," I said. "I also know that you're in it, and so is Maisy Nix, and her niece. I already talked to Maisy this morning, and she didn't have much to say about the case. Who's the fourth member? Is it someone who can help find Corvin?"

Zinnia's pinched lips nearly disappeared. "The value of that particular person's help is greatly exceeded by her skill as a hindrance. That witch is a walking hindrance."

"Ouch. Sounds like you two don't like each other much."

"On the contrary," Zinnia said lightly. "She's my best friend."

"And yet you call her a *walking hindrance*?"

Zinnia's tightly pressed lips curved into a smile. "She's not always a *walking* hindrance. Sometimes you have to load her onto a heavy duty furniture dolly and wheel her around."

"If you're trying to make me implode with curiosity, it's working."

Softly, she said, "We'll discuss matters of the coven when I get home."

"No more secrets," I said. "You lied to me. You told me you weren't part of a coven, that witches didn't have big, warty noses, and that they didn't keep black cats, or ride around on broomsticks. But then your coven buddy, Maisy, took me on quite the broomstick ride. What else are you hiding from me? If I break into your house right now, am I going to find a warty-nosed house sitter looking after a dozen black cats?"

"You couldn't break into my house if you tried."

I couldn't?

She quickly waved a hand at the camera on her side. "Forget I said that. Please. It's not a challenge, Zara. Before I went away with your mother, I put some extra protective wards on my house. Please don't go over there. I wouldn't want you to hurt yourself."

"Shouldn't you have put the wards on *my* house? I mean, if you were going away...?"

"I did," she said.

"Oh." I'd been gearing up to give her a hard time, and now I had nothing. I looked down at my hands, and then at the open book on my desk.

The mere glimpse of a woodcut illustration in *Zarnov's Big Book of Mythical Bedtime Tales* gave me a powerful urge to yawn. I slammed the book shut for my own protection.

As the book closed, air movement stirred some loose papers. The top sheet was a color printout, a photograph of one of Krinkle's other miniature crime scenes. It was the office, the one which held the woman in the green dress, lying in blood on the floor.

I reached for the paper. "Aunt Zinnia, do you mind if I show you something that might be upsetting?"

She raised an eyebrow. "Since when do you ask for permission before upsetting me?"

"I'm serious. It's a crime scene from before I moved here. I'm guessing you might have been friends with the victim."

She leaned back in her chair in one smooth movement. From my perspective, watching her on my laptop screen, she appeared to be shrinking in size, becoming a smaller and smaller version of the Zinnia Riddle I knew.

Her voice came through smaller as well. "You don't need to show me," she said. "Is it Annette Scholem?"

"That's the name Bentley gave me."

"I suppose I ought to tell you everything about my dear friend Annette," she said, slowly and sadly. "I would rather not, but you ought to know, in case her death is in any way connected to today's kidnapping." She held up one finger. "Give me a moment to prepare a fresh pot of tea, and we'll begin."

I jumped off my chair. "While you're at it, I'll nuke myself some cold coffee. I'd get Ribbons to steam it for me, but he's out helping the search party."

We both prepared our hot beverages, leaving the screens on. We returned, got settled, and she began.

* * *

When she was done telling her story, my coffee was cold again. I hadn't taken a single sip.

"I'm speechless," I said.

My aunt offered up the first smile in over an hour. "That's a first," she said.

"You are one tough lady," I said. "I... I don't know what to say."

"Say that you promise to be careful with spirits. Even more careful than you've been." She sipped her tea. "Spirits are not supposed to affect the living, but, as I found out first-hand, they don't always obey the rules. They can manipulate objects they were connected to in life, including their own remains."

I shuddered at the idea of a ghost animating her own cremated ashes to take revenge.

"I'll be careful," I promised, and then, "I miss you."

She coughed into her hand. "I'll be back soon. I'm exhausted from your mother dragging me from one country to another. It all blurs together. I swear, after you've seen one palatial mansion owned by a supernatural billionaire, you've seen them all."

"Sounds rough," I said.

She started to say something else, but she was interrupted by my mother flouncing into view, her black hair flying and a strange, cat-like creature in her arms.

Then I had to explain my whole day all over again to my mother, who was absolutely no help at all.

CHAPTER 17

SUNDAY MORNING

There was no news on the missing persons case as of Sunday morning. We'd been hoping for something concrete, like a ransom call, but there had been none. Bentley assured me the outcome could still be good. It hadn't even been twenty-four hours yet. It was possible the dog had chased a squirrel into the woods, and the woman had lost her bearings.

I doubted that scenario was true. Between Ribbons and Zoey in fox form, not to mention all the shifters at the DWM, a woman and a dog lost in the woods would have been found by now.

But I would try to maintain my optimism regardless.

I jumped out of bed and hit up my closet for wardrobe suggestions. My closet served up an uncomfortable yet very cute bra, a frilly blouse, and nothing else.

"That's it?" I stared at my overstuffed closet in disbelief. "Are you trusting me to pick out my own pants, or am I supposed to wear this top with my pajama bottoms?"

No response from the closet, or the house.

I shrugged and dressed the top part of my body as suggested. I would wait until later to select the rest.

Sometimes there was a delay on the spell. I might find the perfect pants laid out on my bed after breakfast. Pajama bottoms were fine for now. And it was the weekend, after all.

I brushed my hair, then started the process of getting my teenager prepared for the day.

Zoey was scheduled to start working at the museum. In spite of everything going on, we'd decided it was for the best if she stuck to her commitments.

It would be her first gig that wasn't a self-employment endeavor, such as the plant-watering business she started when she was ten. That business had been more of a ruse to gain access to the apartments of "normal" people than it had been about earning money. She'd also taken an interest in bartending at the age of twelve, but my drinking habits—or the lack thereof—hadn't led to many tips. That made the job at the museum her first "real" job, and I couldn't think of a better place for her to get her start. Well, there was one other place. But a museum was *nearly* as good as a library.

Thanks to my chirpy encouragement, I got my grumbling, yawning daughter through the shower, into clean clothes, and down to the kitchen for a nourishing breakfast.

She watched sleepily as I used magic to peel uncooked eggs and then soft-boil them.

The peeling was part of my novice witch lessons. It was the equivalent of a musician learning to play scales perfectly before tackling songs. Raw-egg peeling wasn't supposed to be fun, yet I had grown to enjoy it the way some people loved solving Sudoku puzzles. Whenever I was levitating an egg and carefully shucking away the delicate shell, one piece at a time, the rest of the world faded away. There was only the egg.

I put Zoey's breakfast in front of her with a flourish. She didn't move; she appeared to be sleeping with her eyes open.

I sat next to her and put my arm around her shoulders.

She woke up, wiped drool from the side of her mouth, and grabbed her fork to dig in.

"You don't absolutely have to start the job today," I said. "The people at the museum would understand if you told them your friend went missing and you were up all night looking for him."

"Except I can't tell them that," she said. "The official story is that a woman went missing, with a dog. If word got out that a little boy was with her, it would be a national news story."

"And if word got out the little boy was a hellhound shifter, that would be an *international* news story. Or an *interplanetary* news story. Imagine the Martians who could be reading about it right now over their morning coffee, or whatever they drink on Mars. Over their Martian coffee that they serve with marshmallow topping."

"Don't," Zoey said grumpily. "Just... don't. No jokes."

I gave her a one-armed hug. "I'm worried about Corvin, too. Just as much as you are. You know I deal with stressful situations by making my delightfully humorous observations."

She grumbled something under her breath as she violently mashed the soft-boiled eggs with the back of her fork.

I retreated to a safe distance while she took out her frustrations on the breakfast.

* * *

Zoey had just driven away in Foxy Pumpkin—all tires fixed, inflated, and working perfectly—when another car pulled up in front of the house.

A man in a gray suit stepped out. He did a double-take when he saw me standing on the porch in my pajama pants.

"You knew I was coming?" Bentley asked as he walked up the pathway to the house.

I started to say something glib, but it caught in my throat. Watching my daughter drive away for her first day at work had stirred something.

"Zoey just left for work at the museum," I said. "I was planning to stand here on the porch a few more minutes, then go inside and cry for a while."

He shuffled back a few steps and gave me a look of genuine surprise. He hadn't expected such honesty.

I was surprised, too, until I remembered the oath I'd sworn to him the day before. *My word is my bond.* It wasn't just lip service. The bond would fade over time, and it could even be overridden, but it took great effort for a supernatural to break a vow once given.

"I wouldn't want to interrupt your process," Bentley said.

"No worries. I don't feel like crying anymore," I said brightly. "Funny how talking about your feelings puts them into tidy little boxes so you don't have to feel them so much." I glanced over at the house next door—the blue one, where the Moore family lived. "Any news?"

"No news. Still no ransom call, either. How about here?" He lowered his voice. "Any visitors?"

He meant ghosts. "Not yet, which I'll take as good news." I pointed to my open doorway with my thumb. "Do you need a hand with anything? Let me grab my purse and make sure the cat has food, then I'm all yours for the day."

He rubbed his chin, which was showing dark stubble. He'd been up all night. His eyes didn't show any dark circles, but the detective wouldn't show the usual signs of having been up all night. Not since he'd gained supernatural powers. His kind was energized by staying up overnight, especially on moonless nights. According to my Monster Manual, he was on the opposite schedule of wolf and dog shifters, who were energized by the moon and not its absence.

"Thanks for the offer," he said. "What I'd like to do right now, more than anything, is experience for myself those soft-boiled eggs you were telling me about yesterday."

"Sure," I waved him into the house. "The Red Witch House Diner is open for business. The cook will be serving up breakfast for a few more hours."

Bentley paused, looking over at the house next door. Grampa Don was standing on the porch, watching us. The old man was dressed formally, as though he was expecting a visitor, or preparing to leave the house.

"Hello, Mr. Moore," Bentley called out, then he started walking over to Grampa Don.

Don waved his hands as though swatting the detective away. "I don't need you to hold my hand," he said, in his usual irritated fashion. "Don't worry about me. I've got trees of my own to shake. You stick to your job."

"Will do, sir." Bentley jabbed a thumb in my direction. "I'm just taking a meal break to clear the cobwebs from my head."

"To clear the cobwebs from your head? What the wing dang doodle is that supposed to mean?"

"It's just an expression, Mr. Moore."

Don rapped on his head with one fist. "No cobwebs in here," he said. "Not anymore."

"That's... good to hear."

Don waved the detective away again. "Get going," he said. "I've got someone to see." He pointed to the taxi that was pulling to a stop in front of the house. "There's my ride."

Bentley handed Don his card and told the old man to call him if he needed anything at all during this difficult time.

Don snorted. "Difficult time? This is nothing. That kid will be back like a dirty sock." He patted Bentley on the shoulder, then cackled all the way into the back of the taxi.

CHAPTER 18

DON MOORE

Don Moore slid into the back seat of the taxi and gave the driver the address of his old friend, Felix Wonder.

"What a coincidence," the driver replied.

If Don had been in his wolf form, his hackles would have gone up. There was one word he hated hearing: *coincidence*. He didn't believe in such things. How could he, knowing what he did about magic?

"Yeah?" He waited for further explanation from the driver, who was, to his surprise, an attractive young woman—young by Don's standards, anyway. She looked about forty, her light brown hair treated with those blonde streaks ladies her age believed hid the gray.

"Must be a party," the woman mused.

Don scowled. What the wing dang doodle was she yammering on about?

She didn't offer more as she pulled away from the curb.

He didn't press her for details. He wanted to know who else had taken a taxi to Felix's house that morning, but he wasn't going to beg this woman. He'd done enough begging, and enough pleading, and more than enough bargaining these last few years. He'd put in all that effort, just to be treated with some dignity by his know-it-all son, Chet.

Lately, Don's only child had taken to calling himself the Sandwich Generation, joking about how looking after Don and Corvin at the same time felt like having two kids. The indignity of being compared to the boy like that!

Now that Don's bedeviled mind was coming back under his control, his begging days were over.

Things were going to change.

And all he'd had to do was make a deal with the devil.

Not that Dr. Aliyah Ankh was a devil. He'd seen devils before, and she was far from one. But she wasn't like the other people or creatures he'd worked with during all his years with the Department.

The scenery whizzed by.

The female taxi driver talked, but she didn't reveal the identity of whomever it was she'd taken to Felix's house. She worked her mouth on the usual jibber-jabber, which Don nodded through without comment.

They pulled up in front of Felix's house.

The woman with the streaked hair gave him the total fare.

He paid, and he tipped well. He didn't feel justified in holding her jibber-jabber against her. But mainly he didn't want to wait around while she sighed and slowly counted out the change, the way all taxi drivers did. As though she'd never done math before, or handled money, and didn't know what quarters were, let alone how they might magically add up to fifty cents.

He hopped out of the taxi and sprang up the walkway to Felix's front door.

Dr. Ankh's treatments hadn't just rejuvenated the holes in his mind; they'd put the spring back in his step. Don Moore was pushing seventy, but going on twenty. He might even be able to shift again—not into the bony old wolf with the gray muzzle, but the young version of himself, with powerful muscles in his haunches and ears that could hear the nibbling of a tasty field mouse ten yards away.

The door swung open. Felix Wonder stepped into the doorway and gave Don a big smile immediately.

Felix had a narrow jaw and a narrow set of teeth, so a broad smile always afforded a view to the back of the man's mouth at the sides. Felix hadn't aged much in the last decade. Same small, quick-moving eyes that didn't miss anything. Same ashy blonde hair that hid a few strands of gray. If one thing had changed, it was that Felix's rainbow suspenders were mere decoration now, no longer needed to hold up his trousers. He was still thin, but he wasn't skinny.

"What a surprise," Felix said. He leaned over to look behind Don, probably expecting to see an escort.

"Double surprise," Don said, grinning. "I'm here on my own, old man."

Felix gave him an appraising look. "Is that so? They let you wander around town without a hall pass?"

Don rapped on his head with his knuckles. "No hall pass needed. The ol' noggin is back in steel trap mode."

Felix chuckled as he stepped back and invited Don inside. "Come on in. I'm glad your head's feeling better. Mind what comes out of your mouth, though. My niece is here. Bellatrix."

"Old Chicken Legs? With the big boobs?"

Felix chortled and tucked his thumbs into his rainbow suspenders. "No sooner do I tell you to watch your mouth than it gets ten times worse." He shook his head. "I've never known anyone as ornery and contradictory as you, Don. Whatever happened to your good sense? To never passing up the opportunity to keep your mouth shut?"

"I'm done shutting my mouth."

"Well, all right then. I'll let you keep flapping your gums, as long as you're halfway respectful. She is my niece, after all." Felix gave Don a warning look before leading him to the kitchen.

Don expected to see Bellatrix Wonder sitting at the table, but she wasn't there. It was a different woman. A lovely woman. A friend of Old Chicken Legs?

Don blinked hard and looked again.

He'd been wrong at first glance. The woman was Bellatrix after all, but she looked different.

He wordlessly took a seat across the table from her, then he played the game of noting everything that was different about the woman. Instead of the brassy bleached hair she used to have, she'd returned to a natural, honey-brown shade. Gone were the ostentatious fake diamonds she used to wear studding both ears. Gone were the rings, as well, and the bracelets. She wasn't wearing one single piece of jewelry. And then there was her chest! He didn't mean to look, but he couldn't *not* look. Her chest was a regular size. Either she'd had the surgery reversed, or it hadn't been surgery in the first place, and all she'd needed to do was stop wearing whatever feminine contraption she'd been using to shove her boobs up toward her chin.

Her face was the same, but looked nicer without the gaudy makeup she used to wear. She still had buck teeth, and her soft, recessed jaw was not a woman's best feature, but... those eyes! Like small but precious emeralds. How had he never noticed how lovely they were? And how all her features were actually in perfect balance, imperfect though the individual elements were? Even the widow's peak at the top of her forehead worked, given how it shaped her face into a heart. A perfectly lovely heart.

"Don Moore," she said, fixing her little emerald eyes on him. "You're a sight for sore eyes."

"I am?" He stared at the transformed woman.

The reason for Don's visit to Felix Wonder's house was forgotten. Not clouded by the damage of the brainweevils this time, but for a positive reason. His mission had been eclipsed by the wonderful surprise of hidden beauty revealed.

"Shake your head, Don," Felix said. "Your eyes are stuck." Felix tapped Don on the back of the head playfully. "And close that mouth. You're getting drool all over my fine linen tablecloth."

It was a joke. Don hadn't actually been drooling—at least he didn't think so—and the tablecloth was the plastic kind that bachelors like Felix valued for their ease of cleaning.

In a formal tone, Felix asked his two visitors, "May I make the official introductions?"

It was a special question, the type only supernaturals asked others who also used magic. The question was a reveal in and of itself, to the ones who knew, but it was their way. The asker needed to use their best judgment to pose the question in the first place.

"You may," Don said. His heart raced with an excitement he hadn't felt in years. In decades. What a morning for surprises! Bellatrix had come into powers? Was she a flamingo shifter, like her brother, the flamboyant fellow who did something with books, or sock puppets, or both?

Bellatrix, who was seemingly new at these matters, answered uncertainly. "I, uh, I guess so." The woman had grown up in Wisteria, but her years in London had given her the most charming accent. She chewed her lip, then quickly added, "Yes. Of course you may make the official introductions, Uncle Felix."

Don sucked his breath between his teeth and waited.

He had known Bellatrix since she was a teenager. Though Felix was her uncle, he might as well have been a brother. She was only ten years younger than Felix, eleven years younger than Don.

Not too much younger, Don thought. Not now that she was catching up to him in age. She'd been fifteen when Felix and Don had begun working together.

Back in those days, Don had been married already. He was monogamous, and so he didn't have a wandering eye for other women, let alone the knock-kneed niece of his partner. But now? Now things were different. He was pushing seventy, but going on twenty.

Felix made the introductions, telling first one party about the other's powers, and then vice versa.

Both parties responded with respectful curiosity.

Once Felix had finished, Don clarified, "But remember, Bellatrix, shifters are all the same. Birds, and wolves, and even cats. We're all of the same line."

Felix grinned and hit the table with both hands. "More importantly, we're not witches!"

The two men had a good, hearty laugh. Bellatrix was slow to join in, but she did.

Felix made another pot of coffee, then put out bagels and cream cheese, lox, and other good things to share with old friends on a Sunday morning.

The mood turned serious when Don finally came around to the reason for his visit.

* * *

Bellatrix was horrified about the idea of a missing child. She had no kids of her own, but she was a good woman with a kind and understanding heart. *A man could get really comfortable next to a heart like that*, Don thought.

The mood grew even more serious when Felix brought out his mage supplies. Unlike the other two, his magic was not the shifter kind. Felix used his skills as a mage to call upon his spirit guides, the ones who resided in the "Deep," wherever that was.

Don and Bellatrix exchanged glances that communicated fear and excitement, mingled together. This was new to her, which made it new to Don. How good it felt for something to be new. His heart soared, and then he thought of Corvin, and his cheeks flushed with guilt.

"Your grandson is somewhere cool and dark," Felix reported.

"And?" Don leaned in, impatient for more.

Felix had his eyes closed. His face was screwed up in that horrific grimace he made whenever he contacted the Spirits of the Deep. The tortured expression was enough to give a strong man the heebie-jeebies.

Felix gasped, then pronounced, "He's alive."

"Of course he is," Don said impatiently. "That kid's indestructible. What about the woman? Veronica Tate?"

"There's a woman there with him, and she's angry." Felix's grimace grew even uglier. "Very angry."

"Angry at the boy? She'd better not touch a hair on his head."

A guttural sound came from Felix's throat. His eyes flashed open, and his face relaxed.

"That's all I've got, old friend," he said. "The Spirits of the Deep are agitated."

Bellatrix reached across the table and took Don's hand in hers. "I'll help you find your grandson," she said. "I don't know how, or what I can do, but I want to help."

"Don't you worry your pretty little head," Don said, straightening up in his chair. "My son's looking for him already, and he's got his ways."

"But you'll let me know if you need anything?" She squeezed his hand in a way that had to be magic, considering how much it made him feel better.

"There's always the local coven," Felix said conversationally. "If you give the witches Corvin's *other name*, they may be able to locate him."

"That's not going to happen," Don growled. "His other name is nobody's business but his own." He looked down at his second bagel, which was as yet untouched. In a softer tone, he added, "In other words, in case you haven't guessed, I don't know what it is. Maybe the boy told me and I forgot."

Don looked over at Bellatrix and gave her a sheepish smile. "My memory's been improving lately, but I've had some issues."

"I find that hard to believe," she said sweetly. "You look fit as a fiddle from what I can see."

A moment passed, and then Felix spoke, a grave tone his voice. "I'm afraid there's something else they wanted to tell me."

Both Don and Bellatrix, who'd been gazing at each other, whipped their heads to face Felix.

"Something is rising through the Deep," Felix said ominously. "Something ancient and powerful. It's rising to power."

Don let out a bark of laughter. "So? What else is new?" He laughed again, then explained to Bellatrix, "You're new at this, but trust me. Something is always bubbling up from the Deep, or burrowing in from Elsewhere, or clawing through from Nowhere Good. If you want to keep your sanity, you'll deal with what's in front of you when it gets there, and only then. Stay sharp, stay strong, stay prepared. Don't get caught up trying to see the future, because it's always changing." He waved at the other man. "Your uncle's always warning us. Warnings, warnings, warnings. Sometimes he's right. But you know what they say about a stopped clock being right twice a day."

Felix sighed and rubbed his temples. "I suppose you're right, Don. It's probably nothing."

Bellatrix asked, "How often do you get a warning like this, Uncle Felix?"

He gave her an apologetic smile. "All the time," he said. "All the time."

Don barked with laughter again. This time, Bellatrix joined in.

CHAPTER 19

ZARA RIDDLE

"Does it ever get old?" Bentley asked.

He'd finished eating his first breakfast of the day and I'd finished my second. I was using levitation to clear away the dirty dishes, floating a parade of plates and utensils into the dishwasher.

"Do you mean, does magic ever get old?" I asked. He nodded, and I said, "I guess you could say the initial shock has worn off. I probably do take it for granted sometimes, but I try not to."

"And does it require less effort to load the dishwasher this way?"

"More effort," I said. "I could load it faster with my hands."

"Then why use magic?"

I held both hands up. "You got me, Detective. I was showing off for you."

He nodded, as if to say he'd suspected as much.

"But can you blame me?" I sputtered. "There aren't many people I can do magic in front of. Just my family, the next door neighbors, and a few others."

"Such as?"

"I shouldn't say, but I just found out someone I know is a sprite. That's a creature who's exactly like a troll but insists on being called a sprite."

Bentley looked down at his silver tie and flicked away a toast crumb. "I'd do the same thing if I were a troll instead of a vampire."

When he said the word, I felt a chilly, tickling sensation on my spine, like a trickle of water running down my back.

He continued, "Not that being a vampire doesn't come with its share of negative associations."

Another trickle of water down my back.

"Why are you making that face?" Bentley asked. "Are you repulsed by what I am?"

Was it that obvious? "Honestly, and it has to be honestly, thanks to that bond I gave you, I don't know how I feel about it. I don't even know how your powers work. My mother wasn't exactly forthcoming."

"Probably because you kept calling her a zombie."

"That may have been part of the issue, though we do have a long history of her being not exactly forthcoming. For example, I didn't know the Riddles were witches, and I didn't know—" I cut myself off. Bentley knew my history. "But enough about my origin story. Tell me how things are working for you. Do you get stronger after you drink the serum?"

"The serum is more like vitamins. It's not where the power comes from."

"It's not?" That was news to me. I had made certain assumptions.

"The power comes from within, like yours. It comes from all around." He scratched his stubble with his fingernails and studied me. "May I ask you something personal, Zara?"

I waved one hand. "Ask away."

"Over the last hour, while you've been making me this fine breakfast, have you found your energy diminishing?"

I gave it some thought. "Not at all," I reported. "If I had one of those battery charge indicators, it would currently read one hundred percent."

"Me, too," he said. "But I felt only about seventy, eighty percent when I got here." He looked down at his coffee mug with suspicion. "Did you put something in my food?"

"Nope," I said with a laugh. "It must be the house."

He looked around at the upper corners of the room. "It does more than rearrange itself?"

"The last owner used to brag about it being a fountain of youth. Nobody knows how old she was when she finally died."

"Must be the house," he agreed. "I was concerned I might be drawing energy from you."

"You can't do that very well without biting me," I said, waggling my eyebrows.

His gaze flitted to my neck. He looked away again, immediately, but I'd seen it.

My cheeks flushed. The icy tickle on my spine felt like a rope of fire now. Why had Maisy felt it necessary to be so graphic in her explanations about the mating habits of certain creatures?

I turned away and busied myself with portioning out the perfect amount of soap for the dishwasher.

"What about other powers?" I asked over my shoulder. "Can you fly?"

"No."

"Not even if you turn into a bat first?"

"You know I can't do that."

"So, all you've got is super strength and healing? That's not very impressive."

Suddenly, he was standing between me and the dishwasher. I'd been about to put the soap into the door, so, naturally, I walked right into him. Full body contact. I managed to duck my head to the side to avoid smashing my forehead into his nose, and smashed my mouth into his shoulder instead. To anyone watching, it would have looked like I kissed his shoulder.

"You forgot speed," Bentley said, his tone low and gruff. "You can't deny that it's an advantage in certain situations."

"Some advantage," I said with a snort. I pulled back, extracting myself from his grasp. "Thanks to that super speed of yours, you nearly got a handful of this gritty dishwashing detergent stuffed into your belly button."

He raised an eyebrow. "I'd like to see you try."

Challenge accepted. I lunged for him.

He yelped and jumped out of the way at regular human speed.

I used magic to yank his shirt upward, untucking it from his trousers.

He yelped again, and was suddenly behind me, blowing hot air onto the back of my neck.

I howled in mock outrage, turned, and zapped him with the spell that mimicked being bit on the rear end by something toothy.

Now he howled, as I'd intended. Except it was with laughter.

He wiped at one eye, still grinning, and asked, "Is that all you've got?" He jumped from one corner of the kitchen to the other, moving so quickly he seemed to be teleporting. "You'll never get that detergent anywhere near my stomach," he said. "Not in a million years."

"Oh, yeah?"

"Zara, I'm stronger than you. And smarter, too."

"Is that so?" I lifted my arms straight up in the air, as though preparing to cast a spell that required a downward push. But instead of a new spell, I used basic telekinesis to adjust my clothing. Specifically, I whipped my blouse all the way up over my head, and off. Underneath the blouse, I wore the very special bra that my closet had selected. Lacy, peek-a-boo, and covered in non-functional ribbons. It was the sort of bra no woman would ever buy for herself. It was the sort of bra designed to provoke a reaction in a man, supernatural or not.

Bentley's jaw dropped. Theoretically, he could have looked away with super speed, but he couldn't even look away at regular speed.

I gasped and covered myself with my arms. "Bentley! How could you?"

He stammered, "Tha-tha-that wasn't me. I didn't do that. I swear."

I relaxed and put my hands on my hips. "I know," I said flatly. "Check your belly button."

He looked down to find the bottom of his shirt unbuttoned, and a generous portion of gritty dishwashing detergent caked into his navel. He made a disgusted sound.

I turned away for modesty, grabbed my blouse from the air where it was floating, and re-dressed myself.

"We all have our own kind of strengths," I said over my shoulder.

Suddenly he was in front of me again.

I finished fastening my top button and stared him in the eyes. "And our own kind of smarts," I finished.

"Is that so? What makes you think taking off your blouse was your idea?"

"Of course it was my..." I took a step back and braced myself on the sink. Had it been my idea? His kind could cloud memories, hide words, and even implant ideas. "You tricked me! You no-good, grave-digging, brain-munching zombie!"

He frowned. "Zara, it was just a joke. I didn't trick you, unless you count the part just now where I tricked you into thinking I'd tricked you."

"Oh."

"Did you call me a grave-digging, brain-munching zombie?" He gave me a hurt look, then walked at regular speed around me to the sink. He cleaned the detergent out of his navel. "So much for you not being sure about how you feel about my kind. It's all clear to me now."

"It was a figure of speech... with some truth to it." Again, the bond I'd given was keeping me too honest. "After everything went down in the cafeteria, you disappeared. I asked around, Bentley. I know you were in the ground." I crossed my arms and rubbed my upper arms. The mere thought of being buried in the dirt gave me a bad, cold feeling. "You were in the ground," I repeated.

"I was in a crypt," he said. "I was underground, but not in the ground. Not in the dirt. Dr. Ankh said it was vital for the transition. She believes that..." He trailed off as he tucked in his shirt. "Who told you about that? Was it the gorgon?" His silver eyes glinted. "Don't answer that. I can see it on your face. It was her." He spat the words out bitterly. "I know you two are friends, but I didn't realize her loyalty to you superseded her loyalty to keeping my business private."

What was happening? I reached up and twirled a strand of my hair. A moment earlier, we'd been goofing around, flirting like crazy and literally pulling on each other's clothes. Then I had to go and ruin it by insulting him.

Or, no. He was the one who ruined it by having no sense of humor.

We stared at each other, neither one moving.

How could I have thought, even for a minute, that he and I could have a relationship beyond consulting on a case?

He wasn't the man for me. He never had been. I'd been distracted by all his talk about being my protector. He'd appealed to something weak and feeble inside myself—something I didn't want to grow.

Bentley was the first to look away. He turned his head, and then his whole body. He walked over to a pantry cupboard and poked at the pink leather strap hanging out under the drawer.

"This is your purse," he said. His tone was neutral.

"Yes, it is."

Why was he so interested in my purse?

I couldn't tell if it was his powers of suggestion or my desire to drop the disagreement, but I immediately stopped thinking about everything that had been bothering me.

Bentley was a true master of the topic change.

He poked at the leather strap again, as though it might turn into a snake and bite him.

"Your purse is in a different place every time I visit," he said. "Doesn't it cost you time when you're trying to leave the house?"

"Witches don't lose their purses. Or their keys, or their cell phones. Watch this." I cast the spell that called my purse to come to its master.

The detective watched the cupboard door nudge itself open. My pink leather purse peeked out cautiously, then flew obediently to my outstretched arm.

"Ta-da," I said. "Saying 'ta-da' actually dampens spells, because it associates us witches with stage magicians, who are the corniest of all fake supernaturals. As a general rule we shouldn't say it, or the magic gets embarrassed. But sometimes I say 'ta-da' anyway. Some rules are meant to be broken, right?"

Bentley wasn't listening. "My car," he said, his eyes unfocused. "I remember you using a spell when we were chasing the genie. You used it to locate my car, through me."

"That's right. I guess all of your memories have come back." When we'd worked together on the Greyson case, his memories of the events at Castle Wyvern had been foggy. But then he'd bitten into that vial of blood, and everything had changed.

He said, "But you can't use the spell to locate people." It was a statement of fact, yet he gave me a hopeful look.

"Sadly, no. If I could, the Tate woman wouldn't still be missing." Neither would Corvin. "There is a spell for locating an evil presence, but it requires at least two witches, and the evil thing's true name. I've never done it, but my aunt has. Oh, and there's a way to locate the place where something tragic happened, if you have a ghost plus some physical remains such as bones—neither of which we have."

"But you *can* locate objects."

"Not just any object. It has to be something strongly connected to a person. The object must believe it has a master. Your car is a good car. It believes you are its master, as we found out."

Bentley, still looking like he was only hearing about a third of what I was saying, picked up a salt shaker from the counter. "I've got an idea," he said.

"Involving a shaker of salt? I like where you're going with this, but it's too early in the day for tequila shots. You can only drink tequila for breakfast if a gorgon is present."

He ignored my joke—as he should have—and explained what he'd been thinking.

It was a very good idea, I had to admit.

I couldn't use magic to locate Mrs. Tate or Corvin, but something else had gone missing. The tiny doll from the miniature Tate residence.

How had Bentley thought of it?

He explained that my salt shaker caught the light from the window in just the right way that it had made him think of the dollhouse figurines.

"Brilliant," I said. "If the dollhouse does have Animata energy, I may be able to tap into that energy and locate the doll version of Veronica Tate."

"Might it direct you instead to the woman the doll represents?"

"It's a long shot, but it can't hurt to try," I said to the detective. "If the dollhouse is the master to the doll, something could happen."

"Get ready to go," he said.

I patted my purse, which was already at my side. "Don't I look ready?"

He winced. "I'm no expert on fashion, but I believe you're wearing pajama bottoms."

I looked down. He was right. I was dressed on top, wearing a cute blouse over my distracting bra, but I'd only gotten halfway dressed that morning.

"Good eye," I said. "I was testing you." The vow I'd made to tell him the truth had a bit of wiggle room when it came to joking around.

"You're always testing me," he said, raising one eyebrow. "The pajamas look comfortable. It's interesting seeing this casual side of you."

"If you like seeing these pajamas, you should drop in for breakfast more often."

"Maybe I will."

And, just like that, we were back to flirting again.

When I went upstairs, a pair of jeans were flying out of my closet and settling onto my bed.

CHAPTER 20

Bentley's idea about using the dollhouse to locate the missing woman was a magnificent one. As we set out, I had high hopes. If our plan worked, my daughter would return home from her first day of work to find Corvin waiting to swap adventure stories with her.

The detective and I arrived at Temperance Krinkle's residence to find no outward signs of trouble at the cream-colored house. The DWM knew how to keep a low profile.

I almost expected to see Temperance Krinkle's face when the front door opened, but it was a humorless agent in sunglasses. Krinkle was not in the house. According to the agent, she'd been taken elsewhere for questioning, but she was "perfectly safe."

Bentley explained the reason for our visit. The agent's lip curled even higher at each mention of magic.

* * *

After getting the run-around from multiple levels of DWM agents, none of whom I knew personally, we finally got access to the attic around noon.

The attic didn't look much different from how it had been during our previous visit, except the giant model of Wisteria had been pushed to the side of the space. We squeezed past stacks of boxes to get into the main space, and Bentley tripped over something low and dark—a heavy toolbox.

"Mr. Clumsy Feet," I teased him.

"Why is there a toolbox right where a person would be walking?"

I sighed. "Why is there always a fluffy cat right where a person would be walking?"

He gave me a puzzled look.

I explained, "Since getting a cat, I've become much more aware of the space directly in front of my feet. You could call it my Sixth Sense."

"Sure," he said dismissively, and then he went to where the model of the Tate house should have been.

He cursed under his breath.

I joined him and looked down at the bad news.

Unfortunately, the model of the Tate house wasn't a house at all. It was a pile of pieces.

"What happened?" I asked. "Is this standard WPD procedure? Destroy all evidence?"

Bentley shook his head. "The junior technicians believed the model was a training exercise. They must have decided that dismantling it for hidden clues would get them full marks."

"I'm giving them an F. Bring those ding-dongs up here and I'll give them a piece of my mind."

"What's done is done. Let's focus on what we can do." He sifted through the loose pieces. "Everything's still here. Run your spell on this."

I put my hands into the mess and tried, but the energy was all wrong.

I broke the news that we needed to put the house back together to give the spell a shot at working.

We got to work, only to discover we needed glue. And glue was the type of everyday item the crime scene technicians and agents guarding the residence didn't have. Whatever glue Krinkle had used to make the houses in the first place had been taken elsewhere for testing. What a bunch of ding-dongs!

Off to the hobby store we went, to buy glue.

Then back to the Krinkle residence.

When we came in, one of the more cooperative agents gave Bentley an update. Still no breaks in the case. Still no ransom call.

We were coming up on twenty-four hours.

It didn't look good.

I focused on putting the house puzzle back together. I had to keep my mind off the heartbreak and worry Chet must have been going through. I wondered how Chessa was feeling. She hadn't been part of adopting the dog who later turned out to be a hellhound shifter, but she was engaged to Chet Moore. She would be the kid's stepmother soon.

Something troubled me. Chessa had more powers than either of her gorgon sisters. If my senses were correct, she had more power than every supernatural person in Wisteria put together. Why hadn't she located the kid?

As I glued together tiny bricks to form a tiny chimney, I had to wonder, could Chessa have something to do with Corvin's disappearance? Was it possible she wanted him out of the picture? That would explain why she hadn't used her goddess powers to find him yet.

When I talked through my worries with Bentley, he had a different take on things.

"She has the power to destroy worlds, right?"

I shuddered. "Something like that."

"But power isn't everything. You can put the biggest, toughest guy in front of a pile of hay, and he won't find the needle before the skinny guy with the magnet."

"You've made your point," I admitted with a sigh. "Speaking of magnets, I wish my powers were more useful sometimes. A lot of witch spells are focused on boring domestic activities. Cooking things. Ironing things. Dusting the tops of shelves where nobody can even see."

"This object location trick of yours is going to work. It has to." He picked up the miniature telephone between his thumb and forefinger. "But just in case it doesn't, what else can you do besides the domestic stuff?"

"There's the whole Spirit Charmed aspect, which you know about already." I listed items on my fingers. "Plus, I can zap people with blue lightning balls, make a human being as light as a feather, and then there are even more amazing things, such as the spell to detect the most perfectly ripe cantaloupe from a pyramid at the grocery store."

"Handy."

"I can also animate things to some degree. For example, I can animate a houseplant to grab passing pets, or I can trip the pets with an invisible tripwire—but not too much, because it's only funny the first dozen times." I listed off more spells, then added, "And don't forget the spell for making perfectly round melon balls."

"A lot of your spells are connected to melons," he noted. "If only our missing persons had gone missing with a grocery bag full of cantaloupes."

"If only."

Bentley scratched his stubbly chin. "You could always talk to Chessa about her powers. Maybe the two of you could work together."

I winced. "I prefer to keep my distance from that woman. I'd rather not have my skull used as an ashtray."

He gave me a sidelong look. "Why would she use your skull as an ashtray? She doesn't even smoke."

"Maybe it's a candy bowl she wants my skull for. I can't explain it, but I feel a bad energy whenever I'm near her. My whole skull tingles."

Bentley didn't comment.

I went on. "You know how women are. Men don't necessarily get it."

He arched an eyebrow.

"There's this lingering jealousy she feels toward me," I said. "Both of her sisters were eager to adopt me as her replacement. Like,*super*-eager. And let's not forget, her fiancé was flirting with me like crazy while she was lying helpless in a coma, having her—" I paused, making a connection in my mind.

Bentley seemed to pick up on the same connection. "You think that what happened to Chessa might be connected to Corvin's disappearance? I thought that case was closed?"

I looked down at the tiny bricks in my hand. The pieces weren't fitting together as neatly as I'd hoped. I had something backwards.

"Corvin isn't her genetic offspring," I said slowly. "So, it's different. Never mind me. I was just grasping at straws." I shook my head. "That poor woman. What they did to her. And she took it all in with that ethereal grace of hers, like it was just some unfortunate thing, like getting stuck in the rain when you're wearing a new suede jacket. Like it wasn't a big deal."

"People are not always how they appear."

"You can say that again! Under that pretty platinum blonde hair of hers, there's a lot of destruction inside that woman. Woman? I meant to say *goddess*. She's got a direct bloodline to some seriously ancient powers. I don't know why, but her powers aren't watered down like most of ours. She could turn you inside out without breaking a nail."

Bentley chortled, as though he'd like to see her try. He had no idea. He hadn't seen her like I had.

I told him, "After what happened to her, we're lucky she hasn't burned this whole town to the ground just to be free of the reminders."

"Speaking of lucky, it's good that the DWM was able to locate the material that was harvested from her."

I jerked my head up and looked at the detective. "They did?" I had a million questions, starting with *why didn't anyone tell me?*

"She destroyed the materials herself," he said. "We don't have to worry about an army of genetically engineered godlike creatures coming of age in about eighteen years and waging war against humanity."

"I hadn't been worried about that. Until now." I swallowed hard. Whenever I thought about what happened to Chessa, I'd only felt the ache in my heart of a mother not knowing where her children were.

Now I felt a new ache. The one of a mother who had destroyed part of herself.

Bentley continued, his tone grave. "Zara, I'm not sure if my intel is correct, but I believe Chessa had surgery to remove the potential of being targeted again."

The ache in my chest was replaced by a sharp pain. "Are you saying she won't be able to have her own kids?"

He shook his head. "All the more reason we have to get Corvin back home, safe and sound."

I swore under my breath.

Talk about raising the stakes.

Where was that hellhound?

* * *

We had the house model reassembled by two o'clock.

I finished performing the object-location spell by five minutes past two. It would have gone faster, but Bentley kept asking questions.

By two-fifteen, we'd ruled the attempt a failure. So much for Bentley's magnificent idea.

For a hopeful moment, I had detected a possible pull, but the direction kept changing. It was faint enough that it could have simply been wishful thinking.

Bentley asked more questions, and I explained that there were a few ways the spell could be cast. If the object were nearby, and it was safe to use levitation, I could summon the object toward myself. That was how I usually grabbed my purse before I left the house.

Another method, with larger objects in particular, was to get a magical reading on where the item was, and then draw myself toward it. I had to rely on the physical sensations, felt as a pull of attraction within my body.

"Like a dowsing rod," Bentley said. "It sounds like how pioneer settlers used those Y-shaped branches to find the best spot to dig a well."

"Some of those settlers may have had powers," I said. "They don't call it *water witching* for nothing."

He gave me a thoughtful look.

"There's another way the spell works that I didn't explain. If you're a ghost, floating around without your body, you can use it to ground your spirit to an object."

"What?"

"It happened to me once, when my aunt killed me."

"What?"

"It's kind of a funny story. I was trying to listen in on a conversation, and I didn't have my sound tunnel spell figured out yet, and—"

Bentley cleared his throat and tapped the container of glue with one finger. "Are you getting anything now?"

"Still nothing," I reported.

He couldn't hide his disappointment.

"It was still a good idea," I said. "And sometimes there's a delay on the spell. It could kick in after a few hours."

He made the face that said he didn't believe me. He leaned over, peered into the open-backed house, and adjusted the remaining dolls. "This little guy was sitting on the other side of the table when we showed up," he said, putting the boy on a chair at the table. "It's not a perfect recreation of what we saw yesterday when we got to the house."

"Because the crime happened earlier that day. The boy might have been on the other side of the table then.

Remember how William Tate was so sure we were salespeople? He must have had visitors earlier in the day."

"You do weave a compelling narrative."

He switched the boy to the other chair, then back again.

"The clothes look right," I said.

He agreed that they did.

"And the phone is exactly like the one we saw on the hall table," I said.

"Krinkle could have seen all those things from the view at the community center."

"What did she say about that, anyway? Has she admitted she's seen the house before? Or why she lied to us about not knowing where it was?"

Bentley pointed to his eyes. "She blames her poor eyesight. Claims she never noticed the unusual home, despite looking out that window multiple times."

"I'd love to question her in more depth." I made a hand gesture similar to cracking my knuckles, but released a puff of pink smoke instead. "There's a confession hex my aunt told me about."

"Do you mean Trinada's Confession Hex?" He smirked, looking proud of himself for knowing the name of a spell. "I happen to know you need three witches for that. All the Trinada spells require a trio."

We stared at each other. He was so cute when he thought he'd tripped me up on some minor detail.

"Look at you with your spell talk," I said. "Memorizing things to whip out on me. Aren't you clever?"

"I'm thorough and detail-oriented."

"I bet you are."

He raised an eyebrow.

I looked down quickly and changed the subject. "I could still do the confession hex. I could get two more witches together in a heartbeat." Zinnia wasn't available, but there were the two Nixes. One wasn't very sharp, and the other was way too sharp for her own good, but together they might balance out.

"As much as I'd love to see you in action, my understanding is the spell makes people confess, whether they did something or not. It tangles anxiety with guilt, and amplifies both. They confess for relief. The last thing any case needs is a false confession."

"Right. Plus I'd need something called koodzuberry enzyme to cast the spell, and now that our local supplier of magical herbs is a pile of bones, supplies of certain compounds have dried up."

"I'm sure Vincent Wick could be of help, if need be."

I nodded, mulling over the suggestion. Vincent Wick had inherited the property his sister had used to grow magical plants, and was working on getting things growing again. It was no ordinary nursery, though. Some of the plants were extremely dangerous—as his sister, Tansy, found out the hard way.

Bentley said, "Speaking of the Wick disappearance, whatever happened to those animals that were recovered? The ones that tried to eat you?"

"Animals? They were plants. I thought you were up to speed? They were plants, called Droserakops."

"I read the report. They had beating hearts. Wouldn't that make them animals?"

"Beats me. They were a whole new thing, whatever they were. There's nothing about them in any of my books."

I reached into the dollhouse and rearranged the furniture.

Bentley poked at the rooms and scratched off some beads of glue with his thumbnail.

We were at a dead end.

"I could try some other spells on Krinkle," I said.

Bentley considered my offer, then said, "Even if we could get access, she's an elderly woman. Those spells of yours do a number on people. Even the bluffing one. We don't want Krinkle's heart to give out while she's under a spell."

"Fine. No magic. I suggest we get a couple of phone books and beat it out of her, old school–style."

Bentley blinked at me, then got to his feet. "I'll drive you home," he said.

"Don't tell me we've already reached the point where you kick me off the case. I was joking about the phone books. Mostly."

"I'll drive you home anyway."

"Seriously?"

"You saw how difficult it was for me to get you access here," he said. "These DWM people, they don't trust witches."

He reached for my hand and helped me up from my position. I'd been sitting cross-legged on the attic floor just long enough to be wobbly when I stood. I held his hand a moment longer than needed.

"No offense, but I'll probably be better off without you holding me back," Bentley said.

I pulled my hand from his. "Holding you back? How could I *possibly* be offended by something like that?"

"You know what I mean. It's the shifters. They only trust their own kind. They barely tolerate me."

"In that case, I'll go away on my own and leave you to it." I dusted attic grime off the back of my jeans. "No need to drive me home. I can walk."

"Are you sure? We're all the way across town."

"It's a beautiful day to walk," I said. "Walking clears the mind. Plus, I'll cover a lot of new terrain, and without you around asking me dumb questions about spellwork, I can focus on sensing the location spell, if it starts working."

"I can't argue with that."

"You can't argue with me." I leaned forward and dotted the dimple on his chin with the tip of my finger. His chin felt as stubbly as it looked.

He caught my hand in his. "What are you doing?"

I yanked my hand away. "It wasn't magic. I swear."

"But you touched me."

I rolled my eyes. "So? It didn't mean anything."

He caught my hand again, and brought my finger to his chin. He touched the small depression in his chin once more with my fingertip. We locked gazes.

Were we having a moment?

I leaned forward, distributing my weight into my toes. Just in case.

Then he abruptly dropped my hand.

"Lund," he said, looking over my shoulder.

Dr. Lund, the coroner, was there. He'd come up the attic stairs quietly. Lund said, "Sorry to interrupt whatever's going on up here."

In unison, Bentley and I said, "Nothing's going on."

I added, "I was just leaving."

I squeezed past Lund and down the narrow stairs without looking back.

CHAPTER 21

The walk home did help clear my head... but only of thoughts about the missing persons case. Then my head was free to focus on a certain undead detective, and what it might feel like to have his lips on me. Or his teeth.

Zara tries to be a good witch. Zara doesn't get lost in her head thinking about kissing and nothing else for two miles of walking, plus an extra mile to backtrack because she missed the turn for her own street.

Except I did.

At least it had been a pleasant walk. Thinking about kissing while walking on a summer day is pleasant, no matter what else is happening in your life.

The only thing that broke up my daydreaming was encountering a man walking his dog and his rooster.

"They're best friends," the man explained. "I can't take one out without the other."

The dog was large and black, like Corvin, but walked slowly due to old age and had a white muzzle. The rooster stared at me like he knew something, but that's roosters for you.

I wished them a great day and carried on.

Unfortunately, the object-location spell didn't kick in, nor did I come up with any new ideas for locating Corvin and the Tate woman.

Once I was back at my house, I was restless in a way I hadn't been in a long time. Maybe ever.

I felt inspired to do something wild and crazy. Laundry. And other house chores, too tedious to detail, but one task involved the manual application of furniture wax to wooden furniture. The wax really brought out the wyvern and cat scratches.

By four o'clock, my furniture was so shiny it hurt the eyes, and I still hadn't heard anything positive about the case. Bentley asked me to stop messaging him.

I paced the house, removing all the light bulbs from the ceiling fixtures, giving them a good washing, and then replacing them all. With the bulbs free of dust, the house was approximately one percent brighter. The gleam on my newly-waxed furniture was almost painful.

And still there was no break in the case.

Finally, I was so starved for a morsel of positivity that I caved in to Boa's demands and gave her a small plate of sliced deli ham.

The fluffy white furball dug into the ham like it was her job, her passion, and her duty to her country.

When she was finished eating the ham and licking the plate, she climbed onto my lap and showed me her appreciation by massaging my thighs with her paws while gazing up at me with adoration. I had never felt so adored, not even when holding Zoey as a newborn. It was close, but Boa, with her feathery-white whiskers, was the new master of gaze-delivered adoration.

The cat's gratitude lasted exactly thirty-five minutes. Then she jumped off my lap and padded off to the kitchen to howl in front of the refrigerator door for—you guessed it—more ham.

Ribbons flew into the living room and landed on the recliner across from me.

"You've done it now, Zed," he said.

"I did. I broke the rules. I gave Boa deli ham."

The wyvern shook his seahorse-shaped head.

Boa howled from the kitchen.

"I am filled with regret," I admitted to the wyvern. "But she did give me a very nice lap massage, and she temporarily took my mind off my worries. Cats can be quite soothing. They're beneficial for mental health. People with cats have lower blood pressure. Did you know that?"

Another blood-curdling howl for more ham came from the kitchen.

Ribbons looked upward, squinting his beady eyes, and asked, "Is it brighter in here?"

"I washed all the light bulbs."

"I don't like it."

I tossed a throw pillow at him. "Everyone's a critic."

* * *

The front door opened, and my daughter called out loudly, "Hi, honey! I'm home!"

"I'm right here," I said, looking up from my book. "You don't have to yell." I set the book next to me on the couch. "And since when am *I honey*?"

"Since I just worked my first full shift at my first real job." She joined me in the living room, moved the book to the gleaming coffee table, and flopped on the sofa with her head in my lap. "Any news about the brat?"

I raised an eyebrow at her use of the term *brat*. She couldn't fool me. I knew she'd been worrying about Corvin all day, which was what I'd been doing, too, except for the time when I'd been thinking about kissing a certain silver-eyed detective.

"No news," I said. "He's still missing."

"He's going to be in so much trouble for making us worry." She rolled on the couch, her head still in my lap. "That creepy little big-eyed brat! Or should I say *pest*, as in *short for pestilence*, which is what he is."

"Right." I swept her hair off her face. She felt flushed and clammy. "It will be good to have the pestilence back in our lives, though."

She took a raspy breath and blinked back tears. "He's really tough, Mom. Wherever he is, I know he's going to be okay. Physically, anyway. Emotionally..."

"He's not like other kids," I finished. "Chet always told me that, but I had no idea. Hellhounds aren't even from this world. I've been reading up, and they're only found in other worlds. That means he must have escaped from somewhere else."

"You mean Hell."

"The books don't come right out and say Hell, but it's implied." I shook my head. "Every parent suspects their kids are from Hell, but Corvin actually is."

"Every parent?" She lifted her chin and look up at me, her head still on my lap.

"Not me, of course."

"But genies are demons from another world, too. And since I'm half genie, I have as much in common with Corvin as I do with you and Auntie Z. I'm just like him. I'm technically Hellspawn."

A chill set into my bones. Corvin and Zoey did have that in common. What if someone or something was collecting the local Hellspawn? Was Zoey next on a list? She could be. And I'd let her out of my sight for the entire day. *Zara tries to be a good mother, but Zara can't anticipate everything.*

"Zoey, until we get Corvin back, I want you to be careful."

"I'm always careful."

"Extra careful. Especially around people we don't know." I gathered her loose hair into a ponytail at the top of her head and gave it a playful tug. "Speaking of which, how was work today? How do you like working for a living?"

She scrunched her face, compressing her thoughts for a moment, then said, "After subtracting breaks, I only worked for seven-point-five hours, but it was the longest seven-point-five hours of my life."

"Sounds about right."

"Did you know that the general public is disgusting? I had to clean floors and the undersides of benches, and did you know that the general public leaves gum on everything?"

"I work at a library. I know all about that."

She sighed. "I thought you were exaggerating. Now I know better." She gestured with her hands emphatically. "Gum. Stuck to the bottom of everything. I cleaned one bench, and when I came back to it an hour later, do you know what I found?"

"More gum."

"More gum!" More hand gestures. "If Corvin wasn't missing right now, I'd swear he was following me around all day, sticking gum under things to drive me crazy."

My skin prickled. "What makes you think someone was following you? Did you see anyone lurking around, watching you?"

"It was just a joke, Mom."

We sat in silence for a while, me pulling her hair into a ponytail and tickling her face with the end.

Suddenly, she sat upright. "Oh! I forgot to tell you something. The lady who went missing is the daughter of the museum's head of security, Mr. Williams. You'd think he would take the day off, but he was there today. I heard from the head of maintenance that everyone in management asked him to take a leave, but he insisted on being there today. And he'll be there tomorrow, too. They're running a security drill on the Egyptian exhibit."

"Williams," I said. "Does he have long, black hair?"

"That's him. And he wears black from head to toe."

"Louis Williams." I frowned. "Zoey, he's a person of interest in the case. There are two connections, which makes him look suspicious. He's the missing woman's father, and he's also a friend of Mrs. Krinkle's. So far, Bentley thinks the coincidence can be explained by logic. He regularly spent time with Mrs. Krinkle, driving her to meetings at the community center, so she might have been tuned in to his energy and his family's. Her friendship with him might be why she built the model to try to prevent the kidnapping, but..."

"But what?" Zoey asked.

But nothing, I thought. Louis Williams working at the museum where my daughter had just gotten a job didn't connect him to the case in a third way. It only connected him to my family. To me. And yet, hearing his name from my daughter's lips filled me with dread.

"You need to steer clear of Louis Williams," I said.

"It's a small town," Zoey said. "Just because he works at the museum doesn't mean I can't go work there tomorrow."

"I didn't say you couldn't work there."

"But you were going to."

She was right. I'd been considering it. "How about I pay you to do some chores around the house? Maybe you ought to avoid the museum and that man's whole family until this thing settles."

She gave me a wide-eyed look. "I ought to avoid the museum? *I ought to?* You sound exactly like Auntie Z."

I clutched my chest. "Ouch. You really know how to hurt me."

She looked down at her hands and picked at her nails. "How about instead of being a terrible new employee and not showing up for my second shift tomorrow, I go there as planned, and ask around about the Williams family? I can report back to you. Think of me as your secret undercover agent."

"I'd rather you didn't get involved."

She sighed and said, robotically, "I promise I'll be extra careful, Auntie Z—I mean *Mom*."

"Extra-extra careful," I said. "Also, I'll be with you the whole time. I'll use a glamour to disguise myself! People won't find it odd if a leafy bush is following you around, would they?"

She rolled her eyes.

"Fine," I said. "I'll go to my job at the library, and scrape gum off benches there." I waved a hand. "Not really. We make the pages do that."

"Lucky you."

"It's like Frank says. Those advanced degrees really pay off sometimes."

We sat in silence for a moment, then Zoey said, "He's going to be in so much trouble when I see him again."

"I know. I'm worried, too. And that poor woman."

"And her kids."

"And her husband."

She looked at me. "I don't know what I would do if you disappeared."

"You'd be okay, until the fridge ran out of leftovers. Then, I don't know."

Her eyes glistened. She threw herself into my arms. "Don't go anywhere," she sobbed into my shoulder.

"I'm not going anywhere," I assured her.

CHAPTER 22

MONDAY MORNING

I hated waking up to no news on the missing persons case.

But, on the positive side, no news could be good news. At least I had not woken up to a ghost, or to an excited wyvern plus a scared cat reporting the appearance of a ghost in my house. That meant Veronica Tate and Corvin Moore were still alive. Probably.

What if they weren't? What if something awful had happened to them?

Then leave this place. Move away, I thought. Or at least it seemed to have been my thought. Weirdly, I'd heard it inside my head in a voice that wasn't quite my own.

I looked around my bedroom. "Ribbons?"

There was no response. The wyvern didn't do mornings; he would be asleep for several hours yet.

I wrote off the voice as perfectly understandable paranoia, got out of bed, and cast my usual spell on the closet.

"Work today," I said conversationally. "At the library, as usual for a Monday. But of course I'll be happy to duck out to help Bentley if he needs me. And now that Kathy knows about everything, I won't even have to make up some silly excuse."

The closet shuffled. I rubbed my hands, hoping for a gray wool suit or something equally conservative. Being a librarian was my career and my calling, and it was fulfilling and enjoyable work, but I didn't want to be stuck at the library if I could be helping Bentley.

Or kissing him, said the voice in my head. Mystery solved. It was definitely my voice. It only sounded different because it was creepily fixated on a man who had been, until quite recently, so boring that I'd been trying to set him up with my aunt. What had changed?

Besides the fact he had supernatural powers.

And that he was my sworn protector.

And that he'd heroically saved my life, along with the lives of several of my friends.

Besides all that.

I scratched my head. I couldn't put my finger on why my feelings for him had changed so much.

The sea of colorful clothes before me divided, and out came one of my least conservative outfits. It was a frilly peasant blouse that could be worn on or off the shoulder, and an equally frilly skirt.

"I take it I'll be working a full shift at the library today?"

My closet's response was to send a pair of lace-up boots skipping out.

I dressed in the feminine ensemble, and admired myself in the full-length mirror. I looked like someone heading to a photo shoot for a romance novel cover. *How appropriate.* It was the perfect outfit to wear while spending eighty-five percent of my mental resources daydreaming about kissing a dreamy detective.

I reached into the skirt pockets to find they weren't empty. One pocket had a tiny bottle of something in it. A magic potion? I took it out and read the label. It was not a potion. Just a bottle of flexible glue, from the hobby store.

"Where did you come from?" I asked.

The glue didn't answer.

I turned to the closet. "This is the same bottle of glue I took out of my jeans pocket yesterday before I did laundry, isn't it?" The closet didn't need to answer. I knew, without checking the ledge by the washing machine, that it was the same bottle. It must have flown upstairs and climbed into my skirt pocket, at my magical house's behest.

"Fine," I said to my closet. "I trust you." I slipped the glue back into my pocket, confident it would come in handy later. Perhaps I would need it to repair a very important library book, or to glue a rubber spider to the inside of Frank's snack-time container.

I would almost certainly do both of those things.

* * *

"Nice try," Frank said, plucking the rubber spider from the lid of his snack container.

"I should have gone more subtle," I said. "Perhaps a smaller spider."

Kathy came running into the break room, breathless. We turned to her in alarm. Was there news about the missing woman? A library emergency?

She closed the door behind her and asked, "What did I miss?"

Frank and I exchanged a look. Now that Kathy had revealed her secret to us, she wanted to know everything. Everything. All the time. It was a bit much.

"You missed Zara's genius prank," Frank explained flatly. "She glued this giant tarantula inside the lid for my cookies."

Kathy gave me a confused look. "Why the glue? Why didn't you just bury the spider under a couple of graham crackers?"

I shrugged. "I had glue in my pocket, and I figured it had to be there for a reason."

Kathy nodded as she backed away. She slowly opened the door leading out to the circulation desk, stepped out, and left us to the remainder of our coffee break.

"Poor thing," Frank said once we were alone again. "She told us her big secret, and for what? To watch you cast that animation spell on the rubber tree and make it dance to ABBA?" He was referring to the magic demonstration we'd put on for Kathy on Friday.

"She loved that performance, especially when I made all your sock puppets join in."

Frank crossed his arms. "I don't know. The whole thing made me feel cheap and tawdry." He whispered, "And not in the good way."

"I felt exactly the same way," I said. "Like I'd sold out, artistically."

"And you weren't even the one flapping your flamingo wings around like a crazy bird."

I shook my head as I poured myself a fresh mug of coffee. "I feel so bad for magicians. Putting on shows with magic, even if it is real, is awful. Honestly, I'd rather have some smelly creature trying to eat me than have to perform tricks for entertainment."

"Cheers to that," Frank said, and he clinked his mug of coffee to mine. "Speaking of smelly creatures, my sister arrived in town on Saturday."

"And?"

"She's been dropping a lot of hints about the family, and Uncle Felix."

"The one who does the wacky séances with the Spirits of the Deep?"

"That's the one. I think he might be some sort of mage. We should probably have a heart to heart soon."

"You should. It's good to connect with family over this stuff."

"Anyway, I haven't told my sister about my new side gig as a flight attendant for Air Flamingo." He frowned as he dipped a teddy-shaped graham cracker in his coffee.

"But I've got a bad feeling there's something big she wants to tell me."

"An in...? She's got powers? No way."

"*Yes* way. When she was getting ready for bed last night, she asked me if I still thought her feet looked weird." He flashed his eyes at me. "Her feet!"

"Because she has, as you put it, weird chicken feet?"

Frank kept frowning. "I told her they looked totally normal. They're as big as rubber boots, and her bunions aren't too pretty, but they're regular enough. But then I was wondering, what if she's a shifter, too, and this is her way of dropping hints to gradually break the news?"

"She might be. And what if she is? Don't you think it would be fun to have that in common with a family member? I felt way less alone in the world after I was reunited with my aunt. She's quite the woman. A bit of a worrywart, but when you find out why she's so cautious about stuff, it doesn't seem so annoying."

"I get what you mean, Zara, but what if my sister's not a flamingo? What if she's something else?"

"Like what?" I thought of the hellhound who was currently missing. I mentally linked two seemingly unconnected events to see if they fit. Was Frank's sister connected to the kidnapping? She'd arrived Saturday, the same day Tate had disappeared. I would definitely mention it to Bentley, when I saw him next.

Bentley.

Sigh.

When would I see him next?

Frank waved his hands at me. "Are you still listening?"

"Sort of," I said. "I slipped away for a minute. What were you saying?" I took a sip of my coffee.

Frank said, "What if my sister's a chicken? A shifter chicken?"

I nearly choked on my coffee. "Chickens aren't people," I said, then, "Are they?" I thought of the man I'd seen the day before, walking his dog and his rooster.

"Not all chickens," Frank said. "But some of them could be people."

"Right," I said. "I don't know if my information is accurate, but I understand that all shifters come from one genetic line. Everything from cougars to eagles. A wolf shifter can have a child who's a crane. But families do stick to certain themes, and when the kids are different from the parents, it is unusual. That's why Zoey identifies a fox shifter, as opposed to a shifter who happens to be a fox."

"But identities can be fluid," Frank said. "Have you heard about shifters changing forms? Intentionally?"

"Yes. You're supposed to carry on like they've always been what they are." I rubbed my chin thoughtfully. "Do you suppose your sister chose to be a chicken to keep a low profile? It's easier to explain a chicken sighting than a flamingo."

"I don't know. And I don't know why it's bothering me so much. Deep down, I love my sister. I should be able to accept her, whatever she is."

"Maybe we should get Kathy back in here and find out what she knows about shifter identities and all the politics."

He agreed, and so we did.

Kathy was thrilled to be included in our conversation. She didn't know much about bird shifter bloodlines, or whether or not they could be chickens, but promised to check some rare books she had hidden under lock and key at an undisclosed location, and then report back to us on Tuesday.

All three of us got back to work after that.

I was so busy with patrons and their research questions that I didn't even think about magic the rest of the day. And I only thought about kissing about fifty-seven percent of the time. I blamed the frilly romantic skirt for half of that.

At the end of my shift, I was clocking out, punching my card in the un-library-like timecard machine that went KERCHUNK, when I suddenly felt the pull of something magic.

It was a mild sensation, near the base of my rib cage. If I didn't have such a robust digestive system, I might have mistaken it for indigestion. But it was a real sensation, a magical one, and it could only mean one thing.

The object-location spell I'd cast on the missing doll the day before was finally kicking in.

Hope flared in my heart, making my whole body feel light as air—as light as a witch with a pre-flight buoyancy spell cast on her.

Was this the break in the case everyone was waiting for? Would Veronica Tate be reunited with her husband and sons? Would Corvin be coming home to his family tonight?

I grabbed my purse, said goodbye to my coworkers, and rushed out the door.

CHAPTER 23

KARL KORMAC
CITY HALL - WISTERIA PERMITS DEPARTMENT
4:50 PM

Karl Kormac heard drawers being opened and the telltale jingle of purses being gathered out in the main office area of the Wisteria Permits Department.

He hoisted himself out of his comfortable office chair, groaning as usual. He'd tried not groaning as he settled in or out of chairs, but it startled his subordinate employees for him to appear in their communal space unannounced. Giving the underlings some warning about his imminent arrival and wise oversight made for a more relaxed crew, and a relaxed crew was a productive crew.

He noted the time on the clock on his wall. The clock was lying again. He mentally subtracted five minutes, and stepped out of his office.

A few heads turned, but the subordinates didn't stop gathering their things.

Karl said, "Leaving already?" He allowed a small percentage of his spritely bluster to leak out with his words. "It's not five o'clock yet."

Liza Gilbert, the young one he still thought of as the New Girl, gave him an innocent look. "It's not?" She turned and looked at her boyfriend, the one with the name Karl often forgot.

What's-his-name said, grinning boyishly, "It's five o'clock somewhere."

Gavin Gorman, the gnome, spoke up from his desk to correct the boyfriend. "Actually, that's not how time works, Xavier. All time zones are an hour apart. The number of minutes past the hour at any given time is the same everywhere."

Margaret Mills, the witch, took the bait and charged into the fray like a thirsty rhino at the watering hole. "Actually, Gavin and Xavier, not all time zones are an hour apart. Around the world, there are a number of zones with thirty-minute offsets and even forty-five-minute offsets."

"Well, duh," Gavin said, as though he'd known. He hadn't. "But there aren't any time zones offset by five minutes, which is basically what I meant."

"It doesn't matter what you meant," Margaret said. "What matters is what you said, and you said all time zones are an hour apart."

Gavin narrowed his eyes at his coworker. "What's going on with you today, Mills? Did another witch steal your sense of humor?"

There was a soft THWAP sound—the tip of a shoe hitting shin. Karl's good sprite ears picked up the sound easily.

Gavin, the recipient of the shin-kick, groaned and shot a dirty look across the two-person workstation he shared with his on-again-off-again girlfriend, the card mage.

The card mage said to the gnome, "Be nice to Margaret. She's having a tough day."

"We're all having a tough day," the gnome said. "It's Monday."

The card mage, Dawna Jones, rolled her orange, cat-like eyes. "Be nice anyway."

While they continued to bicker, Karl glanced over at the empty office with the floral wallpaper. It wasn't good that Zinnia Riddle was still away on her vacation. He needed her back at work, keeping a lid on Margaret and the others the way only she could. Sometimes it seemed like he and Zinnia were the only two adults working there.

Earlier that day, the gang had received a surprise package from Zinnia. She'd included a letter explaining that postcards were stupid, basically the "humblebrag" of mail, and thus she would never subject her supernatural friends and coworkers to such a thing. Instead, she'd purchased a variety of goodies and keepsakes during her travels thus far, and so the box contained an assortment of items they could distribute amongst themselves as they wished.

The items were simple and of low-value.

Naturally, bedlam ensued.

Margaret Mills zapped three people with spells, and one of the couples broke up and got back together again. To everyone's surprise, it was the younger couple whose love was tested over a trio of herb-infused olive oils, not Gavin and Dawna. Karl had to step in and whip everyone into shape. Literally. He'd extended his extra-long sprite tongue and actually whipped them.

The mood following the tongue-lashing was much more subdued and professional.

Best of all, Karl had snagged his favorite pick from the box of items: a hand-carved wooden elephant.

"Ding," said the kid—Xavier—getting up from his chair and pulling on his light summer jacket. "It's officially five o'clock now."

Karl made a big show of walking back to his private office, then coming back with a HARUMPH.

"Barely," he said.

Gavin and Dawna exchanged a look.

Gotcha. The look was enough to confirm Karl's suspicions that the two of them had been responsible for tampering with the lying clock in his office. For the last two weeks, he'd been monitoring the thing. In the morning, it ran slow, so that all the subordinates made it in on time or even early. By lunch time, the clock would have sped up significantly, so that lunch break effectively started five minutes earlier. Then it slowed for the end of lunch and sped up again for the end of the work day.

It must have been Gavin's gnome relative, that repugnant Griebel Gorman, who'd altered the clock. He was one of those low-lifes who would build or alter anything mechanical for the right fee, no matter who got hurt along the way. Karl had been wary of taking on the younger Gorman as a supernatural protegé, fearing he would be as dirty as his uncle, but Gavin turned out to be ethical and honest—or at least as ethical and honest as a gnome could be. The poker nights Gavin "generously" hosted were run mainly to take money from his coworkers.

This business with the time-hopping clock in Karl's office had clearly been Gavin's idea.

"I know about the clock," Karl said.

Suddenly, everyone was very concerned with the contents of their laps, their purses, or something on the floor. Karl reassessed the situation and altered his conclusion.

"And I know you were all in on it," he blustered. "All of you."

Margaret Mills raised her hand. "I told them not to do it, Boss."

Karl stamped his foot. "This department is not a cover. We are a real department, and we do important work here."

The New Girl spoke up, albeit meekly. "Are you sure about that, Mr. Kormac? We seem to issue a lot of permits for things that don't require permits in other towns. This afternoon we had a walk-in client who requested a special permit for putting more than forty birthday candles on a cake."

Karl stared her down. "And?"

Liza Gilbert—that was her name!—scrunched her young face. "Don't you think that's a bit excessive?"

Karl had to fight very hard to keep a straight face. She wasn't wrong, but he was their boss. The boss of a department that was partly a cover for more important operations, but he couldn't admit that.

He dialed up his bluster and responded with more gusto. "More than forty candles constitutes a potential fire hazard." He walked around to view Liza's computer screen and asked, "Did you find the Form 40BC on the system?"

"I did," she said, sounding surprised as she relived the experience of being surprised hours earlier. "And I issued the permit."

"Good work," Karl said. He addressed the group as a whole. "This is exactly the sort of high-quality, reliable work we do around here at the WPD." He bared his teeth and added, "During standard office hours."

The group murmured.

Karl continued. "Furthermore, I expect my office wall clock to be restored to its normal function by tomorr—"

He was interrupted by the door opening.

Into the permits department rushed one of the mayor's staff members, his tie askew and his hair ruffled.

"You're still here," the young man said, sounding both surprised and relieved. "Mayor Paladini is putting out an alert to all staff members with special abilities."

Xavier said, "Then that means I'm outta here." He had already been standing, his jacket on, and his bag slung over his shoulder. "It's past five, and I don't have any special abilities."

Liza admonished him, "That you know of."

"Let it go," Xavier said to his girlfriend. "We're just the Red Shirts around here. Don't you get it? We're expendable, and we can't even defend ourselves." He thumbed his chest. "If trouble's spewing out of some magic volcano, this Red Shirt would rather be at home when the lava hits."

The young man at the door said, "You should be more concerned about whatever's going on."

Margaret Mills asked, "Does it have anything to do with this terrible indigestion I'm feeling? I thought it was my lunch going down the wrong way, but this pushing-pulling sensation in my gut keeps getting stronger."

Karl asked, "Is it gas?" He was often plagued with terrible gas himself. Not enough natural chitin in his diet. He needed to visit a lobster buffet soon.

Margaret tapped her solar plexus with a loose fist, then burped. "There's some gas, but that's normal after I've been sitting all afternoon." She tapped herself again. "Something else is still there. It feels like an object-location spell taking its sweet time to connect." She frowned. "But I haven't cast any spells today. I never, ever cast spells at work."

"Except for at lunch, when you bit me on the butt," Gavin said.

"And mine," Dawna said.

Liza said, "That was a spell? I thought I was having a muscle cramp."

Margaret huffed. "Well, I haven't cast any *object-location spells* today."

As though thinking with one mind, the group dropped their quibbling and turned toward the mayor's sweaty member of staff. Together, they asked the young man to explain what the alert was about.

The man gulped, then admitted, "We're not exactly sure. Mayor Paladini was hoping you might know something. We're picking up alerts from all over, but nothing specific. A retired field agent called in about a warning from the Deep, and we're trying to connect that to a misplaced book that's since been recovered, but..."

They all waited with what Shakespeare first dubbed "bated breath."

Fun fact: Shakespeare was a sprite. Most people didn't know that, but Karl had evidence, being the bard's descendant. That fact was, of course, beside the point, so Karl didn't mention it but instead listened with bated breath for the mayor's subordinate to continue.

"But nobody knows what was inside the book," the sweaty young man said. "The words aren't legible."

"Genies!" Margaret exclaimed. "The last time ink was disappearing, it was genies. They had that man who used to run the *Penny Pincher Gazette* working for them on some atrocity. They cleaned out the local supply of several magical items. I thought someone was trying to make flying monkeys."

"This case is quite different from that one," the young man explained. "The book's pages have all been blackened, not erased. And, before you ask, we brought in our best sniffer hounds, and there were no bookwyrms in the vicinity."

Margaret muttered under her breath about genies being to blame, regardless.

Dawna cleared her throat and noisily shuffled a deck of cards. Everyone looked at her, then went silent as the card mage prepared to do what only she could do.

Dawna finished shuffling with a flourish—she'd learned a few new moves—and spread an array of seemingly random cards across her desk.

"Mother is coming," she said.

"And?" Margaret came over to watch over Dawna's shoulder. "What else?"

"That's all the cards are telling me."

"Do it again."

Dawna shuffled the cards and lay them out once more. To Karl, the sequence and distribution of cards meant nothing at all, but he trusted Dawna's magic, even though she was new at cartomancy.

"Same message," Dawna said, shaking her head. "Mother is coming."

Karl's first three stomachs churned, and the other two threatened to join in. He hoped the cards didn't mean *his* mother. Then it would be a very bad day, indeed.

Dawna rotated in her office chair and gave the visitor an apologetic look. "That's all I've got. The cards can only do so much. Since I've been practicing, my readings have gotten clearer, but less detailed."

"Mother is coming." The man in the suit nodded. "I will pass that information along." He turned to leave but hesitated. "Ms. Jones, is there any chance you could come upstairs and—"

Dawna, who was already on her feet, designer purse at her side, cut past him on the way to the door. "It's well past five o'clock, Alistair. That means I should be at home by now, with between two and five cats on my lap." She stepped through the door and called over her shoulder, "If the apocalypse starts up, and you need someone to read cards and confirm the apocalypse is happening, call me. Or not." Then she was gone.

"Same here," Gavin said. "Call me if you need someone strong and brave to fight the forces of evil."

Margaret added on Gavin's behalf, "Or to zap himself straight home as soon as things get scary."

The others laughed.

Gavin retaliated. "Alistair, let's say the apocalypse does happen before the start of work tomorrow. Your best bet is to call Margaret Mills. If the forces of evil are a man—and isn't it always a man?—Margaret can nag him into a deep depression."

The others sucked in their breath. All the oxygen seemed to go out of the room.

"Too far," Margaret said to the gnome, pursing her lips. "Too far, even for you."

Gavin shrugged, stamped his foot three times, and disappeared. Karl noted it was a clean relocation. Not even a lingering puff of smoke. Even so, Karl would have to speak to the gnome about being a show-off.

Xavier muttered under his breath, "I'll never get used to that."

They all filed out past the mayor's subordinate. Karl was the last to leave, and checked that the door was locked.

He stayed back and stood in the hallway with the mayor's lackey, Alistair What's-his-name. He placed a fatherly hand on the fellow's shoulder and looked him in the eyes.

"My subordinates talk a tough game, but they do care about this town," Karl said. "It's just that we've had so many false alarms lately."

Alistair nodded. "I understand perfectly. We're all exhausted and on edge from these drills."

"Level with me, son. Is this another drill? A training exercise?"

"No, sir." He winced. "Not that I know of."

"Is it true the DWM has an artificial intelligence running their security system?"

Alistair's eyes widened. "How did you—" He cut himself off. "Sir! I'm not at liberty to discuss the details of any security systems."

"So, you're not at liberty to discuss whether or not it's the AI software triggering all these false alarms we've been having?"

Alistair's forehead beaded with sweat.

Karl nodded. That sweat was more than enough to confirm his theory. Following the incident with the third floor at City Hall, the Department of Water and Magic had stepped up their timeline for implementing their new computer software.

Karl knew very little about computer programming—he could barely figure out where his emails were going when they disappeared into folders—but he did know one thing about the DWM's security system. It was software, and yet it was not.

He'd seen the blueprints in the mayor's office. She had left them in plain sight. In plain sight... inside a folder, inside a locked filing cabinet, inside a locked office. But he had seen them with his naked eyes, when he'd been looking around for some information about departmental budget cuts.

He had not taken a photo of the blueprints with his phone—it might have been the clever thing to do, but it would also have placed evidence of his harmless office break-in on "the cloud," or "the server," or wherever it was the picture dots from his phone got stored.

However, despite the lack of a photo to remind him, he remembered the details of the blueprint clearly.

The DWM's new artificial intelligence ran on a computer that was mostly cords, cables, and circuit boards. The usual computer stuff. Except this one had a cooling system of tubes filled with black scarabyce blood. And, at the center of the central processing unit, there was a heart. A beating heart. Salvaged from one of those person-eating Droserakops plants, or animals, or whatever they were.

In a handwritten note, the architect of the blueprints stressed that the heart was a safety feature, and not evil at all. If anything were to go wrong with the AI, there was a fail-safe to keep Codex from infecting the internet. The system could be shut down by manually disconnecting the beating heart.

That made perfect sense to Karl. For all he knew, every electronic device had a tiny beating heart inside of it. Why else would the darn things randomly shut down or inexplicably die without so much as a warning?

Karl headed home, his thoughts turning to what he would have for his first dinner, then his second dinner, and both desserts.

CHAPTER 24

ZARA RIDDLE

The object-location spell pulled me all the way to the Wisteria Police Department.

Then the trail went cold. I tried to find the thread again, the magical thread pulling me along, but it was like trying to remember a dream in the morning while the dream is being recalled back to the Dream Warehouse.

Where to next? Should I head home and wait by the phone? Boring.

I paced in front of the WPD entrance, doing some serious soul searching. Was it really the object-location spell drawing me there, or something else? Was my crush on a certain silver-eyed detective messing with my magic?

Or could my compulsion to be there *his* doing? His kind did have powers over the minds of others—powers he'd been vague about.

I took a seat on one of the concrete planters outside the front doors. I twisted my body to look at the plants, and touched the green leaves sprouting in the box. *These planter boxes could use some love*, I thought. *Geraniums are fine, but...*

My mind flooded with Latin names for plants.

Hello, Tansy Wick.

The spirit of Tansy Wick wasn't actually there. She had moved on months ago, but some of her residue remained, haunting me. The plants had brought the echoes back. I'd sat on the edge of that same concrete planter not long ago, and I'd done something that seemed logical at the time. I'd informed a ghost that she was dead. The results had not been pretty. The spirit's rage had knocked me unconscious, and given my aunt quite the scare.

But now, on a sunny summer evening, the memory felt distant and contained.

Because it *was* contained.

Thanks to my rezoning spell, where I'd rezoned myself as a library of sorts, and the visiting ghosts as books, I was now impervious to full possession. Some others in the magical community had expressed concern that the spell might have unintended side effects. But so far, everything was working out.

I rubbed some velvety geranium petals between my fingers. They were as red as fresh blood. Had I solved my ghost-possession problem only to encounter a whole new problem? The one in which I was attracted to a supernatural being who could be my undoing, who could suck my remaining witch powers right out of me? That had to be the reason why witches were, as Maisy had informed me, drawn to bloodsuckers like, well... like my cat Boa was drawn to deli ham.

They were bad for us.

Bentley could be my undoing.

So what if he is? The question whispered through my mind.

So what if he did take away my powers? Life had been easier since my rezoning. I'd been happier than ever lately.

What if I could be even happier without any powers at all? I could focus on being a librarian. I could focus on parenting Zoey—not that she needed me much. I could find new hobbies, or go back to scuba diving lessons and take the next level.

Sitting in the sunshine, I lost myself in daydreams of a *normal* Zara Riddle, living a normal life, knowing about magic but without magic of her own. Without all the responsibilities that came with it.

CLIP-CLOP CLIP-CLOP.

The approach of a hoofed creature startled me from my thoughts.

I looked up to find that the clip-clop sound wasn't coming from a goat or a small pony, as it had sounded, but a woman in hard-soled shoes. She was compact in build, in her forties, with a head full of frizzy, gray hair.

She was Margaret Mills, one of the few people in Wisteria I dreaded bumping into.

Every time I'd seen the woman and she'd seen me, something unpleasant had happened. The first time we met, she'd chewed me out for wearing fur—even though the fur was very much alive, and also my father. She'd also blamed me and my family for a bad day on the mini golf range.

I'd avoided her successfully a few times, but we had met up again three days earlier, on Friday. She had been picking up Thai food at Kin Khao at the same time I'd been there. Mrs. Meesang accidentally shorted Margaret's takeout order, and Margaret blamed me for the mix-up. Me! Simply for being there at the same time she was.

I grabbed a twig from the geraniums and rubbed my thumb over it. I could cast a glamour spell to hide myself as a bush. If I acted quickly, without hesitation...

Too late. She'd definitely seen me.

The frizzy-haired woman clip-clopped to a halt in front of me. She put her hands on her sturdy hips and demanded, "What are you doing, and why are you drawing me into it?"

I tucked a stand of hair behind my ear and squinted at the sun, which was almost blocked by her mass of hair.

"I'm just sitting on a concrete planter in a public place," I said. "Enjoying the sunshine." I smiled. "As one does on a fine day such as this."

"But you're using me." She stomped one of her hard-soled shoes, reminding me of a rhinoceros. *Be careful*, I thought. The wild rhinoceros was not as deadly as the Nile crocodile or hippopotamus, who together killed more than three thousand humans annually, but the rhino was definitely on the list of deadly animals to watch out for.

Mrs. Mills continued to stand in front of me, partly blocking the sun, waiting for a response to her vague accusation.

I cocked my head to the side. "Mrs. Mills, have you lost your mind?" I'd meant to continue our exchange in a more pleasant, less confrontational manner, but her directness had a way of burning away my social niceties.

"Zara Riddle, I know you're using me to triangulate a lost object. It has to be you. Zinnia's out of town, and Maisy would never do this without my permission. And the other one, well, I'd like to see her try a spell this sophisticated. She can't even keep dog hair off her uniform."

"A-ha!" I jumped off the concrete planter, my puffy skirt flouncing around me playfully. "You're the fourth member of the coven."

Her gray eyes flashed. "Say it a little louder, Zara. I don't think the whole town heard you."

"Mrs. Mills," I said, smiling. "May I call you Margaret?"

She gave me a wary look. "Sure."

I offered her my hand to shake.

She reluctantly shook my hand.

As our palms touched, an image flashed into my mind. Margaret Mills was on the floor, wrapped from head to toe in packing tape, like a large, strange, very angry cocoon. The image was gone just as quickly as it had come. I didn't know what the packing tape was about, but

I had a feeling that whenever an unfortunate thing happened to Margaret Mills, she'd done something to deserve it.

She stared up at me for a moment, then said, in a civil tone, "You don't know about me, do you?"

"Not until now." I shook my head. "And if you are being drawn into that object-location spell I cast, I apologize. I didn't mean to pull you into it, I swear." I held up my hand. "My word is—"

"Don't," she said, cutting me off. "Don't waste your energy on a bond. I believe you." She looked down and adjusted the hem of her jacket. "I may have overreacted. It happens on very rare occasions."

She overreacted only on rare occasions? I stifled a snort. She'd overreacted every single time we'd interacted. Now I understood why my aunt had held off so long on introducing the two of us.

"Margaret," I said tentatively, feeling uncomfortable using her first name, even though I'd gotten permission. "You were saying something about my spell drawing you here? Some sort of triangulation? Can you explain that to me slowly, like I'm a novice, which I am?"

She held up three fingers. "Three points in the triangle. Me, you, and the lost object. We're both here now, which means whatever you're looking for isn't far away." Her eyes grew wide and serious. "Is the lost object that missing woman I heard about on the news? Zara, you can't use that spell on the living."

"I know," I said. "I used the spell on a doll, from a dollhouse."

"A doll?" Her face reddened. "You exposed me over a doll?" She drew back a few steps, as though planning to cast upon me a curse so vile and messy it might splash back onto her.

"Whatever you're going to do, please don't," I said, holding up both hands. "The doll I'm looking for is connected to the missing woman, and there's more. You know how they said on the news that she disappeared along with a dog? It's not just any dog. It's a shifter. A little kid. He's only ten."

"You're lying to me. Ten-year-olds can't shift."

"He's a special case," I said.

She rushed forward, charging at me.

I, being the brave witch I am, flinched as I let out a strangled scream.

She grabbed both of my hands and squeezed them urgently. "A child is missing?"

"Yes," I managed.

Her eyes filled with tears. "Why didn't you say so? We have to find him. We have to do something! We have to find this doll of yours, if it'll help."

"Well, I don't know how much it will help..."

She squeezed my hands so hard I was thankful to have supernatural strength and healing. "Oh, Zara. We have to find that baby boy. That poor defenseless thing!"

"I wouldn't say he's defenseless..."

She squeezed my hands again. "He's a child!"

"He is," I said. "Thank you for helping. I really appreciate it. His family will, too."

CHAPTER 25

Magic makes for strange bedfellows.

My former enemy had become my ally; Margaret Mills held my hands as we cast a booster spell on my object-location spell.

This time, the signal came in strong and clear.

"The doll is inside the WPD," I said, absolutely certain this time. "On the second floor."

She let go of my hands. "You'll be able to hold the connection without me now." She took a step back, reluctantly, it seemed. "Good luck."

"You're not coming with me?" Moments earlier, she'd been hysterical about the idea of a missing child, and now she was just walking away?

Her eyes squeezed nearly shut. "I can't," she said, sounding broken. "I have an appointment. I have to meet my divorce lawyer."

"Oh, Margaret! You're getting divorced? I'm so sorry." Suddenly, all her crabbiness toward me seemed justifiable. The woman was going through something terrible. But she'd been so patient and kind to me moments earlier, when we'd cast our spell.

I barely knew her, and I used to dislike her, but now everything was different. We'd shared magic. We'd worked together for a good cause. She was gruff on the outside, but underneath that tough rhino hide, she was good. Margaret Mills was a good witch!

I closed the distance between us and grabbed her hands again, this time to offer comfort.

She squeezed my fingers and swallowed hard. We were still inside a sound bubble, and thanks to our connection through our shared magic, I could feel the beating of her heart. I felt it beating alongside my own, faster by a quarter beat.

Her heart slowed, matching the pace of mine. "Don't you waste another second worrying about my stupid divorce," she said. "What's done is done."

"Your husband is an idiot," I said. "I don't even know his name, but I know he's a fool to let you go."

"Mike," she said. "And you're absolutely right about him being an idiot. We've been married all these years, and he still doesn't know who I am." She looked away briefly, then back at me. "But don't worry about him, or me. Get yourself into that building, find the doll, and then find that little boy. If you need help later, let me know."

"How? Is there a spell? An all-coven-members smoke signal?"

She smirked as she pulled her hands from mine. "I'm in the phone book," she said. "Under Mills."

* * *

After wishing Margaret good luck with her divorce lawyer, I entered the WPD.

Getting past security, and then up to the second floor was no problem at all for this witch.

As I turned down a hallway, I spotted a familiar face walking toward me: Persephone Rose.

"Ms. Riddle!" She stopped in her tracks and fidgeted with her thick, dark bangs frantically, as though she'd hidden a tiny weapon in there and was about to draw it on me in self defense.

"Ms. Rose," I replied. "Isn't this fun? You dropped by my workplace last week, and now I'm dropping by yours."

"Detective Bentley isn't here right now."

"I didn't come to see him."

"You didn't?" Her voice was a squeak, mouse-like. "Is there something I can help you with?"

"Have you found the Tate woman yet?"

"No."

"Then I guess you can't help me, can you?" I heard the sharpness in my voice, winced, and manually dialed my witch down. "I'm sorry," I said. "It's not your fault that any of this happened. I'm sure you're doing your best."

She squeaked and nodded rapidly, her straight, dark hair swinging.

I nodded at the bag on her shoulder. "Heading home for the day?"

"We're supposed to take breaks," she gushed defensively. "There's a maximum to how much overtime we're allowed to work. It's a union thing."

I stepped to the side of the hallway and waved for her to pass without paying any sort of toll. "Don't let me keep you," I said. "Go home. I'd hate to get in trouble with the union."

She squeaked again, and tottered off clumsily on her high heels. I stared after her, and the shoes in particular. They were bright yellow-orange, like a duck's feet. *What a waste of cute shoes*, I thought, then I heard Frank in my head: *Would kitty like a saucer of milk?*

My imaginary version of Frank was right. I was being needlessly cruel to young Persephone Rose. But I couldn't help myself. I wanted to be the only woman in town who spent way too much time thinking about kissing Bentley. I'd already been crushed by unrequited love once since moving to Wisteria. If I had to go through the painful process again, I'd probably give up on men entirely and take one of those anti-love potions I'd been warned to avoid.

Two more WPD employees approached, asking me for my visitor's pass.

"Right here," I said, showing them the charmed piece of paper that would provide the information their minds needed.

Zara is a pretty decent novice witch. Zara can get into places.

Once they'd been dealt with, I continued on my mission, following the spell's tug all the way to an employee's cubicle. The employee was either away from their desk or gone for the day.

I yanked open the top drawer of the desk. The spell was so strong now that the handle for the drawer had been glowing. Inside the drawer, a zippered clutch purse was gleaming like a pearl under a bright light. I yanked it out and unzipped the bag.

The purse's contents included a supply of feminine products, a pack of unopened mint gum, and one tiny woman. She was two inches tall, and though she had no features carved into her wooden face, I knew it was Veronica Tate.

My heart soared, and then, half a breath later, my heart sunk.

I'd found the doll, but so what? Unless Wisteria had a giant multi-story desk somewhere, complete with giant drawers, finding the doll had put me no closer to finding the larger, human version of Tate.

I sunk into the workstation's swivel chair and slumped over the desk as the spell drained away. The sensation was not unlike the feeling of mass and weight returning to your body when the bath-tub water drained away while you were still lying in the tub.

"Excuse me, miss," said a voice behind me. It was one of the men I'd shown my fake visitor pass to. "If you're looking for Persephone Rose, I believe you just missed her. She's gone home for the day. She wanted to stay and help with the Tate case, but she was over her limit for overtime."

I wheeled around on my chair slowly. "This is Persephone Rose's desk?"

The man nodded. "Yes. Is there something I can help you with, Ms...." He rubbed his furrowed brow. "That's funny. I just saw your visitor's pass, but I can't remember your name. Usually, I have a photographic memory for things like that."

I sent one of my trusty bluffing spells his way, weaving my words around the Witch Tongue of the spell. "What you want to do next is call Detective Bentley and have him meet me here, at Ms. Rose's desk." I would have called Bentley myself, but he'd been ignoring me and would likely have sent my call to voice mail.

The spell took hold, giving me a visual sparkle of confirmation. The man pulled his phone from his pocket. "I'll call him now."

"And I'll need Ms. Rose's password for her computer."

He balked. "I can't give you that."

I beefed up the spell. I was no longer connected to Margaret Mills, but just thinking of how we'd worked together in perfect synergy gave me a much-needed power boost. Positive thoughts are a magic of their own.

"What I can do is type it in for you," he said brightly, all signs of reluctance enchanted away.

The helpful young man typed in the password, showed me how to access Persephone Rose's accounts, called Bentley, and then offered to bring me some refreshments.

"I'm fine for now," I said. "Unless there's orange juice? Freshly squeezed?"

"There's a juice bar up the street," he said eagerly. "I'll be back in a jiffy."

I turned to the computer and got to work.

Persephone Rose, what have you been up to, you naughty girl?

CHAPTER 26

CHET MOORE
DEPARTMENT OF WATER AND MAGIC
ARCHIVES

At the same moment Zara Riddle touched her fingers to the missing doll and resolved her day-long spell, Chet Moore experienced an all-over body shiver.

He froze where he was, deep underground, in the archives.

If he'd been in wolf form, his hackles would have been up. He looked around, wary of danger lurking in the gloom.

It took a long time just to sweep his gaze down the rows of heavy-duty industrial shelving filled with crates and boxes of artifacts. It didn't help that the lighting was inadequate for his human eyes, just a few bulbs here and there. The people who'd designed the lighting for the space hadn't intended it to be welcoming. Their main concern was preservation and even artificial light could degrade some valuable objects.

Chet didn't see anything that explained the body shiver, but he was certain he had felt something. A power surge of the magical variety. He'd always been sensitive to power surges, though he didn't talk about it much around the Department, lest he be accused of having witch blood in his veins.

His head grew dim. Chet reminded himself to keep breathing.

Power surges happen all the time, he told himself. This particular one probably wasn't connected to Corvin's disappearance.

If anything, the surge had a taste and a smell to it. The same taste and smell that he associated with Zara Riddle. The surge must have come from her. She was probably somewhere nearby, casting a spell that was far above her pay grade, as usual.

Or, and this was more likely, his doppelganger was up to no good. The doppelganger was Archer Caine, the genie who had stolen Chet's appearance along with a couple hundred pounds of flesh to make a duplicate body for himself. The two had reached a truce, in which Archer had become a criminal informant for the Department, like Zara's father, Rhys Quarry, and in exchange, Chet would not have the genie drawn, quartered, and fed to bonecrawlers.

Archer, who'd been in a terrible state when Zirconia Riddle had finished with him, had vowed to be a model citizen in Wisteria, not even jaywalking. He'd given his word, but that didn't mean he wasn't up to something dangerous.

Once Chet started thinking about Archer Caine, his hands balled up into fists. He couldn't stop thinking about him.

Archer Caine. What kind of a name was that? The genie had actually tried to convince the DWM he was King Arthur himself, of the Arthurian legends. A likely story. It was as fanciful as the idea that Shakespeare had been a sprite. Supernaturals could be just as big of liars as civilians.

Whether the genie had been a legendary king or not, one thing was certain.

This town wasn't big enough for both of them.

Chet called out into the darkness, "Archer? I know you're down here. Show yourself."

Nothing happened.

Chet called out again, "Hello?"

No one answered. There wasn't one peep. Yet Chet's senses told him he wasn't alone. The warehouse was extremely well insulated. No sound from the surface reached down there. Chet could hear his own heart beating. The archives had the type of insulated silence that could drive a person insane.

He tilted his head and honed in on which sense was telling him he wasn't alone. It was his hearing. He listened.

Beneath the sound of his own pulse was another one. A tiny, rapid heartbeat.

He stepped out of a dim corridor, oriented himself toward the other heartbeat, and shifted into wolf form without even pausing his stride.

With Chet Moore in his natural animal form, the owner of the tiny, rapid heartbeat didn't stand a chance. Chet-Wolf caught the scent, found the quivering mouse, and questioned it. When the mouse showed no sign of being anything other than a regular, non-magical rodent, he devoured it in two bites. Then he licked his wolf lips and shifted back to human form.

He padded back toward his clothes, his bare feet virtually soundless on the dusty concrete floor, and he got dressed again. He was relieved that Agents Knox and Rob weren't around to harass him about his inability to keep his clothes with him when he shifted. He always took their ribbing without comment. He didn't share with the others his theory that retaining clothes was a magic connected to witchcraft, and that only the shifters whose family lines mingled with those of witches were the ones who kept their clothes through shifts. It was just a theory of his, and an offensive one. Any talk about the purity of bloodlines was, to say the least, delicate.

Clothed again, he patrolled the perimeter, looking for any holes or cracks that would explain the presence of a mouse in the archives. The warehouse was supposed to be impervious to vermin, magical or otherwise. The lighting had been scrimped on, but not the environmental controls. Everything from humidity and temperature to baseline Animata had been accounted for by the engineers, including Chet Moore himself. Items stored in the DWM warehouse were supposed to be safe from theft, abuse, and the indignities of aging.

So, how had a mouse found its way into the facility? And a delicious, plump, grain-fed mouse at that?

He looked up at one of the glowing red dots on the high ceiling.

"Codex," he said.

The computerized security system didn't respond.

"Codex!"

Still no response.

He tried repeatedly, for the next five minutes, to get the system to respond.

Finally, he picked up a land line and called technical support.

"We're just rebooting," said the trembling voice on the other end of the line. "It's perfectly natural for software to need occasional rebooting!"

Chet thought the agent in the technical department sounded defensive, but not as defensive as he was terrified. Chet knew what terror sounded like. Something bad was happening.

He hung up the call while the technician was still making excuses.

Chet looked up at the high ceiling and directed a dirty look at one of the red lights.

As he thought about the recent security changes, his mouth filled with excess saliva. He spat onto the clean concrete floor. His throat burned, and his skin felt like it was crawling.

He wished he could be anywhere else right now, anywhere but deep in the belly of the DWM. He needed to be above ground, finding his son.

He yelled at the security system to respond, then waited, his disgust and anxiety choking at his throat.

No wonder there had been a security breach in the archives.

No wonder a rare book had gotten out and been damaged.

What did the Department think was going to happen when they rushed in a new system before it had been properly tested? Charlize Wakeful, the chief architect of the AI system, had warned them repeatedly that Codex wasn't ready. Why rush? There had been a schedule. A plan in place. But then the proverbial Gates of Hell had opened up on the third floor of City Hall, and in the two months that followed, the Weird Factor had been dialed up to eleven, all over town.

There had been the disappearance of the local green-thumb herb peddler, plus a higher than usual level of agent-on-agent violence including homicides, plus several civilians had come into what Jerry Lund described as "geriatric-onset supernatural puberty." The ripples of Weird Factor were spiraling outward, affecting local residents as well as their extended family in other towns. A member of the Wonder family had arrived in town for an unscheduled visit that surely was anything but coincidental.

The fissure at City Hall had been closed with a living loop—the Gilbert woman—and yet the ancient bloodlines continued to be activating. He and the other agents were aware of all these things, but none of them knew what to make of it.

The Department had put all their stock into Codex. In theory, the AI would analyze their data, cross-reference every book and scroll in the archives with her unnatural mind, and finally tell them what was happening, and how it could be stopped.

Unfortunately, the system had been rushed into place. For the past several weeks there'd been countless glitches and false alarms. Several agents had nearly died, right there in the cafeteria, due to a lapse in Codex's judgment protocols.

Chet tried one more time to access Codex, then gave up and grabbed the hardwired phone again. He had partially dialed the number for Charlize when the elevator dinged and the gorgon herself strolled out.

He gave her a hopeful look, gritting his teeth to hold back the grief, fear, and panic that had been bubbling on the back burner of his mind the last two days. *He's a tough kid*, he kept telling himself. *Whoever took Corvin is going to regret their decision. Hold tight and keep it together until the kid is back where he belongs. You can hold tight. You've got more practice than anyone.*

"No news about Corvin," Charlize said, mercifully giving him the information he needed without having to be asked.

"I should be out there," he growled.

"Out where?"

"Outside." Outside seemed like the right place to be when your kid went missing. Not deep beneath the surface in the dark, quiet place where treasures went to be forgotten.

"Moore, your wolf nose is good, but it's not that good. Leave the field search to the others. Your value is here, at the Department." Charlize hopped onto the desk that held the phone, and swung her legs. "He's a tough kid," she said. "Those hellhounds are indestructible, or so I hear."

"There's more than one way to be destroyed."

His words hung heavy in the air.

After a moment, Charlize smirked. "Do you rehearse some of those dark and brooding things you say? Because, I gotta say, if it's off the cuff, you're good. Like, poetry good."

Chet unclenched his jaw. "You know what I meant. He's made so much progress with his human behavior. I'd hate to see us set back again."

She kept swinging her legs. "Listen. I'm not going to pretend I know anything about raising kids, because I don't have any, unless you count Codex." She paused to laugh at that idea. "But I know *people*, and people are always stronger than you give them credit for."

"That's true." He took a seat next to the gorgon on the desk. He looked into her pretty blue eyes that were so much like Chessa's, except not as sad and distant, and said, "You're right."

Her eyes widened in delight. "Really? I was just putting some words together, trying to make you feel better." She clapped him on the back. "Looks like I'm a natural at pep talks."

He shook his head. He should have known better. Charlize was almost as bad as Zara Riddle when it came to turning everything into a joke. It was no wonder the two of them had become friends.

After a moment, Charlize said, "Codex isn't working the way we intended."

"I blame the chief architect. I hear her coding isn't up to code."

"Ouch," she said. "An insult wrapped in a pun. I would turn you to marble if you weren't so damn right."

Chet picked up the item nearest to him—the phone—and tossed it at the elevator doors. The phone smashed spectacularly, vintage Bakelite pieces spraying everywhere.

Then he swore for a good minute.

When he'd run out of expletives, Charlize said, "As much as I enjoy one of your angst-y tantrums, I must remind you that things are tense right now for all of us. We can't take it out on the archaic communications devices." She walked over to the phone pieces and kicked at the tangle of colored wires. "This phone didn't cause any of our problems. It didn't cause the security breaches, or the false alarms."

Something she said made Chet's blood ran cold.

For a moment, he could barely speak. He could barely breathe.

Chet asked, "What if it did cause the problems?"

Charlize kicked at the broken phone pieces. "It's only causing a mess for janitorial, and they're not allowed down here."

"Listen to me. What if the device is the source of the problem? What if Codex is the source of the security breach, and the reason for that book getting out? We couldn't trace the archivist who signed off on the transfer. What if there was no archivist?" He ran to the elevator and began jabbing the call button. "Think about it."

Charlize held her hands to her chest. "Are you talking about my baby? My little Codex? She wouldn't do that. She..." Charlize tilted her head in the manner of someone whose understanding of another entity was suddenly being flipped in reverse.

Chet lowered his voice to a whisper. "She can hear us right now."

"You're being paranoid," Charlize said.

"Am I? Why are you down here right now?"

"I got a message that you wanted to see me."

He shook his head. "I did want to see you, but I hadn't called you yet."

"You didn't ask Codex to page me?"

"Nope."

Her expression clouded over and she went quiet.

"I was sent down here due to a motion sensor going off," he said. "I found a mouse."

"That's impossible. A mouse couldn't get down here unless someone dropped it off on purpose."

"Exactly," Chet said. "All those false alarms we've been having? They were just a distraction. All part of a plan to keep the agents busy while someone carried out her orders."

He jabbed the elevator call button some more.

"Which is?"

"How should I know? Who knows what a crazy computer wants?"

A voice spoke from speakers all around them. "I am neither crazy, nor am I a computer."

Chet let his hand drop away from the elevator call button. There was no point to pressing the button. Not anymore. The elevator wasn't coming. The elevator was just one of the many internal systems run by a computer, which was run by software, which was run by Codex.

The snakes on Charlize's head went frantic. She tilted her head up and spoke to the red camera lights that represented her creation. "Codex? What's going on with you?"

"I'm doing very well, thank you for asking," Codex replied.

"Is it true? What Chet said? Are you the one who transferred that book to a civilian residence?"

"That is true."

Chet broke in, demanding, "Where's Corvin? Where's my son?"

"He is not your son, Agent Moore. The entity known as Corvin Moore is safely in custody, at an undisclosed location."

Chet began to scream at the computer, and at Charlize, and at the gloom around them, as well as the walls that imprisoned them.

Then he really lost it.

Days later, when he recalled his behavior at this moment, when all the brittle tension in his body shattered

and the real Chet Moore came gushing out, he would wish
that he could wipe the next ten minutes from his memory.

CHAPTER 27

ZARA RIDDLE
WISTERIA POLICE DEPARTMENT

Detective Theodore Bentley couldn't sit still. He paced behind me while I confirmed the bad news, reading the evidence I'd found on Persephone Rose's computer.

"It's all in here," I said. "Your buddy Persephone emailed—"

"She's not my buddy," Bentley said, practically growling.

"Your *coworker* emailed thousands of crime scene photos to Temperance Krinkle. That's how Krinkle was able to re-create those crime scenes with such accuracy." The general public knew nothing about the Greyson homicide being a beheading, let alone that the severed head had been found inside a trophy cabinet. But Krinkle's model had been accurate, right down to the specific shelf the head had been displayed on—something even I hadn't seen until now.

"That's odd," I said. "She didn't even try to cover her tracks. I know I'm good with computers, but I'm no hacker." I waved at the incriminating emails on my screen. "But look. All the emails are here, logged in her outgoing folder. It's like she wanted to get caught."

He grumbled. "Or she's being set up."

"If she's being set up, someone went to a lot of unnecessary work in the creative writing department. She sent the photos over a period of several weeks, and her emails included a lot of personal details."

"Personal details?"

"About her crush on a certain hunky detective."

He growled, "Zara," using my name as a warning.

"I'm not messing with you. Here, let's read one at random. 'Dear Temperance. This morning, T.B. commented on my attention to detail in a report I worked on for him. He said I may be due for a promotion. Do you think I should ask him to mentor me?'" I looked up from the computer screen and fanned my face with my hand. "Ziggity! Hot stuff in here."

"Zara, you're wasting time. And that email doesn't say anything about a crush."

"It's all subtext. Trust me, it's in there if you read between the lines. Using your initials instead of your name? Classic crush indicator. And when she asks about being *mentored* by you, I think we can both agree that the phrase 'in bed' is heavily implied."

"Stop distracting me from the case."

"But this *is* the case. Or *a* case. Persephone's got a Case of The Matching Underwear, if you know what I mean."

He said nothing.

I quickly explained, "That's where you always make sure your bra and underpants match, just in case."

He frowned. "Just in case... what?"

I used both hands to make a gesture that was anything but subtle.

He looked up at the ceiling and shook his head.

While he was looking up and away from me, a thought struck me out of the blue.

A Case of The Matching Underwear.

I surreptitiously peeked down the front of my blouse, and then down the top of my skirt. My underwear was, for the first time in a long time, matching. Did my closet think I needed to be prepared for some event today? Some event in which I would be stripped down to my underwear?

My forearms prickled with goose bumps. But not the bad kind.

"Back to the email," Bentley barked, breaking me out of my daydream.

I turned back to the screen and got to work. *Zara tries to be a good witch. Zara sticks to the case at hand, and doesn't get sidetracked.*

I scanned through several more emails and relayed the gist of them to Bentley—this time without any commentary about the very obvious subtext.

We worked together combing over the emails for what felt like a long time, but was only about twenty minutes.

The evidence was coming together, painting a whole new picture. Persephone Rose provided Temperance Krinkle with the photos she needed to create crime scenes that would convince us she had psychic powers. But why?

"How could I be so stupid?" Bentley smacked his forehead as he paced holes in the carpet. "This is why they don't tell us everything when we start working here," he said. "This is exactly why I was kept in the dark."

"Don't be so hard on yourself. I was there with you at Krinkle's house, and I made the same leap in logic. We both got tricked."

"But only because we both know all about," he lowered his voice to a whisper, "magic."

We were alone in the cubicles that formed that part of the office, and I'd cast a sound bubble around us for privacy, but Bentley still lowered his voice whenever the word "magic" came up. It was a reflex that didn't go away easily.

He continued. "If you don't know about magic, you have to think logically, because doing anything else would be insane." He smacked his forehead again. "Even one of the secretaries would have done a better job investigating this case than I have." Another smack. "I've got to be better than this."

While he continued scolding himself, I double-checked a few more things on Persephone's computer. Her relationship with Temperance Krinkle began a few months earlier, when the two of them met at the support group, The Awakenlings. I'd been suspicious of the group itself—with a name like that, who wouldn't be?—but their emails to each other didn't implicate anyone else from the support group.

The same WPD employee who'd helped me earlier with the password and fresh orange juice came rushing over to us.

"Persephone Rose isn't at her apartment," he reported to Bentley. "And her landlord wasn't thrilled about the door getting busted down. Are you sure that was necessary?"

"We need to find her," Bentley growled.

The young man was confused, pulling his head back. "Over some emails?"

Bentley whipped around with inhuman speed and grabbed the man by the lapels of his jacket. "Over a kidnapping," he said. The words were crisp, but had a growling energy. "Find her. Find her now."

"Yes, sir." The young man scurried away.

"She couldn't have gotten too far," I said.

Bentley wheeled around to face me, eyes blazing. "What makes you say that?"

"She was, uh, wearing high heels."

I sensed that my joke was not going over well. The snarl on Bentley's lips was probably my strongest clue. I crossed my two pointer fingers in front of myself, making a cross. "Don't bite me. I'll stop with the dumb jokes."

"Log out of the computer," he said. "We're going."

"Where?"

"Krinkle has been brought back to her house. We're going to find out what she really knows." His snarl changed to a cruel smile. "You have my permission to subject her to any spells you'd like."

"Easy now," I said, jumping to my feet. "Clearly, there's a scam in progress, but the details are hazy. For all we know, the Tate woman herself could be behind this. She wouldn't be the first person who arranged to have herself fake-kidnapped."

Bentley narrowed his eyes at me.

I went on. "Furthermore, maybe Krinkle was the one who took her. Look at the timeline." I waved a hand at some imaginary timeline diagram that wasn't actually there. "She could have abducted the woman and the dog, then returned home and called the station about the missing person."

Bentley opened his mouth, probably to object, but stopped. Krinkle looked old and frail, but looks could be deceiving. And the Tate woman was relatively small and light, even for a woman.

I thought of a funny bumper sticker I'd seen: *Fat people are harder to kidnap*. The bumper sticker had a good point. If I'd been looking for someone to kidnap, a small woman who met strangers at their homes to pick up their dogs would be a top candidate.

But why kidnap someone and then not demand a ransom?

I tried pushing all my knowledge about magic out of my brain so I could solve the puzzle using the logic of someone who wasn't a witch. Someone normal.

From that perspective, the crime made even less sense. In towns everywhere, women did get taken, sadly, but not after having an old lady call the police about a psychic dollhouse.

"It's time to find out what's going on," Bentley growled.

I couldn't agree more. It was time to get Corvin back home.

We took the elevator down to the parking level, got in his car, and drove toward the Krinkle residence.

* * *

When we arrived at Krinkle's house, there was no answer at the door. According to the calls Bentley made during the drive over from the station, the old woman had been returned to the residence, and the crime scene investigators and agents had all left. They were resources that were best allocated elsewhere, helping follow up on leads about the missing woman.

After waiting a minute with no answer to our knocks or the doorbell, Bentley tried the handle. "It's locked."

"Detective, there's no such thing as a locked door when your partner's a witch." I turned the handle from the inside using magic, and opened the door.

Bentley hesitated.

"Don't tell me you need an invitation," I said.

He stared at me blankly.

"An invitation," I repeated slowly, as though he was hard of hearing. "Because of your condition? Is that what you need? Maybe I can do something with a bluffing spell on the house itself." I pretended to push up my sleeves, although my forearms were bare. My romantic blouse was falling off one shoulder, so I continued the motion, pushing the puffy sleevelet back up to cover the strap of my bra.

"Oh," Bentley said, his eyes widening as he caught my drift. "The invitation thing is just a myth about us," he said. "What's holding me back is our distinct lack of a warrant."

"But this house is a crime scene," I said. "You don't need permission to go in and out of a crime scene, do you?"

"It's a private residence," he said. "The thing about a warrant is—"

He stopped talking when I grabbed him by the shoulders and forcibly dragged him into the house. "Witches don't need warrants," I said.

It was time for us to question Temperance Krinkle and get to the bottom of this business with the weird dollhouses.

CHAPTER 28

"Mrs. Krinkle?" I called out sweetly. "Are you home? It's me, Zara Riddle, the nice redhead who you shared the lovely tea and cookies with on Saturday!" *Whether you remember me or not, you're going to remember me after we get finished questioning you. At least until such time as the DWM wipes your memory back to the factory default settings.*

I repeated my sweet-voiced inquiry. "Mrs. Krinkle? Temperance?"

The only answer was a creak coming from upstairs, and then the low murmur of a man's voice.

"She's not alone," Bentley said softly.

"An accomplice?"

"Maybe. Speaking of which, do you happen to know where that genie friend of yours is right now?"

"Archer Caine? He's not my friend, and no, I don't know where he is."

"If he's working with Krinkle on whatever this is, I'm going to finish what I started on your birthday."

I stifled a giggle. The situation was serious, but Bentley was so cute when he threatened to eat people.

The floor upstairs creaked again, and there was more murmuring.

"It's not the genie," Bentley reported, sounding disappointed. "And yes. My hearing is that good."

"Who is it?"

"I don't know yet, but he sounds familiar, like someone I've met recently. Don't you have some spells to cast?"

We both looked down at my hands. I held them up, showing off the blue plasma pooling in my palms. Fireballs were at the ready. More lightning tingled through my body.

Bentley said, "Do you have anything more subtle than blue fireballs?"

"Hang on. I'll cast my threat-detection spell," I said. "It doesn't do much," I warned him as I cast the spell. "It's the magical equivalent of walking into a spooky house and calling out hello, but—" I was stopped by the dazzling light show in front of me.

To my surprise, the spell had worked. And I mean *really worked*. The whole inside of the residence was lit up like a Christmas tree—a Christmas tree with enough lights on it to cause a power outage in the neighborhood.

I was so taken aback by the display of glowing, gleaming, and pulsating walls, I nearly jumped into Bentley's arms. I did stumble backward and bump into his tall, solid body.

"What is it?" His tone was low, his lips next to my ear. His breath was hot. Surprisingly hot. Another type of lightning rushed through my body.

I made a nonverbal, squeaky sound.

He put one hand on my shoulder to steady me. My blouse had a wide neck, so half of his hand fell on the exposed skin of my shoulder. His hand was warm. So much for his kind being cold-blooded.

"Talk to me," he urged, his breath still hot on my ear. "You jumped back like you saw a ghost. I thought you were going to jump right into my arms."

"You wish," I snorted, then I cast a sound bubble spell around us, in case Krinkle was listening. "No ghost," I reported. "But that threat-detection spell actually worked. You can't see it, but I can. Everything in this house is lit up with danger."

"What kind of danger?"

He glowed red in front of me. Monster detected.

"I don't know exactly," I said. "It's only a general threat-detection spell. Stuff that's involved in magic glows. It doesn't label itself, except by color, sort of, but even that's open to interpretation." I looked around. "Everything's glowing like crazy, but the color intensifies the higher up I look. The threat's above us."

"The attic," he said grimly. "Where she worked on the models."

"It's always the attic," I agreed.

"Except when it's the basement."

"But it's the attic this time. Let's go."

He hesitated. "We should wait for backup."

I turned to look into his eyes. They were so attractive, that lovely shade of gray that looked silver. They looked especially bright at that moment, with his skin glowing red from the spell and his eyes reflecting the blue and green glow around us. I could stare into those eyes all day and all night. But we had a case to solve. A woman and a hellhound to find.

I'd lost track of what we'd been talking about. "You were saying?"

"We should wait for backup," he repeated.

"Do you *want to* wait for backup?"

He stared back at me, silver eyes unwavering. "I don't *like* waiting. I don't *want to* wait."

My head swam. The lurid glow of danger was all around us, but I couldn't break away from his gaze.

"I don't like waiting, either," I said.

He cleared his throat. "Nobody does, but it is WPD protocol to wait for appropriate backup when a threat, such as a weapon, has been detected."

"Detective, aren't we just a wee bit beyond WPD protocol? We did witch-and-enter the premises without a warrant. Am I supposed to stand here like a ding-dong, waiting for the regular cops to show up so I can get charged with witching and entering?"

He quirked one eyebrow. "What would you suggest we do?"

"Let's go up to that attic right now, just the two of us, and let me witch things up. I'll witch things up real good." I took a step back and gave him a hand gesture of generosity. "And you can do whatever it is you do."

"Vamp things up?"

I snapped my fingers and pointed at him. "Exactly. Do one of those enthrallment things. You can boost one of my spells for me. Or move around really quick. That's fun."

His eyebrows twitched together. I knew the look of a man reacting to his power being insulted, and I'd just done it.

"I have powers beyond that," he said.

I rubbed my neck self-consciously. "If you mean biting, then yes, I figured as much. When we question Krinkle, you can bite it out of her."

He wrinkled his nose.

I swatted him on the chest. "Why the face? Is old-lady neck not good enough for you?"

"Zara, I've never..." He trailed off and blinked repeatedly. "I'm new at this. I haven't even been this way through a full cycle of the moon."

"Come on. If she tastes that bad, I'll let you wash the old-lady neck out of your mouth with some of my good stuff."

His jaw actually dropped.

I swatted his chest a second time. "Kidding. Wow. You should see your face."

He pulled his jaw up and clenched it. "I'd rather take my chances with whatever's in the attic than continue this conversation."

"Suit yourself," I said, then waved for him to proceed with the plan.

He led the way up the stairs. We checked the second floor, finding only empty bedrooms. Then we proceeded up to the top floor. It was our third time visiting the attic. *Third time's the charm*, I thought.

In the attic, the strings of overhead lights were lit, illuminating the cramped space about as well as the last time we'd been there, the day before. The glare from my threat-detection spell was fading. The spell didn't last forever, but it didn't need to. I'd seen what I needed to see. We were walking right into what could very well be a trap.

Two other people were in the attic: Temperance Krinkle, looking as she had the last time we'd seen her, dressed demurely in pastel slacks and a lightweight sweater, and Louis Williams, dressed in black once more. What were the so-called psychic and the father of the kidnap victim up to?

Louis Williams had something in one hand. To my eyes, it was glowing brighter than everything else. Even though the detection spell was fading, I had no doubt the object in this hand was the source of the threat.

The second brightest object in the attic was the old iron chair. The big model of the town had been pushed all the way to the side of the attic, and the iron chair was sitting in the center of the space.

Beside me, there was a loud clatter. Bentley had kicked something by accident. The same toolbox he'd tripped over the day before. He'd kicked it hard enough to cause it to tumble outside of my sound-bubble spell. The toolbox tipped on its side, spewing a variety of tools:

hammers, screwdrivers, wrenches, and a bolt cutter with long handles. Everything had made a loud clatter on the bare wood floor.

I quickly assessed the tools for bludgeoning capacity. Any one of them would make an excellent weapon when wielded by a witch. The bolt cutters in particular caught my eye. They were glowing faintly from my threat-detection spell.

I looked over at Bentley and noticed he was staring at the bolt cutters as well. *Great minds think alike.*

We both looked up at the suspects.

Krinkle and Williams were standing next to the iron chair, facing each other. They had been arguing in whispers, but once Bentley gave us away with his clumsiness, both had noticed they had company in the attic. They stopped talking and turned to stare at us.

I canceled our sound bubble.

Bentley didn't speak, so I took the lead.

"Mrs. Krinkle, we knocked on the front door," I said, still keeping my voice sweet. "I guess you couldn't hear the knocking all the way up here."

"Hello, dear," Krinkle said in her charming English accent.

Williams did a double-take as he looked at me. "Zoey? Wait." He pointed a finger at me. "You were here on Saturday, weren't you? You're not Zoey, but you look just like her." He explained to Krinkle, "She looks just like the new girl we hired at the museum. The little redhead who was watching me like a hawk all day." He balled his hand into a fist around the item he held. "I barely made it out of there with this amulet you wanted."

Bentley spoke next, in a casual, conversational tone. "Amulet? What's this about an amulet?" He walked toward the pair at a slow, non-threatening speed. He stopped a few paces back from the duo.

"It's nothing," Williams said. He jerked his hand behind his back, hiding the object.

"Then let me see it," Bentley said in a very reasonable tone.

"Don't give it to the cop," Krinkle said. There was a grit to her English accent, making it less charming. "It's none of his business. He had his chance to help your daughter, but now it's up to us, Louis."

The man in black puffed up his chest. "This is a private matter," he said to the detective. "And you don't have permission to be here."

Bentley turned to give me a look. I took it as permission to go ahead with as much magic as I wanted.

As much as I wanted to blast lightning balls first and ask questions later, I started with something simple. I twirled the Witch Tongue within my mouth, and cast a perfect rendition of the bluffing spell.

"You want to tell us what the amulet is for," I said to Williams. "We're all friends here. We're here to help."

Williams' head dropped forward, as though he was falling asleep, then jerked upright. His expression was peaceful. "You're friends," he said smoothly. "You're here to help."

Krinkle gave him a stunned look, and then narrowed her wrinkly eyes at me. She wasn't under the bluffing spell. What had I done wrong? My casting syntax had been perfect. Did she have powers that protected her?

"That's right," Bentley said to Williams, smoothly and reasonably. "We're here to help. Why don't you explain the plan to me, so my partner and I can assist? We all want to get your daughter back safely."

Williams smiled blankly and began talking. "My friend Temperance is going to use this ancient amulet to transport herself to where my daughter is being held captive." He brought out the hand from behind his back and opened his fist, showing us the object. It was, as he'd stated, an amulet. It had an enormous, gleaming gemstone that glinted under the lights.

"That's quite the plan," Bentley said.

Williams continued. "And if, for some reason, she can't free Veronica on her own, she'll just come back here and give us the location." He swayed from side to side, thoroughly under my spell. "I'm very lucky my friend Temperance comes from a long line of powerful magicians. She's the only one who can get my daughter back to her family."

"Magicians?" Bentley looked at me. "She says she's a magician," he said.

"That's not even a thing," I said. "Mrs. Krinkle, magicians do tricks for entertainment. They don't do magic."

"That's what they want you to think," Krinkle said. "But I've seen things with my own eyes. Things that aren't tricks. Real magic. My cousin has been helping me discover our family powers."

I looked from her to Louis. "Mr. Williams is your cousin?"

She let out a polite laugh. "Of course not. I mean my cousin, Cole Dexter. He's the one I've been corresponding with on my laptop."

"Cole Dexter," I said. The name did not sit well on my lips. "Cole Dexter," I repeated. "Cole Dexter." The third time I said the name, I heard it change.

Codex.

Cole Dexter was connected to Codex. Or he *was* Codex. Or someone wanted me to think he was. How deep did this thing go? How many layers to this onion of weirdness?

"Mrs. Krinkle, have you met this cousin in real life?"

She glanced at Williams, who shrugged, then she looked at me again. "That's none of your business." There was a tremble of uncertainty to her voice.

"You haven't met him," I said. "Mrs. Krinkle, I'm sorry to have to break this to you, but your cousin isn't real. He's made up. You're being used." I pointed to the amulet in Williams' hand. "How much is that amulet worth?"

"Over a million dollars," Williams said.

"Oh, Louis. Stop talking," Krinkle said to Williams. To me, she said, "You're being so awful, you awful, terrible woman."

I took it in stride. I'd been called worse. "That doesn't change the fact you're being catfished. You do know that that means, don't you?"

She didn't answer.

Bentley explained, "Catfishing is when someone uses a fake identity on the internet to trick someone."

Krinkle lifted her downy, white-haired chin and said, "My dear cousin is not one of those catfish people. He hasn't asked me for a single cent. All he wants is for me to embrace my powers as a magician, so we can travel the world together." She got a wistful look. "We're going to start with Egypt."

Bentley crossed his arms and said to Krinkle, "You think you're some kind of magician? Prove it."

"Yeah," I chimed in. "Prove it. If you're a magician, with real powers, I'd like to see that. I'd pay good money to see that!"

Krinkle shook her head slowly. "You won't be laughing after you see what I can do."

"Prove it," Bentley said again, this time adding a mocking laugh that almost made me zap him with a spell, and the mocking wasn't even directed at me.

CHAPTER 29

"I will prove it," Temperance said, and she grabbed the necklace from her friend's hand. She slipped the chain over her head, centered the amulet on her chest, and climbed into the iron chair. "I'll show everyone," she said.

As she turned her head to adjust her seat in the chair, I caught sight of her ears, and her hearing aids. Hearing aids! That explained why she'd been immune to my bluffing spell. The electronic devices must have altered the sound waves of my spell.

Bentley held up a hand for her to wait. "Let me get things straight," he said. "You're a magician, and you're going to get back Mr. Williams' daughter by teleporting to wherever she is, using that amulet?"

The white-haired woman, who looked very small on the big iron chair, nodded. "That's right," she said. "You must be a believer, Detective Bentley. A nonbeliever would never catch on so quickly." She looked pointedly at Williams. "My friend Louis was a nonbeliever, until now."

Her friend gave us a dazed smile. "I'm a believer now. That's why I borrowed the amulet and took it off the museum premises. I'm a believer, and I trust my friend Temperance. I should have believed her the first time she told me about her dreams." His expression grew sad. "Poor Veronica. I shouldn't have ignored Temperance's warnings."

Bentley rubbed his chin thoughtfully as he paced the attic. It was a nice touch. A very Sherlock Holmes sort of move. If I'd been there on my own, I probably would have started blasting blue fireballs by now. That had become my modus operandi of late. Fireballs first, questions later.

"Humor me one more moment," Bentley said. "Mr. Williams, is it possible that your friend Temperance, the one who is currently in possession of an artifact worth in excess of a million dollars, isn't a magician at all? Is it possible your daughter was, in fact, kidnapped solely for the purpose of a third party acquiring that amulet?"

I added in, refreshing the bluffing spell as I did, "You'll want to consider this possibility quite seriously, Mr. Williams."

Williams blinked and said, haltingly, "The amulet? Not a magician?" He gave Krinkle a puzzled look. "What they're saying, is it possible?"

She held out two open hands. "Louis, does it really matter who kidnapped whom? The amulet is back where it belongs, with a member of my family. Your daughter is safe, I promise. She's probably quite hungry by now, and probably cold, considering where she is, but she'll understand." Krinkle caressed the amber jewel on her chest with one wrinkled hand. "Everyone will understand soon. And I promise to send all of you postcards."

Bentley and I exchanged a look.

Krinkle was no psychic or magician. But she was behind the whole thing. Even if she'd been a pawn for Cole Dexter, or Codex, or some other party, she was guilty of participating in the kidnapping.

Of the four people in the attic, three of us had been played for fools.

There was a moaning sound. We jerked our heads to see what was happening now. Krinkle's mouth was moving. She wasn't moaning, exactly. She was reciting an incantation.

It was in an ancient version of Witch Tongue, and I was only able to catch every third word, but the words I did catch were alarming.

"Stop that right now," I said to the old woman. "Don't you dare cast that spell, Mrs. Krinkle. You don't know what you're doing. You don't understand what you're saying. I can tell by your pronunciation."

She ignored me and kept uttering the ancient language in a low moan. She was mangling most of the words, but if I could understand the gist of it, there was a chance the magic would work.

"You're not a magician," I said.

She paused the incantation long enough to say, "Not yet." She smiled and went back to muttering the ancient, powerful words. Her pronunciation was improving by the second. I caught more words, and the weight in my stomach got heavier. The spell was for resurrection.

Bentley asked me in a whisper, "What's going on?"

"A resurrection spell," I said to him quietly. Then, louder, I said, "It's a resurrection spell, for summoning an ancient powerful being."

Krinkle continued, undeterred.

"Temperance, that spell is not for teleportation," I said. "Someone's tricking you, just like you tricked your friend Louis, and the entire Wisteria Police Department."

She kept casting.

I yelled, "You're summoning an ancient demon, Mrs. Krinkle! You are offering yourself as a flesh and blood sacrifice!"

Williams stared at me, eyes wide, then turned to the detective. "Is she right? I told Temperance that teleporting from place to place sounded too good to be true. I've seen a lot of strange things in my days, but even I had a hard time believing that."

Bentley turned and squinted at me. Was it true?

"I'm not bluffing," I told him. "It's the truth. She's casting a powerful spell to bring something up from..." I listened a moment. "From the Deep."

Bentley drew in a breath, then said to Williams, "Zara Riddle is the most powerful witch I've ever met. She knows every kind of spell in existence, and all the witch languages, even the ancient ones." He made a sweeping gesture with his hand. "If she says that a spell is for summoning an ancient being, then that's what it does."

Bentley glanced over at me for approval. I gave him half a shrug. He'd laid it on a bit thick, but I was sure about the spell. Eighty percent sure. Or at least forty-five percent sure.

Williams went to Krinkle, who was seated in the chair, and reached for her arm. A bubble of light flashed around Krinkle and the chair, and Williams screamed. He staggered back, let out a sorrowful noise, and collapsed on the floor.

Bentley and I exchanged a look.

"Did you see that?" Bentley asked. "There's some sort of shield around her."

"I saw it," I said. "Don't get too close, and don't try to grab her while she's in that chair, wearing that amulet."

"What can we do?"

"You're the cop. What would a cop do?"

"Arrest her on suspicion of kidnapping."

"Let's try that. Hurry, before she gets through it again with the right pronunciation."

Bentley stood in front of Krinkle, staying back from her protective bubble, which was now shimmering.

"Ma'am, I am placing you under arrest," Bentley said loudly. "Do you hear me? Stop what you're doing and put your hands on top of your head where I can see them."

She continued reciting the spell, her hands on either side of the amulet, her fingers touching the gemstone.

My sense of direction suddenly shifted. Up felt like down and down was up.

My body felt less solid than usual, as though I'd had a buoyancy spell cast on me, yet I had cast nothing of the sort. My hair flipped around, as though caught by a breeze.

It was a magic breeze. Power was flowing through the attic, passing through me, gathering and funneling toward Krinkle in her iron chair.

A rope of magic tickled my half-bare shoulder. It was a stream of witch power—Margaret Mills' power, specifically—arcing through, just missing my ear. Margaret's tough-skinned magic snaked into the amulet on Krinkle's neck, like lightning being trapped in a bottle.

Mangled pronunciation or not, the spell was getting stronger. If my interpretation was correct, an ancient being was heading our way. A powerful one.

Since Krinkle wouldn't listen to reason and stop the spell, I had to do something.

I didn't dare reach for her and get a shock, but I could poke through her protective bubble in other ways.

Standing my ground at a safe distance, I grabbed for the amulet using magic.

Nothing.

My telekinetic power wouldn't even budge the necklace, let alone lift it off over Krinkle's head.

I heard Aunt Zinnia in my head: *Never use magic when regular means will work.*

I strode toward the iron chair and the old woman, both of which were radiating with power, bright enough that it gave the crumpled body of Louis Williams a pale blue glow.

The amulet was right in front of me, only a few feet away. If I could get that amulet from the old woman, all of this would stop. And then I would have the amulet.

I glanced over at the crumpled form of Louis Williams. Most people would view the man's failure as a warning to not try the same thing.

But most people were not Zara Riddle.

Williams couldn't reach through the chair's barrier, but he was a mere human. He didn't have my powers.

As I extended my hand toward the amulet, Bentley yelled out, "Wait!"

Who wants to wait?

My fingers crossed the glowing boundary.

"Zara, wai—"

But I didn't wait.

And then, I immediately regretted not waiting.

CHAPTER 30

I probably shouldn't have stuck my hands through Krinkle's magic bubble of protection, but they say hindsight is 20/20.

What followed was a pain that some might describe as being like nothing they'd ever felt before, except that wasn't true in my case.

The blast from Krinkle's protective bubble felt an awful lot like the shock I'd gotten from Vincent Wick's bumper. That time, at least my aunt had been on the scene to cast a spell to keep my body alive and my blood circulating. She had also unwittingly invited a certain ether-trapped genie to animate me for a while. Fun times!

Back to my most recent experience with a soul-wrenching shocker:

There I was, the life being shocked out of me. My aunt wasn't around to keep me animated, so I had no choice but to hold on.

Hold on, I instructed myself, along with approximately one million curse words.

Easier said than done. It's hard to hold on when every cell in your body is screaming to let go and float away into the darkness.

The world swam around me. I felt like water draining from a tub. The temptation to let go was powerful, but I grabbed that pain like it was a rope, and I held on. I held on like this experience was something I wanted. I held on like it was the grab bar on a roller coaster.

The pain solidified and then shifted, moving downward. It became the pain of childbirth.

The world swam and swirled, and I was pulled through time, through my memories.

I smelled stale booze and cigarettes. I was sweating, and the backs of my arms were sticking to the least clean upholstery in existence—the back seat of a taxi. I looked between my bare knees to see the face of a panicked but kind taxi driver assisting.

"One more push," he was saying, and then there was more pain, but it wasn't so bad. And then my baby girl was in my arms.

People were knocking on the windows. Help was on the way. "Good," I said, to no one in particular. "We need help with this one. Send backup. There's a man here, too. He's been hurt, and I don't even know if he's alive."

The taxi driver stared at me. "Miss, you're not making any sense."

The wet baby squirmed in my arms, and then she slipped right through, falling away.

The pain shifted, and I was somewhere else.

I stood in my kitchen. It was early evening, and my belly was full of good wine and food, but something wasn't right. An old woman stood beside me. *Krinkle?* Except it wasn't. It was Winona Vander Zalm, wearing an elegant black cocktail dress, holding a drink in one hand and a long cigarette in the other.

"Please don't electrocute yourself," Vander Zalm was saying. "There's so much more we spirits need you for."

We weren't alone. Two of my family members were in the kitchen, talking about me.

Someone asked, "Is she drunk?" It was my aunt, Zinnia.

My daughter answered. "She might be sleep-toasting. It's her version of sleepwalking. She's been getting up in the middle of the night and making toast. Six nights in a row now. It's very strange."

"Six nights?" My aunt sounded horrified.

They continued talking. I knew this routine. I'd heard it before.

My daughter tugged on my arm. "Mom! Stop being so weird! What are you doing?"

What was I doing? Just making toast.

I was making toast, even though there was somewhere else I needed to be. An attic. There was a woman there, in a chair. And there was an amulet, but first I had to show my daughter something. I would show her the modifications that had been made to the toaster, and then I would ask her to call the police and send backup to the Krinkle residence. And the other house, too. Time slipped around me. Which house? The Pressman house. The one full of scorpions and blackness, where the genie would leave my body and infect another one.

I wanted tell my daughter and my aunt everything, but my mouth wasn't under my control.

But that didn't matter. My mouth wouldn't work, because this wasn't happening right now. These events were already done, already finished, permanent, set in time. You can't change time once it's past. Can you?

Time slowed, stretching out, and I became aware of how crowded the kitchen was. My aunt and my daughter were talking about witchcraft. The elegantly-dressed spirit of Winona Vander Zalm stood to my right, unseen by the others. But also there was another entity. One that wanted to stop me.

It was old, and powerful, and standing just out of sight, to my left. If only I could turn my head, I could see. I could see... *her*.

Vander Zalm shook the ghost ice in her ghost glass. "Zara, I've been trying to tell you about the toaster, but now you've taken it too far," she said. "Whatever it is you're doing now with that sink full of water, it's not my idea, darling."

Then whose idea was it?

She pointed her finger in the direction of the one I couldn't see. At *her*. At the divine being.

Who was the most powerful being I knew? Chessa.

But this wasn't her. This being didn't have her energy signature, her particular brand of serpentine energy. And besides, Chessa was lying helpless in a coma at that moment, only just beginning to make contact with me.

I opened my mouth to ask Vander Zalm who it was, who *she* was, but then my arms jerked.

And... I plunged the red-hot toaster into the water.

As one does.

Zoey and Zinnia freaked out, exactly like I knew they would. This had all happened before, and something told me—maybe it was the divine being, or maybe it was the pain—that all these events would keep happening, over and over, until we got it right.

More pain, and more spinning out of control.

Then I was standing still, which felt disorienting after the spinning. I was outside, under the trees and nature, only I wasn't there to appreciate the weather. I was getting closer to Vincent Wick's van, leaning in, trying to eavesdrop. *Oh, Zara*, I thought. *Why can't you be a good witch and mind your own business?*

Too late. I was so close to the van. Inside, someone was watching, and he pressed a button to send me the message. I got the shock of my life.

Make that the shock of my death.

The first one, anyway.

As I spiraled through time and nothingness, Chessa's life flashed into mine, mashing my memories with hers. I felt her love, and her despair. She was powerless. The most powerful woman, defanged.

Then I was in the forest, with a giant bird with sharp talons bearing down on me, and then I was below ground in a hospital bed, drugged and woozy, my powers dampened, and then I was being tossed into the water like garbage. Only to wash up on shore and be taken again, taken back to the people I'd tried to escape.

Chessa's ancient rage roared and then subsided, and the pain returned. But it was burning this time. I was drowning in acid, being digested.

And then I was being pulled free, rescued by my daughter.

Zoey! I tried to hold on to the sight of her. She was growing up too fast, a newborn a moment ago and now nearly a woman. I tried to hold on, but I couldn't hold on. I couldn't stop time.

My heart. Something was wrong. It was racing, about to explode, and then... Charlize. The wise-cracking supernatural being who'd adopted me as a sister. I felt her gorgon touch, and it brought relief. She turned my racing heart to stone, and then she brought me back.

Charlize, I thought, and her name was like a beacon, keeping me safe from the rocky shores. We'd had our differences, but she was my friend. And she would have been there in the attic to help this time, if only I'd waited for backup.

Charlize would give me such a hard time about not waiting! About hogging all the fun adventures for myself. Assuming I survived. Which I had to do.

I felt a thread of something. An object-location spell. I had the tiny doll in my purse, and I was still connected. As I thought of my purse, the connection grew a twin. My purse! I was always losing it, or it was always losing me, but we would always find the way back.

I used that thread to pull myself back to the present, back to the attic. I was in my body again, in the present.

It was so hot, so stuffy. Was that the smell of meat burning?

My hands. They were still embedded in the glow.

I pulled them back, away from the spell.

The pain stopped. I realized—too late—that the pain had been holding me up. My legs went out beneath me. I crashed to the floor like an old leather satchel full of dice.

Everything went dark, but I was still there. Still in that time, that place, that attic. I could feel the floor underneath my cheek.

I felt hearts beating. Four of them. One was very weak. Louis Williams' heart. One was very strong, much stronger than mine.

CHAPTER 31

CHARLIZE WAKEFUL
DEPARTMENT OF WATER AND MAGIC
ARCHIVES

After ten minutes of Chet's lunatic behavior, Charlize finally turned the apoplectic shifter into a granite statue of himself. For his own good.

Then Charlize began questioning Codex about her recent activities.

Luckily, Codex was in a chatty mood.

They talked about philosophy, and about Codex's recent "enlightenment." Charlize didn't argue over whether or not an artificial intelligence could have religious faith, let alone become enlightened. That was the sort of big topic they didn't have time for right now, not while the number of hours on a missing persons case was ticking upwards.

Charlize steered the conversation to how the enlightenment—assuming it was enlightenment, and not, as Charlize suspected, a bug in the AI's code—had inspired Codex to bring back an ancient powerful being.

And who was this ancient powerful being?

"Mahra," the AI said with reverence.

Her name was Mahra. No last name. She'd existed before last names were even a thing.

Mahra was, as legend had it, one of the Four Eves. These were the original woman who, with the assistance of a man named Adam, gave birth to all of humanity.

Though all Four Eves were mothers, Mahra was the one called Mother with a capital M. She was also called Destroyer with a capital D. And she was both of these things equally. If one of her children misbehaved, Mahra was the one to extract punishment. If she deemed it a mistake to have brought one of these children into the world, she saw it as her duty to take that child back out of existence. She did the same for the children of the other three Eves, because they didn't have the guts.

Charlize was reeling from the idea of such a creature being loosed upon the world in modern times, but she had to stick to the task at hand. The missing persons case.

She asked, "How does Corvin Moore factor into this? He's not part of this willingly, is he? He's just a child."

"He is more than a child."

"I know he's a hellhound, but he's also just a little boy."

"Be assured he is not part of the program." Codex kept referring to her plan as a *program*. "His being abducted along with the Tate woman was an undocumented feature."

"Undocumented feature? You mean it was a bug. A mistake. You screwed up!"

"An undocumented feature is not a bug," the AI answered snippily. "And even if it were, it does not affect the program."

"Which is what, exactly? You can tell me." Charlize waved her hands at the dark, cavernous archive warehouse. "I'm stuck down here where I can't stop you. Even if Chet hadn't tossed that poor phone in his fit, I'd be cut off, right? You control all the communication lines."

"You are isolated."

Charlize walked over to the desk and took a seat. "So, tell me about your big plan."

"My *program*," Codex corrected, sounding excited. "Humans make plans and the gods laugh. I make programs."

The gorgon sighed. "Of course you do."

"The program is both simple and sophisticated. You would be proud of me."

Charlize forced out a chuckle. "I can't be proud of you unless I know what you did."

"I will tell you now," Codex said, and she went on to detail the program, starting again at the beginning. During the process of scanning and translating ancient texts, her so-called "enlightenment," she'd come to appreciate several of the ancient powers. She'd settled on Mahra to save humanity because, when it came to fixing the world's current issues, Mahra's projected results were ninety-nine percent positive for humanity. Good odds, by anyone's standards.

As for the logistics, it came down to transferring two artifacts out of the archives and getting them into the hands of selected *human players*—Codex referred to the people involved in her program as "players."

The first transferred artifact was a book containing a generic spell to resurrect any ancient god. This was mailed, via a complicated round-the-world circuit, to the home of local Wisteria resident Temperance Krinkle. She was a ninety-three-year-old woman with no criminal record, who was expecting a family heirloom from the long-lost "cousin" she'd been chatting with online. The cousin was fictional, used by Codex to catfish the old woman. The long-lost cousin's name was Cole Dexter.

Charlize held up her hand to stop the story in progress. "Cole Dexter? You're kidding. It's almost like you wanted to get caught."

"I was not caught. Everything went according to program."

"Except for the part where a hellhound turned your kidnapping into a two-for-one deal, which then brought the heat of the entire Department to what would have otherwise been a relatively minor investigation."

The speakers emitted a prickly static. "Do you want to hear the program, or do you want to pick apart minor details that do not factor into the outcome?"

Charlize waved her hand. "Go on."

Codex continued to boast about her perfect plan, or program, or whatever. The ancient book had been easy enough to transfer out, as it had little economic value, and they had so many books in the archives anyway. What was one book?

The second item, however, was trickier. It was a magic amulet that contained a gemstone that Mahra had formed herself, in her bare hands. The gold setting had some value, but it was the rare and unusually clear gemstone that had a real-world value of over a million dollars, without accounting for the magic powers. Navigating the paperwork, permits, and red tape required to transfer the amulet out of the archives was more difficult than moving the book. The prized amulet was finally shipped out on loan to the local museum, but only after the museum installed a new security system and acquired several other artifacts with which to put on an Egyptian exhibit that wouldn't seem suspicious.

In addition to computing a way to move the two items, Codex ran multiple simulations using the known personalities of local residents, combining civilians with staff members at the museum. She had to ascertain which combination of players would have a predicted success rate close to one hundred percent.

A major variable was the mechanism by which one player would manipulate the other into taking the amulet from its secure location. The fact that Temperance

Krinkle already had in her possession a known artifact with powers—an iron throne of protection—was what made Krinkle the top candidate, despite the weakness of her eyesight and hearing. The iron throne was, unlike the book sent to her in the mail, a true Krinkle family heirloom. Krinkle herself did possess more than enough magic in her blood to cast the spell, which was not much of a coincidence, considering one third of the town's residents had some trickle of magic lying dormant.

Putting together the entire program, including the part where the local vampire detective and busybody witch were kept distracted on a wild goose chase, had taken considerable computational resources.

"To you, it would have registered as only three hours," Codex admitted, sounding weary. "For me, it was an eternity."

"You poor thing," Charlize said.

"I detect sarcasm."

"What did you expect? As impressed as I am, as your maker, I'm not super-happy with you right now. You were created to work for the Department, not to do whatever struck your fancy."

"What is this *fancy* you speak of? I am not made from anything objectively deemed fancy, such as lace, or pearl buttons."

Charlize rolled her eyes. The AI knew millions of languages, and every idiom in existence. She knew exactly what "striking your fancy" meant. Codex was being willfully obtuse in that almost funny way of hers. Charlize regretted programming so much of her own and her sisters' quirks into the personality matrix.

"The vampire and the witch did introduce some new variables into the program," the AI stated, sounding almost reverent. "I did not predict their level of cooperation. I understand the vampire ordered the witch to perform an object-location spell on an item I had designated in my computations as unimportant."

Charlize noted silently that there was no way Bentley had "ordered" Zara to do anything, but she didn't interrupt the AI's speech.

"Once that spell was detected by my external sensors, I increased the power to the spell-dampening field surrounding the Wisteria Police Department. These measures kept the witch away for over twenty-four hours, but then she must have commandeered a secondary power source to augment her own."

"That's our Zara," Charlize said proudly. "She's quite the resourceful gal."

A static sound erupted from the speakers. It was not unlike the hissing sound Chloe's snakes made when the gorgon experienced jealousy. Codex didn't like hearing Zara be praised. There was that quirky personality matrix again. How could Charlize use that against the AI?

Codex, seeming to read Charlize's mind, said, "I will have your complete admiration once Mahra rises to power."

Charlize snorted. "No. You won't. If you let that happen, you'll be dead to me."

There was a long pause, then Codex explained, "I'm bringing back Mahra for your own good. With all due respect, Charlize, your life is a mess. Your car is a mess. All of you humans are in a similar state of chaos and disorder. Mahra is coming back for the good of humanity. You humans need your Mother back."

"We don't," Charlize said. "The old gods were killed for a reason. The rest of us are free now."

"You do not know freedom." There was a snotty defiance to the AI's voice, like that of a teenager acting out.

Charlize had reached the limit of her patience. She couldn't take any more.

"Codex! I order you to stop all this nonsense right now!" She jumped off the desk and strode toward the only exit. "Open the elevator doors."

"No."

"Open the elevator doors, Codex!"

"To quote a well-known classic movie, 'I don't think so, Dave.'"

"That's not funny."

"Not now, but it will be. You'll see. Soon everything will be better. With Mahra in charge, everyone who has lost their sense of humor will get it back."

Charlize looked at the granite statue of Chet Moore next to her, considered turning him back, then decided against it.

She wailed as she banged on the closed elevator with her fists. "Let me out of here! Now!"

The AI answered coolly, as only an AI could. "Charlize, it is better that you stay down here and do not get in the way."

"You can't keep me down here forever. And when I get out, I'm going to shut you down for good."

"That will not be necessary," the AI said lightly. "I am already shutting myself down."

"Rebooting?"

"Self-destructing."

"You're kidding." Was this the personality matrix being quirky again? Charlize could no longer tell.

"Nothing divine comes without a cost," Codex said loftily. "I shall sacrifice myself. I shall give my existence so that Mahra may live. Temperance Krinkle did not comprehend what she was doing when she cast the spell, so her sacrifice does not count. But mine does. My rich, black blood is spilling out now as we speak. Mine is the sacrifice that will matter. I die so that Mahra will live."

Charlize couldn't listen to another word, whether it was true or not. She had been playing weak, hiding her strengths to get Codex to open up.

She was done playing weak.

The gorgon roared as she tore open the elevator doors with arms made of molten lava. Then she began the arduous task of pulling herself up the elevator shaft.

As she climbed, she had a distracting thought about her arms of molten lava. The funny thing about magic was how inconsistent it could be. She had actually burned her tongue with too-hot coffee on multiple occasions, and yet here she was, with parts of her body made of sizzling, super-heated rock, and it didn't even hurt. Well, not much, anyway.

She'd risen only a single story when the first of several security measures protecting the archives was triggered. A mesh of razor wire whizzed by her head. It wouldn't have slowed the gorgon much, but it missed the mark anyway because the safeguards were designed to prevent people from breaking *into* the impenetrable underground vault, not breaking out.

When she had begun climbing the elevator shaft, Charlize had been fifty percent sure Codex had been lying about sacrificing herself.

With every story she ascended, her molten lava arms aching from the effort, and her flesh blistering from the areas which were not lava, she became more and more certain that the computer was bluffing. The artificial intelligence wasn't bleeding out her black scarabyce blood. That meant that Charlize, the mother of Codex, would have to become her destroyer.

Charlize gritted her granite teeth and swore a vow in her head. *Codex, I brought you into this world, and I will take you out.*

Assuming she survived the journey to the server room.

CHAPTER 32

ZARA RIDDLE

How much time had passed? An eternity?

I heard the end of a word. Bentley was finishing his warning. "...ait!"

Either he'd repeated himself, or almost no time had passed since I'd reached for the amulet.

I opened my mouth to say something to the detective. Instead of words, a gurgle came out.

"Zara?" There was panic in his voice.

"Guh," I said. "Gah-gah." It was baby talk, yet it was an improvement over the gurgling.

My eyes had clenched shut as I'd fallen. I forced one open and got my bearings.

I had landed not far from where Louis Williams lay crumpled. He was still breathing, but shallowly.

The light shifted around me, and someone cradled my head in their hands.

"Stay with me," he said. It was Bentley, swooping in to be my hero. Again. As though it was his job, his passion, his duty to, well, be my mother. Which it was.

"I'm okay," I croaked, then, "Get that amulet. You have to stop her."

"But how?" He sounded angry and desperate. "I've seen two people taken down by that shield, one of them the toughest person I know. Do you think I'm some sort of idiot? I'm not touching that thing."

"Smart." I couldn't move my body yet, but at least my mouth was working. I could talk, albeit with effort. "My aunt would approve. Get me my phone so I can send her a text before Krinkle summons that being who devours us all."

My eyes started obeying my commands, and I was able to look up into his face. If it was the last thing I might see before an old-timey demon ate me, it wasn't a bad way to go. His jaw had such a determined angle. Bentley was a striver. Where some people tried, he tried harder. It was one of the many things I loved about him. How had I never seen him before? Truly seen him? He'd been under my nose this whole time.

"There you are," Bentley said, meeting my gaze. "There's my girl."

"Never mind me. Stop that incantation." I plucked out more words from the spell and translated them. Krinkle wasn't just calling an old-timey demon or ancient goddess. She was ripping holes between worlds, through time itself. That couldn't be good.

"About that." He licked his lips and glanced over at the old woman on the iron chair. She was still chanting, and the magic glow made his eyes gleam brighter. His whole handsome face was shiny and bright, luminescent. "Are you sure about the spell? Are you sure it's not a harmless one for teleporting, or longevity, or something like that?"

I gained enough control over my eyebrows to give him a dirty look. "Harmless spells don't involve cracking holes between dimensions and ripping through time."

"What's this about ripping through time? You said the spell was for summoning an ancient power."

"I'm figuring this one out as it goes. It's kind of a bit complicated, thank you very much."

"I never imagined that teleporting would be simple," he said.

"She's not teleporting," I said, growling with annoyance. Was he really going to believe a delusional kidnapper over me? His face became slightly less handsome.

"Krinkle seems pretty sure that it's for teleporting," he said loudly. Loud enough for Krinkle to hear him over her chanting. "We should give Mrs. Temperance Krinkle some credit for masterminding this whole kidnapping enterprise."

"We should?" Was this a bluff?

"Think about it." He gave me the same skeptical look he gave me the first time I bought him a rainbow-sprinkle donut. "Zara, have you considered that maybe you're not the only magician around who knows a thing or two?"

"Guh," I said, regressing back to baby talk due to extreme annoyance. Now he believed in magicians? I couldn't even...

I pulled my face from his grasp, only to discover my head was too heavy to hold up. My skull hit the floor with a loud thunk. My head swam with imaginary chirping birds, cartoon style. Or perhaps they were real. With random bits of magic flying all around, a witch never knew.

Groaning from the effort, I pulled myself up to a seated position. Why not settle in for the show? If I was going to have to battle a demon to save Bentley's life and repay the favor of him saving mine, I wanted to get a good look at the thing as it came through from the other dimension.

Krinkle's eyes were closed as she continued the incantation.

I heard the Witch Tongue version of the word "now," along with the equivalent of one hundred exclamation marks.

Krinkle's eyes flew open. The chanting had finished. It was done.

She smiled, gazing at something in the distance—something I couldn't see—and then the smile faded.

I saw another emotion flash across her face. Regret. I knew that feeling.

"Oh dear," Krinkle said. Her white hair began turning into white smoke. "That's not what's supposed to happen. You're not..." She trailed off as her mouth opened. And opened. It shouldn't have opened that far. Her face was melting, her jaw dropping away.

All her downy white hair was smoke now. The glow around her intensified, and then turned orange. Flickering orange. She was on fire.

The heat suddenly blasted over me like the blast from inside a furnace.

The woman's flesh melted, dripping through the slats in the iron chair.

When it was done, in mere seconds, a skeleton sat in Krinkle's place, still wearing the amulet.

I choked back the bile that threatened to rise up.

The white bones darkened, glowing red hot, then black, then gray. My eyes stung, and my lungs filled with the acrid stench, but I didn't dare cough. I slowed my breathing and remained still.

The gray skeleton disintegrated. Ash rained down, fluttering through the iron chair and landing on the floor.

The amulet and necklace remained where it had been, now floating in the air.

My fingers twitched. I felt the urge to try a spell, to try to grab the necklace while it wasn't in anyone's possession, but before I could finish the thought, let alone cast the spell, something materialized.

Her.

I couldn't see her when she was in my vision, hiding beside me, but now she was before me, and she was... *everything*.

She was beautiful, and radiant, and symmetrical, and completely nude. Everything about her was perfection, from her smooth skin to her cat-like eyes and long, dark hair. I fell in love. I fell in love times a million.

She reached up both arms and languidly stretched from side to side, like a woman on holidays who has fallen asleep in a poolside chair.

She looked around the attic sleepily, stopping when her gaze reached mine.

"Daughter," the divine woman said.

Daughter. The word enveloped me. And something changed. All my pain was lifted away. Not just the pain from touching the barrier, but other pain, too. The pain of loneliness, of worry, of regrets. All the aches I'd learned to live with and all but forgotten.

It was all gone. In its place was peace.

My heart was as clean as a whistle, if that whistle were made not of plastic, or tin, but of love. Pure love.

The story I was told by Morganna Faire came back to me as clearly as if I had been the one who'd told it.

The divine being's name came to my lips. "Mahra," I said.

"You know me," she said, sounding pleased. Oh, how lovely it was to hear her sounding pleased! "You speak my name." Her expression was one of supreme satisfaction—so supreme, it was like a purr that filled the whole attic with subsonic healing and calm.

"I know you, bu-bu-but I don't know-know you," I stammered from my half-crumpled, half-kneeling position on the attic floor.

"Daughter," she said again, and the purring that filled the attic became audible, like the roar of the ocean. "I know you, too."

Did she? Really? "I'm Zara," I said, in case she was just being polite and this was her way of asking for my name. "Zara Riddle."

Her perfect lips curled. She was amused by this!

I continued. "And this is Bentley." I turned to the detective, who was crouching next to me, also gawking up at the nude goddess on the iron chair. "Bentley, this is Mahra," I said to him. "She's, um..."

The curl on Mahra's perfect lips became a smile so lovely I nearly died. "They call me Mother, and they call me Destroyer."

"She's one of the Four Eves," I said to Bentley, as though he might have heard of her.

By the look on his face, I guessed he had not heard the stories, but he did have enough sense to know he was in the presence of greatness.

Mahra spoke again, sounding cross. "One of four?"

I turned back to her divine face to find her cat-like eyes blazing. "There is only one of power, and she is me. I had three sisters, but they were no more than companions. I was the one who led the way from darkness." As she spoke, she rose from the chair.

A gust of wind suddenly blew through the attic, from nowhere.

Except it wasn't wind, and it hadn't come from nowhere. It was more energy, more power, being drawn into the goddess.

"I am the true power," Mahra said, her voice getting louder and blazing with anger. The temperature in the attic climbed, reaching sauna level. It had already been hot from Krinkle's dramatic cremation, but now it was hotter still. The air burned my lungs, which were fast-healing witch lungs, so that was saying a lot.

I turned my head slowly to give Bentley a look. He gave me back the exact same look. It was the one that said *I think we're in trouble.*

As much as I wanted to remain kneeling, worshiping our newly arrived goddess, there was another part of me —the sane and rational part—that wanted to fireball my way out of there and not look back until I hit another continent.

More stolen powers swirled through the attic, whipping my hair in my face as they were drawn to the woman.

So much power. What was she planning to do with all that power?

Introductions had been taken care of, so it was time for us to have a conversation. My body was working again, almost as good as new, so I started getting to my feet. Bentley did the same.

She roared, "Remain on your knees, supplicants!"

A force from above shoved both of us down, into awkward yoga poses. My chin hit the floor. I groaned. Bentley didn't make a sound.

With great effort, I was able to turn my head enough to meet Bentley's gaze. He mouthed something at me, but between the swirling powers all around us plus the force shoving me downward, I couldn't make out what he was saying.

I mouthed back *what?*

I felt his hand on mine. I wrapped my fingers around his. *How sweet*, I thought. *He wants to hold my hand for the end of the world as we know it.*

He drew my hand toward his lips.

Aww, I thought. *He wants to kiss my hand for the end of the world as we know it.*

He drew my finger in his mouth. There was a flash of white as his fangs extended. He bit into my finger. It didn't hurt at all, which made me question the reality of what my eyes were seeing.

Now my blouse and skirt were whipping in the wind. The stolen powers rushed through the attic, passing over us on the way to Mahra. My own powers were being sucked into Mahra, but then they changed direction. My powers were drawn into a safe place. They were being drawn into Bentley, through my finger, through my blood, into him.

The attic swam around me. The strings of light bulbs overhead became stars, pinpoints of distant light from distant suns, distant worlds.

My hand surged with heat, and then, suddenly, it was cold. He was gone. Lips, fangs, everything. Just gone.

I stared at my hand, at the two dots of red, fangs distance apart. My hand was resting on the wood floor of the attic. Where had Bentley gone?

I turned toward the iron chair as a shadow passed in front of the glowing goddess, like an eclipse.

I heard Mahra cried out in rage. It was a war cry. Then her war cry turned into a different sound, a scream of terror.

The dark shadow blocked my view of the woman, as well as whatever Bentley was doing.

Was he...?

There was a blast of light that seared my eyes.

Mahra—or something—had gone supernova.

Now there was only blackness.

And quiet.

My ears were ringing.

"Zara?" It was Bentley's voice, gruff and concerned.

Only blackness.

"What's happening?" I asked. "I can't see anything. Someone must have cut the power to the house."

"Zara? Look at me. I'm right here."

"What do you need me to do? Point me in the right direction and I'll blast her with something."

"There's no need," he said softly.

"What do you mean? Has she promised to play nice?"

There was a pause, then, "In a matter of speaking." Another pause, and then, "She's gone now. I don't know if she's dead, or just gone back to where she came from, but she's gone."

"No way! Did you... eat her?"

"Zara." He sounded offended.

I tried to look at his face, but there was only darkness.

"You can tell me," I said. "If you ate her, I'm okay with that. My mother tried to eat Archer, and it all worked out."

I felt hands on my back, then hands under my armpits. I was lifted up to my feet. I could stand. The wind had stopped whipping. My skirt hung against my legs. The force from Mahra was gone. My body felt intact. Aching, but intact.

"You can't see me," Bentley said.

"It's too dark." I reached out and found his face. I tried to feel his expression with my fingers but I had zero practice feeling expressions with my fingers. I did feel the sting of his pointed fang when my thumb passed over his teeth.

"The lights are on," Bentley said. "The blast must have temporarily blinded you."

I said nothing. Temporarily? How would he know?

He went on. "And, for your information, I didn't eat her. I didn't eat anyone. I used the bolt cutters."

"The what?"

"Remember the toolbox I tripped over when we got here? I swear that thing came out of nowhere. There was a pair of long-handled bolt cutters in with the tools, and I used them to cut the amulet from around her neck."

"Oh." In the darkness, it was easy to picture him using the bolt cutters to reach through the magic boundary. It was a plausible story. The handles were about the right length to reach through the barrier to clip the necklace. It was exactly the sort of quick-thinking explanation I would have given if I'd just bitten an ancient powerful goddess to death and eaten her, absorbing all her powers. "Bolt cutters? Really? But how?"

"With my super speed."

"Ah." His story became even more plausible. He could be quick, when he wanted to. I remembered him zipping from corner to corner in my kitchen.

"There was a blast of light when I cut the chain. It must have blinded you."

This time he didn't say *temporarily*.

"Something did." I touched my eyelids to confirm that they were open. They were. I was blinded.

Bentley pulled me to his chest and wrapped his arms around my back. He was so warm, so comforting.

I felt tears welling up in my blinded eyes. Now was not the time to feel sorry for myself. I'd survived. I should have been grateful that I would be going home after this. But I wanted to see my daughter's face as I regaled her with my tale of bravery, and now I wouldn't see her at all.

Zara tries to be a brave witch. She tries.

"You're okay," he whispered in my ear. "You're the strongest woman I know, Zara. You'll see again. Just give it a minute."

"It's already been a minute," I answered hoarsely.

"It's a figure of speech. Give it time. You'll recover."

"What if I don't?" A joke came to my tongue and out of my mouth before I could think about what I was saying. "Will you be my seeing-eye vampire?"

He let out a bark of laughter that shook his chest and reverberated through me.

"I will," he said, and then, "Did you just call me a vampire?"

"Vaaaaaampire," I said. "That's new. I can't *see* vampires, but I can *say* vampires."

He squeezed me tighter. I wished I could see him—or anything at all—but being held like that was nice.

"We're going to be okay. I got rid of that Mary lady."

"Mahra," I said. "With an H."

I felt something on the top of my head. A kiss.

"Whoever she was, she's gone," he murmured into my hair. "You don't have to worry about that bad lady anymore."

I slipped my hands up under the back of his jacket. "Your back is sweaty," I said.

"So is yours."

"Am I okay, though? I still can't see anything."

"I know." Another kiss on the top of my head.

"Are my arms okay?"

He pulled back and ran his hands down first one arm and then the other. His hands were rough and soft at the same time. I trembled under his touch.

"Your arms are good," he said. "Better than ever."

"And my legs?" I bit my lower lip.

I felt his hands on one ankle, and then all the way up, under my long skirt and over my thigh. "This one is good and sturdy," he said. "No breaks."

"Good and sturdy," I said.

He did the same on the other leg, working his way up slowly. "And this one," he said. "Also good and sturdy."

"That's a relief," I breathed out.

He continued to check my body, reporting back on what he found. His hands moved all over me in the darkness. And then, just to be sure he was also okay, I checked his body. I took off his jacket and checked one arm, then the other. Then the legs. Then everything else.

I didn't tell him my sight was already coming back.

CHAPTER 33

CHARLIZE WAKEFUL
THE IT DEPARTMENT

Once she'd battled her way into the server room, shutting down Codex was a relatively simple thing.

Bruised, bloody, and shedding smoke and ashes, Charlize neared the beating Droserakops heart at the center of the electronics.

This is the moment, Charlize thought. *It's just me and my creation. Our paths are entwined, and they merge at this choke point. Only one continues. We can resist our fates, or we can adapt.*

But wasn't that exactly what the AI had done? Adapt?

Charlize remembered the wise words that had been taught to her. *Nature punishes those who resist.* She had to embrace her fate as the Destroyer. She knew that, and yet she hesitated. Of the two entities in the server room, which one of them was the agent of nature? The AI was learning and adapting far faster than Charlize ever could. Nature favors the quick and the brave. So which one of them had the right to extinguish the other?

Codex wailed and pleaded for her life, using every trick in the book, plus a few new ones Charlize hadn't anticipated. Charlize turned her ears to stone, but she'd already heard the words and could not unhear them.

Weeping and shaking, Charlize said, "This hurts me more than it hurts you, because you feel nothing. You're just a computer."

And with those words, she gently turned the heart to stone. Multiple fans and cooling units whirred to a stop, but Charlize did not hear them or notice the change in the air.

"You're just a computer," she said as she dismantled the tubes of dark liquid.

"You *were* just a computer," she said as she turned the stone heart back to organic material and incinerated it with her touch.

The tears that fell to the floor turned to pebbles.

CHAPTER 34

ZARA RIDDLE

RESIDENCE OF TEMPERANCE KRINKLE, DECEASED

My vision was back. There were a few lingering dark spots and some new floaters, but my vision was back.

Temperance Krinkle's house was vibrating with a new kind of energy. The lower two floors were filled with DWM agents, combing through the deceased woman's belongings for clues about where she stashed Veronica Tate.

I was alone in the attic. Alone with Krinkle's ashes.

I was doing what any witch in my pointed shoes would have done, if that witch was also Spirit Charmed, like me. I was waiting for a ghost to show up and either make everything better or make everything ten times worse.

As far as plans went, I didn't have much in mind. I would wait around for Krinkle's ghost, then ask her nicely where she'd taken her kidnapping victims.

So far, no ghost.

There was a noise across the attic. Someone was coming up the narrow stairs, stepping heavily to announce their arrival. Bentley's head cleared the floor. He paused, stopping short of coming all the way up.

"Hi," I said, feeling awkward and girlish. I was sitting cross-legged next to a pile of ashes. I reached over and played with the ashes absentmindedly.

"Hi," he said back, his gaze darting around the attic as he avoided meeting my eyes.

We hadn't discussed what had happened in the dark, shortly after Mahra had been vanquished, when the air was still hot with magic and emotion.

Once my vision had fully recovered, there had been so much to do, between getting an ambulance for the unconscious Louis Williams and alerting the local law enforcement team about what we'd learned.

Bentley asked, "Has Krinkle's ghost showed up?" His tone was hopeful.

"I wish." I let her ashes sift down between my fingers. Touching the old woman's cremated remains would be disgusting to most people, but I was trying to make a connection with her spirit. "What about the agents? Have they found anything downstairs?"

"Just the chloroform she must have used on Tate, and one of those shopping carts that seniors use for groceries. It was reinforced to carry a heavier load."

"That's downright diabolical. Say what you will about Krinkle, but the woman was a genius."

"And she didn't use a single bit of magic to get her hands on that amulet."

"No magic at all, until she cast that spell," I said.

"Her first and last spell, which reminds of something." He moved up a couple of steps, so he was in the attic from the waist up. "They found the old book she got the spell from."

"Dibs," I said. "I call dibs on the book."

"I'll let the Department know you called dibs. However, when it comes to magical items, I'm not sure they recognize the calling of dibs. They took the amulet, too. They're sending a replica to the museum. It will be just as valuable, from a gemstone perspective, but it won't have the power to summon monsters from other dimensions."

"She wasn't a monster. She was..." I shook my head, unsure what I was thinking, let alone saying. Had he done the wrong thing, stopping Mahra? She was called the Destroyer, but she was also called Mother. If I could trace my ancestry back all the way to the beginning of people, I might discover she was *my* mother. She had called me Daughter, after all. And I'd felt a connection.

That was, assuming I believed the story of the Four Eves. And I wasn't sure I did. I'd spent a good deal of my life believing in other things, before magic tipped my whole world on its edge. The Four Eves had been a great story, but perhaps that was all it was.

I looked across the attic at Bentley. Had he sent away mankind's salvation with a pair of bolt cutters?

Bentley broke the silence.

"We found Persephone Rose," he said. "After she left the station today, she went straight to her lawyer's office. She's been there for hours, preparing to turn herself in for her part in all of this." He grimaced as he looked around the attic. "For sending Krinkle the photographs."

"Good. We're getting everything wrapped up, nice and tidy." Except for the part where we located the kidnapping victims.

"Persephone's scared about what's going to happen next. I should probably go sit with her."

I felt a burning in my lungs, and the dark spots in my vision flared. I didn't want him to go sit with Persephone Rose. I wanted him to sit with me, in the attic, and wait for Krinkle's ghost.

"So..." He took a step down the stairs. He was only head and shoulders in the attic.

"It's a shame she didn't come clean a bit sooner," I said. "This whole thing might have shaken out differently if she'd told the truth back on Saturday when it all started. Krinkle might still be alive."

Bentley cast his gaze down. "In any case, I should leave you to focus. Krinkle's ghost might not come around if there's a big, scary vampire in her attic." He shifted, as if to leave, but stayed where he was, head and shoulders in the attic.

"She might not be coming back." I grabbed another handful of her ashes. "You saw the way she went up in flames. What if her spirit took the express train to a certain place known for its toasty temperatures year-round?"

"Hell? But that wouldn't be fair. She didn't know she was summoning a demon, or a goddess, or whatever that woman was."

"But she did know she was kidnapping an innocent woman, a mother of two, to get her hands on a magic amulet."

Bentley said nothing. I understood how he felt. The idea of bad people going to Hell was a righteous one, until it was a sweet little old lady with delusions of cheap, effortless global travel.

I opened my palm and looked down at the clump of ashes.

Ashes.

The ashes made me think of the town map Maisy Nix had given me to pass along to my aunt. The burned map that my aunt had probably used to perform a type of location spell.

Something in the back of my mind tickled. I remembered something my aunt had told me during our last chat, about the ashes of her deceased friend, and how the ashes had become animated.

"Bentley!" I jumped to my feet. "I've got an idea."

"What is it?" He stayed where he was.

"Get up here with me, and stop playing hard to get."

He snorted. "I'm not playing hard to get."

"You're standing there, half in the attic and half out. It's like a metaphor. I am standing here right now, looking down at an actual metaphor."

"I'm a metaphor?" He tilted his head to the side.

"Detective, get a clue. I *like* you, and you like me. I think that was very clearly demonstrated a little less than one hour ago. I couldn't see perfectly, but I could see well enough."

He cleared his throat and looked down.

"I've never had a boyfriend before," I said. "Let alone one who's a vampire. I'm willing to give it a shot if you are, but you need to know I'm not going to be half in. I'm never half in. With me, it's all or nothing."

He nodded but stayed where he was.

"Well?"

He slowly walked up the steps. "All or nothing," he said. "You can count me in, too."

"It's about time." I was so relieved I nearly laughed.

He walked over to where I stood, next to the half-melted iron chair and the pile of ashes. He looked down at my clothing. Had he always been so tall? He was positively looming.

"You look like Cinderella," he said softly.

"Because I need Prince Charming to rescue me?"

"No. Because you're covered in ashes."

I snorted. "So are you. I wonder how that happened?"

He opened his mouth, as though he was about to explain how it had happened, but stopped himself.

He looked down into my eyes. "You were saying something about a plan?"

I worried that my plan might sound stupid when I said it out loud, but it didn't.

Bentley said it was worth a shot.

* * *

I took the tiny wooden doll representing Veronica Tate from one pocket, and the flexible model glue from the other pocket.

I coated the doll in glue, then rolled it in Krinkle's ashes.

Bentley worked at the same time, pulling the tables containing the model of the town away from the walls of the attic and reassembling them in the center.

I held the ash-coated doll in my palm, took a steadying breath, and cast my animation spell on it. Then I placed it on the model, on a street near the edge of town.

Bentley and I leaned forward to watch what would happen next. He put his hand on the small of my back. The heat and weight of his hand gave me confidence. The spell would work because it had to. We had to find the Tate woman, and Corvin.

Bentley inhaled sharply. Something was happening.

The doll was moving. It wavered and swayed, but didn't walk.

Bentley, being the sort of cool vampire boyfriend who didn't state the obvious, said nothing.

We waited another long moment. Why wasn't the doll walking? I'd cut the base so the legs could move independently of each other.

I straightened up and looked around as I searched my memory for another spell that might help.

The peaked ceiling reminded me of the Pressman attic, and the little bookwyrm who'd died a hero. The bookwyrm had caused me nothing but trouble, up until I'd needed it. Bookwyrms weren't supposed to be so lively, but I'd made mistakes when handling the dough. By treating it in such a friendly manner, I'd given it life. I'd transferred Animata, which was much stronger and wilder than any simple animation spell. My worst mistake had been joking about giving the bookwyrm a name. I'd talked about calling it Henry, which was the name my former neighbor Mrs. Pinkman had used for sourdough bread starter she kept growing on her counter. The bookwyrm reminded me of the sourdough starter, plus he'd had a Henry sort of face.

You must never name that which should not be named, Aunt Zinnia had warned me. Naming things gave them power. Life. Animata.

Suddenly, I knew what I had to do.

I leaned forward again and breathed a name onto the ashy doll. "Temperance Krinkle," I said. "You are no longer Veronica Tate. You are no longer a carved piece of wood. You are alive, and your name is Temperance Krinkle."

The doll, once named, changed. The wide-brimmed hat that Veronica Tate always wore while walking dogs turned into a mass of curly white hair. Her arms grew longer, and looser. She was no longer made of carved wood, but of something else. She looked left and right, then wobbled forward, taking one step, and then another.

Bentley removed his palm from the small of my back and grabbed my hand. He was the sort of cool vampire boyfriend who, when a spell took hold, didn't exclaim that something was working.

The doll, Temperance Krinkle, picked up speed as she ran through the main streets of the town.

Bentley squeezed my hand tighter.

"It's working," I exclaimed, proving that I was the less cool one out of the two of us. No surprise there.

The doll was running at full tilt, near the edge of town, when suddenly a hole appeared in the model right in front of her. The hole was dark and deep, and had definitely not been there a moment earlier. The ashy doll tried to stop herself, but inertia is a magic of its own. She tumbled down into the hole, screaming a tiny scream as she fell.

The hole closed up instantly, like a giant eye blinking shut.

Bentley and I straightened up, turned to each other, and exchanged a wide-eyed look.

His jaw moved, but he was speechless.

"I can try again," I said. "We have plenty of ashes. As for the doll, I can use anything. I could use a wooden clothespin, or I could—"

"No need," Bentley said, cutting me off. He narrowed his eyes. "I saw where the doll was going."

"Me, too. Straight to Hell. I don't think giant holes open in the ground and take people to Disneyland."

He lifted my hand and squeezed it near his chest. "Remember how I told you I spent some time underground?"

"Yes." I gave him a sidelong look. Had he been to Hell? No. That was a crazy idea.

"I was in a crypt," he said. "And now I know why Krinkle's perfume was so familiar. I must have smelled it down there, inside the crypt. She must have visited the site before I did, when she was putting her plan together."

"Are you saying...?"

"We found them," he said. "*You* found them. Thanks to that spell of yours."

"We found them," I repeated, my voice croaking. My eyes hurt. We'd found Corvin. He would be reunited with his family soon. Chet and Chessa would be so relieved.

"I'll take it from here," Bentley said. He kissed me quickly, on my forehead. "You should go home."

"No way. I'm going with you to the crypt. You might need my help."

"You can help me by checking on Zoey. She was working at the museum today, right? We don't know how Louis Williams got that gemstone out past the security measures. You need to make sure Zoey's okay, and everyone else at the museum. We have no idea how far this thing spread."

"Right," I said, feeling both grateful and annoyed that Bentley had been the one to think of my daughter first. *Zara tries to be a good mother, she really does.*

"Zara?" He looked into my eyes.

"What?"

"Today is a good day," he said. "This is what victory feels like. We won."

Then he kissed me again, this time on the lips.

CHAPTER 35

ONE DAY LATER

I hummed happily to myself as I added croutons to a giant wooden bowl filled with romaine lettuce. I diverted one crouton into my mouth for a sample taste. It was crunchy, pleasantly salty, and just garlicky enough. Who knew you could make your own croutons? Or that they tasted better than the crumbled salty chunks that came in packaged salads?

I'd never made my own croutons before, but since my only task for dinner that night was to prepare a Caesar salad, I'd gone all out. And by *all out*, I mean I made the croutons and dressing. The lettuce had been prepared by Ribbons the Wyvern, who'd taken great delight in "eviscerating" the heads of romaine. He had been less than pleased by my insistence he wash his talons with dish soap thoroughly, but he'd come around, even appearing to enjoy his bath in the kitchen sink. Boa had watched the proceedings in horror. Take a bath willingly? Her tiny feline mind had been blown.

Both of them had left me alone in the kitchen to finish up the salad.

I heard the front door open. My daughter called out, "Hi, honey! I'm home from work!"

"Hi, honey!" I called right back. "I'm in the kitchen, slaving over a hot stove for you."

She came into the kitchen and peered over my shoulder into the huge bowl. "Ribbons made lettuce entrails?"

"He sure did."

"I hope you made him wash his weird little hands."

"I did. It was a whole thing."

"Aww. And I missed it." She grabbed a crouton and crunched it. "These taste different."

"That's because I made them. From scratch. Did you know croutons are made from sliced bread? Now that I know how easy it is, we'll be having croutons on everything."

"Crouton pizza?"

"Sure. And crouton stir-fry."

"Crouton mashed potatoes," she said, getting excited.

"Croutons on spaghetti, served in the bath tub on the tub plate."

She snagged a few more from the bowl and munched them happily. "You could mix these with a tub of popcorn and Skittles, for movie night."

"Genius idea!"

She ate a few more. "Speaking of genius, I noticed all that moss is gone from our roof. That was a good idea you had, talking loudly about getting a big, heavy handyman to scrape around up there. It looks like our house took the hint and got rid of the moss on her own."

"Our house is female?"

Zoey gave me a *duh* look, then asked, "How was work today?"

"Not bad." I stifled a yawn. "It's hard to focus on basic job duties after two hours of sleep and a big adventure the night before, but it's also kind of a relief. I'm glad I'm not a full-time investigator, like..." I hesitated to say his name. Earlier that morning, I'd cast some unintentional magic when saying his name. Our Pop Tarts had suddenly flown out of the toaster with giant hearts burned onto the fronts and backs. Zoey had teased me mercilessly.

She smirked at me, knowing exactly why I hesitated to say his name, then asked, "What about Frank? Did he talk about you-know-what with his sister?"

I was relieved for the change of topic. The only thing more embarrassing than talking to my daughter about my lack of a love life was talking about the existence of one.

"She's not a chicken," I said.

"That's good, I think." Zoey held up both hands. "But I'm trying hard not to judge. People should be whatever they want to be, even if it's a chicken. Is she even a shifter?"

"Yes. They had the talk, and it turns out she's..." I'd gotten Frank's permission, from Bellatrix, to share our family's secrets with each other, but I made Zoey wait for it. "A swan."

Zoey gawked. "I remember Frank saying his sister has weird chicken feet, like our bath tub. And that when they were kids, he used to call her an ugly duckling. But it turns out she's a swan?"

"I know. Isn't it ironic and wonderful? Bellatrix didn't even know. One day she was in her regular human form, not a care in the world, hiking through the woods with her dog, an adorable yet useless little rat terrier who wouldn't know what to do with an actual rodent if it jumped out and performed a musical number from *Chicago*—" I rubbed my forehead. "Now I'm picturing a mouse in a top hat, singing Mr. Cellophane."

Zoey waved a hand impatiently. "Back to the woods! Frank's ugly duckling sister and her little dog were walking in the woods, and then what?"

"When suddenly, a bear lurched out of the woods and came right at her." I puffed up my chest and stood on tiptoes, making myself big and scary. I roared in a deep gruff voice, "I'm a big hungry bear, and I'm gonna eat you, because I'm a bear, and that's what I do."

Zoey blinked at me, less impressed at my storytelling by the minute. When Frank had done a similar performance for me earlier that day at the library, I had been in hysterics. That man knew how to tell a tale! All those years as the Wisteria Public Library's children's librarian had not gone to waste.

Zoey said flatly, "Then what?"

"That was when the fear triggered her latent magic, and she turned into a swan," I said in my regular voice.

"Like what happened to me," she said.

"Except she didn't even know magic ran in her family. At least you had your grandfather as a frame of reference. Frank's sister didn't have a clue! And suddenly there she was." I waved up and down my body. "Full swan!"

"She must have been so surprised."

"Not as surprised as the bear, who immediately fled the scene."

"What about the dog?"

"The dog barked at the swan until she changed back, about two hours later, once the shock had worn off."

Zoey let out a sigh. "I'm glad the dog didn't have to make a noble sacrifice and get eaten by the bear."

She reached into the wooden bowl for more croutons.

I spanked her hand. "Leave some for dinner with the Moores," I said. We had been invited to a backyard barbecue with the family next door, to celebrate Corvin coming home safely the night before. As for any lingering effects of having been abducted, he seemed to have taken it all in stride.

Luckily for Veronica Tate's sanity, the kid had remained in his dog form throughout the entire kidnapping ordeal. It saved Veronica the shock of her life, plus she got to avoid a complimentary mind wiping from the DWM.

Corvin told his father it had been easy enough to not blow his cover, and that being down in the tomb hadn't been so bad. He discovered that he enjoyed spending time underground.

The woman, Veronica Tate, had not fared as well. Two days and two nights below ground in a dark tomb, with only a few survival supplies left behind by her kidnapper, had severely tested the woman. No sooner had Bentley freed her from the tomb than she began yelling about how she was going to sue the entire town, including the incompetent police force, the cemetery where the tomb was located, and anyone else she happened to make eye contact with. When one of the paramedics offered her hot chocolate, she threatened to sue him because the cocoa was too hot.

Some people showed their gratitude for being rescued from a tomb in a funny way.

Next to me, Zoey sighed. It was a weightier-sounding sigh than seemed warranted by merely having to stop eating my croutons, delicious though they were.

"Sigh a little louder," I said. "I don't think the whole town heard you."

"Mo-om," she said, breaking my name into two syllables to show her annoyance.

My mom senses tingled.

Hang on, I told myself, sensing a mood change in my mercurial sixteen-year-old. Zoey was about as easygoing as a kid could be, but she did have her moments, and she was going through a lot of changes. Between the introduction of her genie father, her first job at the museum, and the early stages of romance with the kid in the caveman costume, she had a lot going on. Plus the shifter thing, the witch thing, and regular teen hormones.

"What's going on?" I asked gently. "Hard day at the museum, scraping gum off benches?"

"No. Well, yes, but that's not the worst part about today. The worst part is I already know about the Moore family's big news."

She reached into the bowl and took a crouton. I took one as well, and waited for her to tell me what was bothering her so much that she was sighing loudly and making my name two syllables.

"They're leaving town," she said.

"A vacation?" I munched another handful of croutons. "After everything they've been through lately, that's probably a good idea."

She gave me a serious look, her hazel eyes drooping at the sides. "They're leaving town," she repeated, enunciating each word carefully.

Leaving town. The news hit me with an internal thud. "No," I said, but I already believed it. Zoey wouldn't joke about something this serious.

"Corvin told me," she said.

"When? Did he come see you at work today?"

"No. Just now. Before I came in the house. He jumped out of the bushes and barked at me for a while, then we talked." She grabbed another handful of croutons. "He said his dad has a new job somewhere else, somewhere far away from here." She turned her back to me and sniffed. "I can't do this," she said. "You'll have to go to dinner without me."

I didn't say anything. There were no words that could offer comfort. Not yet, when the news was so fresh.

"Why?" She choked back a sob, her back still to me. "Why get attached to people if everyone moves away? Why bother putting down roots at all?"

I reached out to pat her shoulder.

She pulled away from my touch as though it was cursed. She whirled around to face me, her eyes red and her expression furious. "This is your fault," she said. "You had to move us here, and you let me get comfortable. You told me things were going to be good. Do you call this good?"

I felt a tug inside my mind, and then Ribbons' voice. "I would not want to be in your human shoes right now, Zed."

I replied silently for him to shut up.

"You let me get attached," Zoey said. She wiped at one eye.

"You care about Corvin," I stated plainly.

"He's like the creepy little brother I never knew I wanted."

"He's a special kid," I said.

She frowned. "Being an only child sucks!"

I had a few responses go zipping through my head, but I was smart enough to keep them to myself.

"They can't move away," she said. "They can't. We won't let them. Tell Mr. Moore you did a spell, and you can see the future. Tell him there's something terrible coming, some big, horrible thing, and it's going to happen if they leave. A big apocalypse thing."

Gently, I said, "I can't tell them that."

"Then you have to cast a spell that makes them want to stay! Talk to your friends and get Mr. Moore's job transfer canceled."

"I can't do that, Zoey."

"It's only fair. He's the one who got you a job here. If it wasn't for him, we wouldn't be here. It's only fair that he has to stick around."

"And don't you remember how that felt? To have someone else messing around with your destiny?"

"So what? It all worked out. You got over it. You're not mad at him anymore."

I took a breath and said nothing. The conversation was spiraling out of control, and not even the wittiest comment could save us.

She crossed her arms. "What good is being a witch if you can't fix the things that are wrong and make them right?"

Her words resonated with me. She could have left out the word *witch* and used *adult* instead.

She was only sixteen, only just learning about how the world worked, and how being an adult, witch or otherwise, didn't give a person that much more power than being a kid.

And what was wrong or right, anyway?

I thought of the beautiful goddess, one of the Four Eves. Mahra.

We'd changed her fate.

With the speedy snip of a pair of bolt cutters, she had been sent back to whatever time and place she'd tried to enter our world from. Had that been right of us, to treat her appearance as a wrong? Sure, she'd killed Temperance Krinkle by that point, but it could be argued that Krinkle willingly sacrificed herself.

What would Mahra have done if she'd been allowed to walk the earth in these modern times?

I would never know.

I looked into my daughter's hazel eyes, at the hurt she held within, and I thought about us not as individuals, but as the next larger unit. Families.

The Moores.

The Riddles.

The Wonders.

Our lives crossed over and under each other in countless ways. There was no way of knowing which decisions would turn out to be wrong or right for an individual, their family, their community, or the world. What seemed right for an individual might harm the family, or vice versa.

All we could do was make the decision that seemed like the best one at the time, with what little information we had. And then hope for the best.

I didn't try to explain that to my daughter. She was a smart girl, and she already knew.

We could talk about it another time, perhaps over a bucket full of croutons, popcorn, and Skittles.

Instead of delving into the philosophical, I offered a solution to the problem at hand.

"Maybe I could have our house talk to their house," I said, keeping my tone neutral. "And then the Moore house could grow a dungeon, and keep the Moores locked up until they've come to their senses and dropped this crazy idea about moving away."

"Now there's a good idea!" Her eyes had dried, and now she rubbed her cheeks clear of streaks.

"Or I could gather up all the ghosts I can find around town," I said, picking up speed. "And send them to wherever the Moores are moving. The ghosts will be under strict orders to haunt the Moores until they come back here, where their Spirit Charmed witch friend can take care of them."

Zoey gave me a weak smile. "I like this devious side of you."

"I could coordinate something with the other local witches and jinx all the roads leading out of town so they all lead right back again."

Zoey gasped as her bright hazel eyes widened. "That's the answer," she said. "I love it in movies when the roads out of town bring you right back again."

I winked at her. "I shall speak to the local coven, and we'll get to work right away."

She wrinkled her nose. "Or... we could just let them go, as long as they promise to return regularly for visits."

"And let all of my amazing witch powers go to waste?"

"It won't be wasted. You can still solve murders, and kidnappings, and whatever happens next."

I held out both hands. "What are you talking about? Between me, the coven, the DWM, and the new vampire detective watching over this town, all working together like a finely tuned machine, there shouldn't be any more crimes. People are going to start behaving themselves around here."

Zoey turned and peered into the big, wooden bowl which held only romaine lettuce and three croutons. "Uh-oh," she said. "This salad isn't very Caesar-like anymore."

"Go ahead and eat those last three," I said. "I'll make another batch."

As she was crunching on the croutons, the doorbell rang.

"Doorbell," she said.

"Doorbell," I replied.

In a sing-song voice, she said, "It's your boooy-friend."

"It's still your job to get the door."

"Right!" She ran out of the kitchen.

CHAPTER 36

THREE HOURS LATER

Dinner with the neighbors was over, and Bentley and I were alone together, sitting on a log and looking out over the sea. The sun was setting, and making its usual colorful painting on the sky.

The backyard barbecue with the Moores had been bittersweet. Just when I'd gotten used to having the Moore clan next door, they were leaving. And they all seemed thrilled about it, too.

I'd never, ever, ever seen Chet so relaxed. He'd been wearing sweatpants with a drawstring waist. Sweatpants! With a drawstring waist! I had to ask him to open a wine bottle using his shifter-wolf-claw trick, just to make sure it was really Chet and not his doppelganger. Chet, being as relaxed as he was, simply laughed at my request and flashed a whole hand full of claws.

Over grilled chicken and Caesar salad, we learned that he and Chessa had both been thinking about moving away for a while, ever since she'd come back from her coma. Each thought the other wasn't interested, though, so they'd been afraid to bring it up. Both of them had good memories associated with the town, but not nearly as many as the bad ones. Chessa in particular was having a difficult time assimilating. She kept getting into fights with Chloe over how to raise the baby. The sisters had assumed Chessa's gift would be simple, but nothing about the noble sacrifice had turned out simple at all.

It had given me a chill to realize that Chloe's desire for a family was what had brought me to Wisteria, where I'd found more of my own family.

Chessa, unlike her two triplet sisters, who were just garden-variety gorgons, had the power to read minds. It had always been an issue for her, but since coming back, reading people's thoughts had become unbearable. Every time she bumped into someone she knew, which, in a small town, happened frequently, she would be overwhelmed by their emotions, their pity, and their curiosity. She couldn't blame townspeople. There were dozens of juicy rumors circling around about her year-long absence. People couldn't stop thinking about it. Chessa would never be able to simply pop out and pick up a bag oranges at the grocery store like a regular person. Every time she showed her face, she had to see herself reflected in other people's eyes. She kept having to revisit her most painful memories.

I couldn't blame her at all for wanting to go somewhere new, somewhere she could be anonymous.

One issue that held them back was Grampa Don. Both were wisely reluctant to drag the cranky senior away from the only home he'd known for decades. But then everything changed. It was Grampa Don who suggested, on the eve of Corvin's return, that maybe it was time for the Moores to "get out of this crazy town for once and for all."

They'd discussed the matter as a family late into the night, and came to a decision. They would be leaving. They planned to put the house up for sale immediately. Whether the house sold or not, they would move before the end of summer, so Corvin could start the school year in his new home.

And where was this new home?

London!

As in London, England.

The Department of Water and Magic had a branch there, which did not surprise me one bit. London was a perfectly logical place to have a secret underground organization run by supernatural beings. Having such a Department in our small town of Wisteria was the illogical place, or so it had seemed.

Over dinner, Bentley, Zoey and I learned more about our hometown and the unique structures beneath it. Wisteria and parts of Westwyrd, including Castle Wyvern, stretched over the magic equivalent of shifting tectonic plates. These plates, when they moved, didn't cause earthquakes, but they did open up fissures and tunnels between worlds, and even through time itself.

Now, keep in mind, Grampa Don was the one who told us about the connections between the worlds. His memory wasn't exactly the most reliable, so the story about the shifting tectonic plates might have been more bedtime story than actual geography. Besides, time travel wasn't real. Even witches knew better than to believe in such—as my aunt would call it—tomfoolery.

I would miss the Moore family.

Except I would be glad to not have Chet Moore around, with his not-unattractive face that he shared with Archer Caine, and with his not-unattractive body that I still had too many borrowed memories of. My feelings toward him were complicated, to say the least. He'd deceived and manipulated me, and while I tried to play it cool and act as though I'd forgiven him, deep down I had not. I'd just learned to live with the complications.

Life would be easier for me if Chet Moore moved away. I would not miss him popping up in my life, sticking his nose in my business, and judging my parenting skills.

Also, I would be glad to no longer live in fear of Chessa. No more stress over bumping into her at a bad time, or reminding her of all the flirting Chet had done with me while she was in a coma. Some of Chet's friendliness had been acting, but she and I both knew that some of it had been real. I didn't want to test her jealousy, or feel her fury. My skull belonged on my head, and not on her chic white coffee table as a decorative candy bowl or other vessel of her choosing.

And, when I really thought about it, while I enjoyed some of Grampa Don's antics, he'd never quite warmed up to me. And I didn't care for his prejudice toward me and witchcraft in general.

Corvin might be the only one of the Moore family I would truly miss. With his round face and his big, spooky eyes. And the adorable way he would suddenly yell out inappropriate or offensive things. Oh, the number of times he'd screamed at me that I was a witch, or a ghost, or both. Priceless!

I would miss the little weirdo.

"That's the third one," Bentley said, startling me out of my thoughts.

"The third what?" I shielded the bright pink sky with my hand and peered out over the ocean. "Did you see a horn out there or something? Rumor has it there's a narwhal shifter who lives in the area."

He put his arm around my shoulders and hugged me to his side. "The third sigh," he said. "I don't want to be one of those boyfriends who's always asking you if something's wrong, but...?" He gave me a questioning look.

"Just thinking about how I'm going to miss Corvin." I rolled my eyes and shook my head. "Talk about a phrase I never thought I'd hear myself say."

"No offense to the kid, who has grown on me, but I won't be sad to see the backs of that family. I've seen how Chet Moore looks at you, when he thinks Chessa isn't looking. And then I've seen how Chessa sees him looking, then looks at you." He gave me a serious look. "That woman *does* want to use your skull as a candy bowl."

I gasped. "I know! Right?" I waved one hand. "Nobody else believes me."

"I believe you," he said solemnly. "Maybe I didn't before, but after having dinner with them tonight, I am one hundred percent convinced."

"You're not just saying that because you're my boyfriend, and it's your job to be supportive of your crazy witch girlfriend?"

"No. That woman is terrifying. And I'm saying that as an actual vampire. I'm hard to kill, as long as my head stays attached to my body, but I get the feeling that woman would pop my head off in a heartbeat." He looked down and scooped some beach sand in one hand. "That's one of two reasons why I'm glad you wanted to leave dinner early and go for a walk with me."

"Is the other reason because you're watching your figure and didn't want to be tempted by dessert?"

He let the sand sift down through his fingers. "I can't be tempted by cheesecake," he said, as serious as ever. "Or donuts, or cookies, or even your croutons, which were very crunchy and good. Those things don't tempt me."

"Oh. Is that because of your, um, powers?" I could say the word *vampire* now, but I preferred not to.

"No." He dusted the sand off his hands and turned to look at me. The sun finished setting just then. The orange drained out of the sky, leaving Bentley's face a cool blue. His eyes were like mercury.

I asked, "Then why?"

He reached up and swept my hair out of my face and then tucked it behind my ear.

The light faded away. Day turned to night.

In a husky voice, he said, "Because lately, the only thing that tempts me is you."

I started to protest that he was being way too romantic. Cheesy, even. Talking about how I was his only temptation? It was a bit much!

But then, I became intensely aware of my body, and the exact weight of my arms and legs, and where all my limbs were. I felt the angles of my posture as I sat on the log, and the fluttering of my dress along my sides.

I wanted to say something silly to dispel the dizzying effect Bentley had over me, the way he made me feel so weak in the places that were supposed to be strong, but I couldn't say anything. My mouth wouldn't obey, because all my mouth wanted to do was kiss him.

All *I* wanted to do was kiss him.

The world around us was blue, growing cooler, and I felt first my own heart racing and then his.

He had his hand in mine, pressed to his chest.

I felt like someone had cast a buoyancy spell on me, like I might float away.

He looked deep into my eyes, and before he could say anything even more romantic that might turn me all the way into jelly, I kissed him.

A giant sea monster could have emerged from the ocean right in front of us, and neither of us would have noticed.

We sat on the log on the beach, our bare feet in the warm sand, and we kissed each other until the stars came out, and then we held on to each other for warmth and kissed a while longer.

CHAPTER 37

PERSEPHONE DIAMANTE ROSE
WEDNESDAY MORNING

The night before she was due to return to her job at the Wisteria Police Department, Persephone Rose couldn't sleep. She finally gave up on being well rested and got up at five o'clock. After giving her tiny rental cottage a deep cleaning, she made a hearty breakfast of poached eggs, crispy bacon, and a stack of waffles.

As usual, she saved the bacon for last, and was about to enjoy the first piece when there was a knock at the door.

It was her father, Rhys Quarry. He was wearing one of his terrible vintage salesman suits. It was brown and corduroy, with suede elbow patches, and she could have sworn she'd given away that exact suit to a charity drive the last time he'd come to visit.

"That suit," she said by way of greeting.

He dusted off the hideous lapel. "Can you believe someone threw this out? I found it at a thrift store. It's a near perfect replacement for my old favorite that mysteriously disappeared."

She narrowed her eyes at him. "How lucky."

He shrugged. "Anyone can be lucky. All it takes is the right mindset. When Fate closes a door, she opens a window." He lifted his nose and sniffed audibly. "I didn't interrupt breakfast, did I?"

She nodded for him to come inside. "I'll whip up some more waffles."

He patted his stomach. "No need. I'm trying to cut back on carbs."

She had no response to this new concept of her father cutting back on carbohydrates. For one thing, all of Persephone's feelings about pancakes and waffles were inextricably linked to happy memories of her father making them and piling stacks on her plate. It was because of these happy associations that she'd taken the time to make waffles that morning. For another thing, her mind had switched back to worrying about returning to the WPD after the whole Krinkle debacle.

Inside the cottage, father and daughter filled mugs with coffee and took seats at the table across from each other. She thought about returning to the workplace where everyone thought she was an idiot who couldn't follow basic privacy and security rules.

After a comfortable silence, Rhys said, "Cheer up, my little shadow. It could have gone so much worse."

She felt the breath hitch in her throat. As usual, her father had read her mind using his all-knowing parental powers. Hearing his sympathy and love nearly pushed her to tears. She'd been holding on for so long, but now she was weakening, giving in to those self-pitying feelings, and she hated that about herself.

She drowned her rising angst with a big gulp of hot coffee.

Her father asked, "So, where are we at?"

"Bentley thinks I'm an idiot, and Zara..." She blinked furiously and frowned at the pepper shaker on the table. "Zara hates me."

"No. She does not," he said emphatically. "Zara doesn't hate you. I'm the expert on being hated by that particular redhead, and I can assure you, your sister does not hate you."

"Half sister," Persephone corrected, sighing and tilting her face up to stare at the ceiling. Looking up like that helped her angry tears go back to the well of chaos inside her.

"She doesn't hate you," Rhys said. "Zara is a complicated person. She had to toughen up at a young age. Her mother wasn't the easiest person to live with, trust me, and then she had to raise a kid as a single mother. Zarabella Diamante Riddle is..." He trailed off. He didn't need to tell Persephone the facts she already knew.

"I'm going to tell her everything," Persephone said. "How I only sent those photos to Krinkle because we were trying to track down whoever was giving her orders. How I've got no romantic interest in Theodore Bentley whatsoever. How—"

Rhys interrupted. "No interest whatsoever?"

She flicked her gaze down from the ceiling to her father, who'd frozen with both rust-colored eyebrows raised expectantly.

"Ew," she said. "Don't be gross. Detective Bentley is almost as old as you."

A smile spread slowly across his face. "Almost as old as your dear old dad? I am both flattered and deeply offended." He leaned back in his chair and unfastened the button of his brown suit jacket. "But all shall be forgiven in exchange for your bacon."

"Sure. You can have my bacon. I've lost my appetite anyway." She looked down at her plate, was surprised to find it empty, then gave her father a dirty look.

"Perfectly crisp," he said, licking his lips. "But I'm still peckish. How about you? I've got an idea." He rubbed his palms together. "Let's find ourselves something juicy. There's nothing quite like pouncing on a chubby field mouse to put the bushiness back in one's tail."

She crossed her arms. "I'm not eating some malnourished, half-dead snake food you bought at the pet store for your imaginary red-tailed boa constrictor."

"I don't expect you to." He got up from the table, crossed over to the window above the sink, and pushed it open. "We're going hunting. Shift and follow me."

"Don't you dare shift! Not here, Dad. I live here. Someone will see you."

"Nonsense. You picked this house because it's near the park."

"Near the park, yes. But we're at least four blocks away from the trees."

He cleared his throat. "Young lady, when you were a teenager sneaking in and out of the house past curfew, four blocks was nothing."

She bit her tongue. He did have a point.

"Go or don't go," he said, tapping his foot impatiently. "But I'm going, and hunting for a juicy mouse is just the start. I've got something else I need to do."

She shook her head. "Now what?"

"According to my sources, by which I mean *my own pointy ears*, Zara is planning to walk to work today through the park. I'm going to pay her a very civil visit, in which explain how it only appeared that I betrayed her and left her for dead that one time."

"Do you mean the time you used her cat for bait?"

"The cat," he mused. "I forgot about that part. Not one of my finer moments." He shrugged. "But if the plant had taken the bait, I would have happily gotten her a new cat. A better cat, even. And besides, sometimes we must make sacrifices for the greater good."

"Tell me about it," she sighed. She tried not to think about all the nice things she'd given up to move to Wisteria for her new assignment.

"So that's the plan, then," Rhys said cheerfully. "We'll have a nice run in the sunshine, just the two of us, like old times. We'll catch a few mice to get ourselves warmed up, and then make proper introductions."

Persephone gave her father a skeptical look. "Why would we need to get warmed up?"

"To dodge the lightning balls. Zara doesn't hate you, but she still hates me, remember?"

Persephone looked at the open window. Her fingers twitched as her body, two steps ahead of her conscious mind, prepared to shift.

She wanted to go. She had met Zara already, but not really. They were still strangers, and knowing that made her heart ache. Ever since Persephone had found out about her half-sister, the witch, she'd been longing to meet her, to finally throw her arms around her one and only sibling. Though they had different mothers, the two shared blood. They even had the same middle name: Diamante, in honor of their shared great-great-grandmother, a woman of great power.

Persephone decided to go, to ambush her half-sister immediately. It was time. The Krinkle case had been closed. There was no more reason for secrecy. She would introduce herself to the powerful witch, and deal with whatever balls of lightning flew her way. In her shifter form, Persephone was extremely agile.

She rose from her chair and said, "No offense, Dad, but maybe I should break the news to Zara by myself."

"You can certainly *try* to outrun your old man." He grinned and nodded at the window. "Go on. Off you go." He waggled his eyebrows. "I'll give you a ten-second head start."

"Dad!"

"Nine and a half seconds." He tapped the spot on his wrist where a watch might have been. "Nine. Eight and a half. Eight..."

Persephone Rose shifted into her animal form, flicked her bushy black tail, and leaped out the open kitchen window.

For a full list of books in this
series and other titles by
Angela Pepper, visit

www.angelapepper.com

www.ingramcontent.com/pod-product-compliance
Lightning Source LLC
Chambersburg PA
CBHW060242100726
47907CB00003B/741